Mary Jean's Red Shoes

To Jan —
Keep moving &
enjoy the arts!
Sandra Strohmeyer

Mary Jean's Red Shoes

A Novel

Sandra Strohmeyer

Sandra Strohmeyer Press

Copyright © 2020 by Sandra Strohmeyer

All rights reserved. No part of this publication may be reproduced, stored in any retrieval system, or transmitted in any form or by any means, electronic, mechanical, photocopying, recording, or otherwise, without the prior written permission of the publisher.

This book is a work of fiction. Names, characters, businesses, organizations, places, and events other than those clearly in the public domain, are either the production of the author's imagination or are used fictitiously. Any resemblance to actual persons, living or dead, events, or locales is entirely coincidental.

Published 2020 by Sandra Strohmeyer Press
ISBN: 978-0-578-72700-4
eBook ISBN: 978-0-578-72701-1

For my father, who always encouraged me to reach high.

"I want music to fill my ears,
a dog curled at my feet,
soft winds caressing my face,
tall trees high above me,
birds singing their love songs,
faces of colorful flowers greeting me.

And one more thing I desperately need,
and that is empathy."

—Sandra Strohmeyer

Mary Jean's Red Shoes

1

Mary Jean opened the door and found a homemade chocolate cupcake on the doorstep of her apartment at the Kingsley Retirement Home for Seniors in Maple Grove, Oregon. A card was lying next to it and she realized someone had thought of her. Someone had gone to the trouble to actually make something, buy a card, and walk it over to her doorstep. She picked it up and carried it inside. She didn't think too long about who the person might be—Charlotte. She was like that with a lot of people at the home. Always noticing whose birthday it was. She put the cupcake on her kitchen countertop along with the balloon she (along with four other seniors) had been given on the last Friday of the month during which the birthdays were celebrated.

Tall but not too tall, Mary Jean was still pretty upright for a ninety-one-year old. True, she had lost a couple of inches, but that was all. She had started using a walker when she went out because she had taken a fall a couple of weeks ago. Her short gray hair had thinned with age, but she went to the salon regularly to keep it looking sharp. No perms for her;

just a simple, short cut that was easy to take care of. Her gray-blue eyes had been one of her strongest features when she was younger. She wore glasses now but still had good enough eyesight to read books with larger print without them. She loved to read and got books on loan from the library regularly. She had lost a lot of muscle mass in the last five years, so her clothes hung loosely on her frame. Gravity always won out at this age. Her face was wrinkled, but her complexion was still fair. She thought she looked paler each year. Part of that was due to staying inside so much.

 Mary Jean did not have many friends. She knew she talked too much at the tables during meals. She didn't like listening to the others. They would go on and on, and she just didn't have the patience anymore to be quiet and to listen. So she jumped in and went off on her own bunny trails while the faces of her table companions got longer and longer, until one of them closed their eyes and took a short nap. One day, she snapped at Mr. Ross because he was butting in and telling the same story he always told during their evening meal. It became real quiet. Lativia started talking about how tough the meat was and how undercooked the peas were until the others started chiming in.

 After dinner, Mary Jean walked down the hallway to her little apartment, the one with the wreath of stuffed fabric leaves her daughter had made for her. It was bingo night, so she had to get herself ready to see how many bingo bucks she could win for things like a new hairdo or a used book. The house cleaners had just left, and her little apartment was all tidied up, not that she got it that messy anyway. They were always putting the pillows back on the couch the wrong way. She fiddled with them, arranging them the way she liked, then got her bingo pad and pencil and headed out the door.

The day before had been her ninety-first birthday. It was September. She loved the warm days and cool nights of fall. Her son, daughter-in-law, and one of her three daughters had come over to take her out to dinner. Her oldest daughter, Abby, had brought her a homemade sweet potato and chocolate cake. Her son, Marcus, brought some photos of her grandson Finley's wedding that they had attended two months ago in July. They all sat around the coffee table, reliving the wedding in the park among the tall sequoias. Afterward, they walked to McMenamins, which was about one block away. The walk was not as hard as she thought it would be. She was slower with her walker but had no difficulty keeping up with the others. She needed a little help with the stairs, especially going down. Once seated, she ordered a pizza but wished she had gotten the trout her daughter-in-law had chosen. Despite her disappointment, she ate half of it anyway. She loved her visits from her children. She was lucky. All of her four children visited her regularly, taking her out to meals or shopping.

It was Sunday evening. Bingo was over, and she had won a thousand bingo bucks. That was enough for her to get a new hairdo. She would have to schedule that next week.

Marcus always called her on Sundays. It was 7:30 p.m., and anytime now, the phone would ring. There it was, right on the button.

"Hi Mom, how are you?"

"Oh, I was working on a puzzle and Lorna took the piece I needed to finish an area I was working on so I decided to try another one but there were too many people at the table . . . . We had brunch at 10 a.m. and ate tuna on crackers and I thought the tuna was stale, then they served a punch that was too sweet and I only could drink a little bit . . . . My hip was hurting so I decided not to walk the half mile around the inside of the building. You know I can't go outside much because my blood pressure medicine reacts with sunlight so I stay inside and try to walk twice a week. Sometimes I go to the exercise class where they show us how to do sit-ups in a chair . . . . Oh, what have you been doing?"

"Well, I rode my bike up Mt. St. Helens—"

"Well, Mr. Landers's daughter just got married and they are moving to Colorado so he won't see them very much and she's pregnant with her first child already. That must have been awkward but I guess kids these days just don't care about that sort of thing anymore—"

"Mom, how does that relate to me biking up Mt. St. Helen's?"

"Well, Mr. Landers used to own a bike store."

"Okay. I see."

"How's Kirsten doing?'

"She's fine. She's been working on a commissioned painting of a dog—"

"My neighbor paints landscapes. I told her she should take them to Art in the Valley and sell them. Your grandpa used to paint barns but I told him they didn't look very lifelike. His cousin painted horses. We have painting classes here and several of the residents like the class."

"That's nice."

"How's Finley?"

"He's doing well. He just got a grant that will support his work for about two years."

"Is that a permanent position? Does he have health coverage?"

"It's not a tenured track position . . ."

"What will Lisa do if he runs out of money? Is her teaching job going to last more than a year? My neighbor's son has a new job teaching at George Fox—"

"Mom, I have to go now. Dinner is ready."

"Well, okay. Thanks for calling, and tell Finley I am real proud of him."

"I will, Mom. Good night."

Mary Jean hung up. She was a lucky woman. Marcus was so attentive. Her daughter-in-law, Kirsten, sent her homemade cards from her paintings, and her three daughters visited her regularly. She was so proud of her grandson, Finley, who also called her occasionally. His wife, Lisa, was already pregnant with her first grandchild. She was so excited about that. She had two granddaughters, too, who lived out of state: one was married and the other was single. Both had graduated from college and found good jobs. So many kids these days still lived with their parents. Some had real troubles, like drug addiction or mental illness, that prevented them from working or barely subsisting. What had this world come to? Mary Jean thought about how hard her kids used to work during the summers. All her children had worked in the canneries and saved their own money to help pay for college. Kids these days didn't want to do that kind of work. Instead, it was largely Hispanic workers who showed up for those jobs.

There was a knock on the door. Startled, Mary Jean stood up from the couch and walked suspiciously over to the door. Who could that be? She seldom had any visitors. She asked who it was, and a man answered, "It's Mr. Weeks." She didn't know a Mr. Weeks, but she slowly opened the door anyway and found a short, stocky man with a scraggly white goatee and vibrant, deep-blue eyes. In fact, his eyes were so intense that she just stood and stared at the man.

"Someone delivered this package to me, but it has your name on it," said Mr. Weeks in a friendly voice. "I live on the other side of the building."

"I haven't seen you in the dining room or anywhere around here. Are you new?" asked Mary Jean.

"No. I am not new. I eat inside my room instead of going to the dining room. I thought I should get this to you. It looks important."

"Well, thank you for bringing it to me, but I never ordered anything. Maybe it's a present from someone, she thought. After all, my birthday was just yesterday.

With that, she took the package, said goodbye, and closed the door. She placed the rather large box on the table. There was something about that man's eyes. It was as though he were beaming with joy. What could possibly be so joyful? She looked at the box and checked the sender's address. It was from Portland, Oregon. The Nike Company. She carefully opened the rectangular box, and there, wrapped up in tissue, was a pair of bright red sneakers. They looked kind of high tech, something her granddaughter would wear to run her marathons. She noticed they were the correct size. How odd. Who would have sent these? She rarely walked outside anymore, and if she did, she had her old, leather walking shoes. She didn't need these and probably would never use them.

She put them back in the box and set them on the shelf. The clock struck eight. The birds sang from the clock. She would have to sleep on this new set of events. She took a warm shower, got dressed in her flannel nightgown, and headed to bed. She decided to read a bit as she did not feel especially sleepy. Her eyes had a hard time focusing, but that was just one more thing to add to the list of what was not fun about aging. Her bowels didn't work as well, she did not sleep through the night, and things just did not taste as good. Her long-term memory was still good, though her short-term memory was fading fast. Don't dwell on it, she thought. Just take one day at a time. "Let me just lose myself in this book," she said to herself. She picked up the book and read a few chapters before she switched the light off. Her thoughts always drifted to the past, and she reminisced about her days working at the local library when her kids were in school, and then the artist co-op when she retired, and the satisfaction she had felt in helping out the artist community.

2

Breakfast the next morning was the usual. Poached egg, one piece of toast with a pat of butter, and some marmalade. She still drank her coffee black. At the table, Milton and Frieda were talking about their grandkids, all grown now. Their kids were all established with good jobs. They never visited but texted them news on what the grandkids were up to. All this new tech stuff. Mary Jean would have none of it. People with their heads down staring at their phones, even at the dinner table. Kids are going to grow up without any social skills, she thought. Across the room, Lativia and Mr. Ross were sitting silently, gazing off into space. She glanced out the window to her left and looked out into the courtyard. It was raining. Nothing new about that. Mary Jean felt a melancholy mood come over her as she finished up her egg and toast.

"My son just texted to say that my grandson got a new job," said Milton. Mary Jean barely heard him as her thoughts were on what she was going to do next after breakfast. She fidgeted with her napkin, rolling it between her fingers. Then she jumped into the conversation and said, "My grandson works at the university and studies how bacteria communicate to each other. He got married in the summer. His wife works as a science teacher at a high school. They knew each other for five years, and . . ."

Milton had stopped listening and was telling Frieda they ought to go now. They excused themselves and retreated to their room. Mary Jean got up from the table and heaved a big sigh. No one listened anymore these days. She walked down the hallway, turned left, and headed to her room. Then she saw Mr. Weeks standing at her doorstep, as if he were waiting for her to answer the door.

She said, "Mr. Weeks, can I help you?" He looked down at his feet, which were clad in red running shoes, and replied, "Would you like to try on your new shoes and come outside for a walk around the courtyard?"

Mary Jean looked at him in surprise. How did he know there had been shoes in that package? Maybe he could tell by the shape of the box? She hadn't given much thought to even trying on those shoes, and she really didn't know him at all. Well, it was unlikely he was a mass murderer, and she couldn't leave him standing outside her door, so she invited him in.

How odd, she thought. His shoes are the same color as mine.

She saw he was waiting patiently for her to get ready, so she pushed her doubts out of her head. She sat down on the couch and unwrapped the shoes. Boy, wouldn't they make a pair, like twins, clad in same-color shoes. She looked up and saw a twinkle in Mr. Weeks's eyes, and it triggered something inside her. What was it? There was a sense of adventure about him. It almost reminded her of Lewis, her late husband. He could always egg her into doing something she didn't want to do. She guessed that was one of the things she had loved so much about him.

"All right, let's see what these crazy things look like on my feet."

She slipped them on. They seemed too comfortable to be called shoes. She still wondered who the heck had sent these to her. Maybe it was that grandkid of hers pulling a silly prank on her. No matter, she figured she could give them a whirl. She walked to the sliding glass door and stepped out onto the balcony to check the weather. It had stopped raining, and the trees glistened with moisture. The scent was so fresh and clean. Birds were singing, and she could hear the band from the neighboring elementary school playing faintly in the background.

"Well, we couldn't have timed it any better," said Mr. Weeks.

Her hip was bothering her again, and now that the sun was out, she knew that if she went outside for a walk, she'd need to cover up so as not to interfere with her blood pressure medication. Mary Jean grabbed her coat and let her worries slide away. Mary Jean reached for her walker, but Mr. Weeks put his hand on her arm. Mary Jean was startled by his touch.

"Don't worry about taking the walker. You can hold on to my arm as we walk," he said.

They took the elevator down instead of the stairs, which were always hard for her to navigate. She signed out at the door. A few residents looked down at their feet and smiled.

Outside, it was cool, and a breeze lightly blew Mary Jean's coat open. She pulled it closer around her body. Together, they walked along the sidewalk that led around the building to the garden area. Each step felt cushioned, yet supportive, and the rubber soles made a squeaky sound on the wet pavement. Along the way, they met no one. It was odd for her to be outside in the cool fall weather. Normally, she would be inside looking out her sliding glass door, sipping tea by herself. She might be working on a crossword puzzle or reading a book. But here she was, walking outside with a strange man she'd just met and wearing squeaky red shoes!

Orange and yellow leaves blanketed the grass under the tall maple trees on the other side of the sidewalk, covering the bright green lawn. She instinctively looked up and noticed the fluffy white clouds against the brilliant blue sky. Soon, they were inside the courtyard and had made it all the way around the building. The garden beds were untended and full of weeds. These raised beds had been planted by the staff in the summer to lure the residents out of their rooms into the sunshine and outdoors. Residents were also encouraged to plant their own seeds, but no one had come out all summer to plant anything at all. That included Mary Jean herself. However, today she felt differently. Perhaps she would get more involved. The thought of growing plants seemed renewing. Something about these red shoes had put an extra bounce in her step and outlook.

At the end of the walk, they returned to the building. Instead of riding the elevator, they took the stairs one at a time, holding the railing for balance. Mr. Weeks walked beside her, supporting her elbow. He seemed to have the energy of a younger man. They stopped at the intersection at the top of the stairs, and he said, "That is number one."

Mary Jean looked perplexed and thought to herself that maybe this man was a little off his rocker after all.

"What do you mean it's number one?"

"That's our first walk of many to come," he said. And with that, he smiled with a wink and walked away toward his room.

Mary Jean watched him leave. Well, that was a strange way to say goodbye. He hadn't said anything about when they were to meet the next time. She still felt like there was something familiar about Mr. Weeks, but she just couldn't put her finger on it. She shook her head and headed back to her room. She had a few hours left until lunch, so she thought she might walk down to the laundry room and wash some things.

As she opened the door, the telephone in her room rang. She shrugged off her coat and answered the phone.

"Hi, Mom. How are you?" It was Shiela, her youngest daughter, calling from work. She worked in a small veterinary clinic in Nelson, about twenty miles away.

"You'll never believe what happened to me today. I went outside walking with a man I'd just met wearing red sneakers from Nike."

"You did what, Mom?" Shiela was sure her mom was finally succumbing to dementia or losing her memory or some such thing that older people experienced.

"You heard right. We walked around the entire building, the shoes were so comfortable, and we both looked up into the sky. The clouds were so white, the leaves were all turning colors, and my hip didn't hurt at all, and Mr. Weeks . . ."

"Who's Mr. Weeks?"

"Oh, he's the man I met yesterday. I don't really know him but he brought over the red tennis shoes, and we don't know who sent them but he asked me to put them on and take a walk with him outside . . ."

"Wow, Mom, that's great. I'm glad you've made a walking friend. It's so important to get outside once in a while."

"Well, I doubt we'll be doing it again since the weather is getting so bad. He'll probably forget about doing it again like he suggested."

"He asked you to go again?"

"Well, he said it was number one of many, which I then assumed to mean he wants to go out again."

"Well, that will be good for you. I have to go now, Mom. Take care."

Mary Jean hung up the phone. She scurried around the apartment, picking up dirty clothes and towels and putting them in a basket. There were carts in the laundry room for those who needed them but Mary Jean could still carry her clothes there and back. She grabbed her detergent and headed over to the laundry room. There were two other women in various stages of cleaning or folding clothes. She sorted her clothes carefully, found an empty washer, and piled in the towels. In another, she put in her dark clothing, added detergent, and set them each in motion.

As she worked, she couldn't help but reflect on the morning's walk. It felt so good getting outside today, she thought. When did I stop going outside?

It was time for lunch when Mary Jean finished her laundry. She hauled the clean, folded clothes and towels to her room and put them away. She really wasn't that hungry and thought about having lunch in her room instead. But she was out of food and needed to go to the grocery store, so she reluctantly went to lunch.

There were three people at her table—Mable, Jack, and Hattie. Mary Jean decided to ask them a question.

"Did any of you plant anything in the garden over the summer?"

They looked at each other and all of them shook their heads, almost in unison. Mary Jean asked a second question.

"If I provided the seeds and we worked together, would you think about giving it a try?"

Mable said, "I'm not sure I could bend over much to do the planting. As long as it doesn't take any bending over, I could do it."

Hattie said, "I don't go outside much anymore. My hips bother me too much."

Jack added, "I used to have a big garden in my home in Corvallis. I use a cane now, and walking on the gravel is hard for me."

Mary Jean nodded. She thought the same of herself. She had too many aches and pains to take up gardening. Too bad there weren't more young people around to help.

Suddenly, that gave her an idea. Why couldn't the school next door send over its kids to help start a garden? Mary Jean thought she might ask the activities director if that was a possibility.

The food arrived—corned beef hash on a piece of soggy bread, overcooked green beans, and some canned peaches. Fresh vegetables would sure be an improvement, she thought to herself. Mable started talking about her win at the bingo game in the morning and Jack argued about how he never won. Hattie chimed in that she never played and thought crossword puzzles were more stimulating. Mary Jean didn't know what to add to the conversation. She began to think that there were more important things to talk about than games.

As she glanced around, Mary Jean noticed Sarah, her house cleaner, across the room, who was serving another table. She knew that some of the employees at Kingsley worked more than one job. When Sarah was done, she approached their table with the tea Mary Jean had ordered. At that moment, Mary Jean remembered something she wanted to ask her friends.

"Have any of you noticed how more residents have been ferried over to the Memory Care Unit this week? I mean people like yourselves who are perfectly healthy," said Mary Jean.

The Memory Care Unit was a part of the facility that gave more support to residents with mental disabilities.

Sarah, who was pouring tea just as Mary Jean spoke, suddenly spilled the tea on Mary Jean's lap.

"Oh, I am so sorry!" said Sarah. She reached for a napkin to clean up the table and handed an extra one to Mary Jean for her lap.

"It's fine. It wasn't very much." Mary Jean dabbed at her lap while her friends grew silent.

Sarah moved to the table next to them to remove some dirty dishes. She lingered while Mary Jean and her friends continued their conversation.

Hattie lowered her voice and said, "Yes. My next-door neighbor was wheeled over there yesterday around suppertime. And the day before that was Wally, three doors down. If he doesn't have all his wits about him, I don't know anyone who does." Hattie looked over at Sarah to see if she was listening. Sarah busied herself with the dishes and hurried away.

"Well, maybe there was something wrong with them that we just didn't know about," said Mable.

"That could be," said Mary Jean. This was the first time she had heard other residents acknowledge the same thing she had noticed. It all sounded rather creepy to her—but also strangely intriguing. She decided she would keep her eyes open. She noticed Sarah looking back at their table with a worried expression.

Mary Jean excused herself from lunch, stood up, and then hesitated. What was it she wanted to do next? Oh yes, she was going to go see the activities director and ask about getting the school kids to help with the garden. She walked down the hallway and knocked on the second door. Miss Harriet opened the door with a smile.

"Hi, Mary Jean. What can I do for you today?" Miss Harriet said.

"I was wondering if we could get some of the elementary school children next door to come help us in the garden. I think that would get more of us outside, and maybe we would actually grow some vegetables." She shifted on her feet. Her bunion was hurting.

"Well, I could talk to the principal and see what happens. I think that's a very good idea. I'll ring her up tomorrow morning and let you know what she has to say."

"Thanks, Miss Harriet. I'll look forward to hearing from you."

3

Mary Jean turned and walked back to her room. As she was turning the corner, she noticed Larry, the cook, talking with Mrs. Lemon, the manager of Kingsley Retirement Home for Seniors. Mrs. Lemon was wearing a blue pants suit with a white blouse. She was in her early forties and had shoulder-length hair that was dyed blond. She looked like she was whispering to Larry. Larry stood a full head and a half taller than Mrs. Lemon, wearing saggy denim jeans and a dirty white apron over his long torso. His blue plaid shirt was only partially tucked in. They immediately stopped talking and went their separate ways when they saw Mary Jean coming. Mrs. Lemon walked straight ahead and didn't acknowledge Mary Jean as she passed. Interesting, thought Mary Jean. That was peculiar behavior.

She arrived at her apartment and found a note taped to the door. She took it down and let herself in. She opened the note. It said, "Meet me down in the garden at once. Mr. Weeks."

What could this mean? Why would he be asking her out again today? She got herself a glass of water, slipped on her green sweater and red shoes, and headed to the elevator. As she waited for the elevator to open, she saw Frieda being wheeled down the hall toward Memory Care! Frieda looked out of it, with her head slumped to the side and her arms slack, hanging down on either side of her body. Had she had a stroke? Yesterday, Mary Jean had had breakfast with her, and she had appeared fine. There sure were some strange things going on, and it was only the afternoon. Things were quickly getting worse.

She entered the elevator and thought about Mr. Weeks waiting for her in the garden. Her heart skipped a beat. Whoa, really? She realized she was anticipating seeing him. Or was she just anxious about his note? She stepped out and headed down the hallway to the garden. It was cloudy outside, and the wind was picking up. Fall was here, and the nip in the air made Mary Jean pull her sweater tighter around herself. She quickly saw Mr. Weeks sitting on the bench in the gazebo. He had on a brown, tweed Irish sweater and a black wool beret that covered his head. Wispy, fine gray hairs showed in the back and side of his head. He looks rather dapper, thought Mary Jean as she stepped up the brick walkway toward where he was sitting.

"Hello, Mr. Weeks. Your note had me worried."

"Hi, Mary Jean. Sorry, I didn't mean to worry you. I've got something important to share with you."

"What is it?"

"Come sit down beside me. We'll be less conspicuous inside the gazebo."

He motioned with his hand toward the bench he was sitting on. Mary Jean thought it a little close, but she complied and scooted onto the bench next to him. His eyes were as piercing as ever and so reminded her of her late husband, Lewis.

"Please don't eat lunch in the dining room."

"Why do you say that? What's happening?" Mary Jean searched his face for answers. His jaw was set and his brows were knitted with concern. She knew this was serious. Again, she wondered who he was and why she hadn't seen him at the new residents' introductions. As if he had read her mind, he said, "I'm going to be completely honest with you. I came to Kingsley to check something out. I didn't want a lot of attention given to me, so I asked for more privacy. So that is why you never saw me during the new residents' introductions."

"What are you checking out?"

"I'll get to that later. In the meantime, if I were you, I would eat your lunch in your apartment."

"Why?" Mary Jean asked again. She felt alarmed, thinking about the lunch she had just had in the dining room.

"I don't know anything for sure. I will share more with you when I learn more."

Did that sound reasonable? Could she trust him? She hardly knew him. But still, she was intrigued by him. He was like a magnet—his soul, his being, his intensity. They drew her in. Being this close to him, she found it was hard to breathe.

"I think I need to walk around. I'm finding it hard to breathe all of a sudden."

Mary Jean put her hand on her forehead. She felt hot, flushed. Mr. Weeks took her hand in his. It was warm. She stood up and gently withdrew her hand.

"I don't even know your first name." She stepped backward one step.

"It's Lewis," he said. He smiled and looked deeply into her eyes as he spoke his name.

Mary Jean felt faint.

"What did you say?" The look on her face mirrored her feelings inside.

"Lewis. Lewis Weeks. What's wrong, Mary Jean? Your face is turning pale."

Mary Jean turned and stared out toward the garden. It all felt so overwhelming. With the residents being whisked away, the hired help acting secretive, and now this mystery man with the same first name as her late husband.

"Look. I've got to go," said Lewis. "Please just eat your lunch in your apartment for now. I'll explain later. Okay?"

"All right. I will. Now I have to tell you something. Your first name is my late husband's name. It caught me by surprise."

"Well, that is a coincidence, isn't it?"

Lewis Weeks winked at her, stood, and walked out toward the garden. Mary Jean watched him go, feeling confused and elated at the same time. *My, today had been full of surprises.* The clouds were becoming darker, more menacing. A light rain was falling while the dead leaves on the ground whirled around, some forming wind tunnels and scattering up into the sky. The strange weather was mirroring the growing sense of unease and mystery at Kingsley. She quickly entered the facility and headed toward the bingo room. If she was lucky, she'd catch the last thirty minutes of the game.

4

The next morning, it rained hard. There was no going out in this downpour. Mary Jean made some coffee and sat in her easy chair looking out the sliding glass door as the rain pounded down on her balcony. At least she wouldn't have to water the flowers today.

The phone rang.

"Hello. This is Miss Harriet, the activities director. How are you, Mary Jean?"

"I'm doing well, thank you, Miss Harriet."

"I'm calling to let you know that the principal has okayed the idea. The school will send some children over with their teacher to help in the garden next summer. They plan to come over in a few weeks' time to introduce themselves. How does that sound?"

"That's wonderful, Miss Harriet. I will look forward to meeting them and hope for a bountiful garden next year."

"Thanks for the good idea, Mary Jean. We can use some of those fresh vegetables in the lunch meal. We really want to encourage the residents to eat more vegetables."

"Yes. I hear that helps us maintain good memory."

"Ahem . . . that's right, Mary Jean. We want what's best for our residents."

"Well, thank you for looking into that, Miss Harriet."

"No problem, we'll talk more later. Goodbye."

Mary Jean hung up. Something was not right. Miss Harriet seemed to hesitate when she mentioned that vegetables help with memory.

Mary Jean heard a scratching at her door. She got up and opened it to find a little black-and-white dog. He sat looking up at her, panting like he was very thirsty and in need of a drink. She looked both ways up and down the hall to see if she could spot his owner. No one was around. Everyone was holed up in their apartments. Well, where had this little guy come from? He had no collar. She found a small bowl and filled it with water and put it in front of him. He lapped it up in no time and looked at her for more. She refilled it, and he drank more. Then he trotted into her apartment.

"Now, wait a minute. You can't come in here."

He looked at her inquisitively and laid down. Mary Jean went to the phone and called the front desk.

"I've got a stray dog here that just walked into my apartment. It is a boy dog, short-haired, with black spots on a white body. And small, like a rat terrier. Do you know whose it is?"

"That doesn't ring a bell. We'll send for the Humane Society to come pick him up."

The little dog trotted up to Mary Jean and stared at her with big brown eyes. He licked her hand that was dangling at her side. He woofed softly as if pleading with her.

"Now, wait a minute. We can't send him off there. That place kills a lot of dogs."

"Well, unless you want to adopt him, I don't have any other ideas."

"Well, I'll think on it. I know I can't keep a dog. I'll ask around to see if anyone will take him."

After she hung up the phone, she thought about what to do. She could ask Shiela if her vet practice knew where to find stray dogs a good home, but she didn't want to bother her daughter. Then it dawned on her—Lewis. He looked like he was a dog person. Her late husband had loved dogs, to her dismay. She hated the hair they shed and how they drooled over everything. Plus, you had to walk them every day or they'd pee or poop on your rug. And she knew how hard that was to get out. Well, for now, she'd let the dog follow her around until she talked with Lewis.

Mary Jean had a whole day to kill. She needed to get ahold of Lewis but realized she did not have his phone number. He had always contacted her. Well, she'd have to remember to ask him for it the next time she saw him. On the agenda today, there was a group going to the public library, then to lunch and the grocery store. That would be fun, but now she had this dog to worry about. She peeked outside and saw that the sun was finally out. Rays of sunshine shone through the curtains, and the birds were busy at the feeder. She had thought it would rain all day by the severity of the morning gale. Mary Jean decided to take the dog out for a short walk, so she took some rope that had been tied around a potted palm in the hallway to keep it standing upright and used it as a leash.

The dog walked right alongside her, heeling like he'd been doing this his whole life. Mary Jean was relieved that her arm wouldn't be pulled out of its socket as it usually was with most dog owners. They walked down the stairs very slowly, the dog waiting for Mary Jean to take the steps one at a time. Once outside, Mary Jean was happy to have her heavier coat on as the air was quite brisk. She kept to the sidewalk that wended its way around the facility. When she arrived at the courtyard garden, there was Lewis, as if by magic, waiting for her by the tall oak tree.

"Now, isn't that a coincidence," said Mary Jean.

"Hello there. When did you acquire a dog?"

"Just this morning. He showed up at my front door, if you can believe it. Nobody knows where he came from. Kind of like you. So since you two have that in common, I thought you should have him."

"You know, I love dogs. What will happen to him if I don't take him?"

"He'll go to the Humane Society where they kill unwanted dogs—at least at this one."

"Well, we can't have that, can we? What's his name? Oh right, you don't know. All the better. I'll name him myself. Come here, little fellow. Let me look at you."

The little dog came over willingly and licked Lewis on his face. It was like they were long-lost buddies who had found each other. Mary Jean watched as the two of them played under the big, sprawling oak tree, with occasional drips of rain falling on their heads.

"We'll have to get him a proper collar and leash. And get him up to date on vaccinations. Let's finish our walk, and I can go register him at the front desk under my name. I think I'll call him Spot because of all the spots he has. Not real original, but what the heck, at least he has a name now."

With that, Lewis and Mary Jean continued their walk with Spot the rest of the way around the facility. They even added an extra block to get to another park nearby where Spot could run a little more off-leash. But Spot stuck to Lewis's side even when they took off the leash. It was uncanny how that dog seemed to know him. Weren't those two a mysterious pair . . .

"I need your phone number," said Mary Jean. "What if I need to call you? I may want you to join me for another walk or ask you to come to dinner with me some evening."

"How nice of you to think of me. But I do not have a phone. I will be in touch with you. I have my ways of knowing when you want to see me. I know that sounds crazy, but trust me. It's necessary."

"Okay, this is getting spooky again. What do you mean you don't have a phone? All the rooms have phones. And how can you possibly know when I might want to contact you?"

"Well, if I told you, you would think I am crazy. Let's just say I'm looking out for you and am working at solving some problems here. I also don't want to blow my cover. You will have to help me with that."

"There's the mysterious man talking again. What 'cover' are you talking about? I'm not sure what to think about you. At least you've taken the dog off my hands, and I know he will have a good home."

Mary Jean glanced at her watch. She wanted to make the trip to the public library, so she'd better get a move on. Her head was swimming with this most recent information that Lewis had just told her. It was crazy. But she felt this burning need to believe in him.

"Look, I have to go. Thanks for taking the dog, I mean, Spot. I guess you'll read my thoughts and know when we will meet again and just show up. See you later."

Ludicrous. Well, right now she did not have the time to take it too seriously. She had to run. As she approached the entrance of the facility, people were convening to board the bus that was parked out front. She joined the line and took a seat. Library, lunch, then grocery store. It would be a full day.

5

Mary Jean returned weary with arms full of groceries and books she'd checked out from the library. She had to buy plenty of extra groceries since she wasn't planning to eat lunches in the dining hall, as Lewis had advised. She hoped this would really be worthwhile. What could be wrong with the meals in the dining hall, and why just lunch? What about the other meals? She shook her head and settled in to putting food away and tidying up the place. She kicked her shoes off and got comfortable on the couch with a new book. She'd no sooner started the first page when there was a knock at her door. She sighed and contemplated not answering it. But then, she remembered Lewis's words and thought it might be him. How foolish, yet . . . . She slowly got up and opened the door.

It was Sarah, her house cleaner. "Hi, Mary Jean. I wanted to apologize for spilling tea on you yesterday."

"Oh, that's all right. No damage was done." Mary Jean wondered if Sarah were here just to give an apology.

Sarah continued, "I hope you are feeling all right.

I just wondered . . . if you felt strange or uncomfortable or unwell after lunch yesterday? Did you suffer any memory loss?"

Mary Jean froze. Did Sarah know something?

"No, I have felt okay. Why do you ask?"

Sarah looked down the hallway and hesitated for a few seconds. Then she said, "Umm, I think there is an illness going around. I think it could be the flu. Umm . . . I just thought I'd check with you. I've got to get going now. I have several rooms to clean and have to wait tables at dinner. I'm glad you are okay." With that, Sarah quickly took off down the hallway.

Mary Jean closed the door. Sarah's questions really worried her. She suddenly felt tired and laid down on the couch, her head swimming, trying to make sense of it all. Who was Lewis, really? What was he trying to find out? And how much did this house cleaner know about what was happening at Kingsley? She tossed and turned until she finally fell into a deep sleep.

Spot was barking and scratching at her door. In her dream, she opened the door and followed the dog down the hall, turned left, and went down another hallway past doors adorned with cards from loved ones, fake flowers, and ceramic dogs. It seemed like a maze. The lights dimmed to the point where she could hardly see. The dog would stop and wait for her as she stumbled about. She tried to keep the dog in her line of vision. It felt like she was walking through a fog. At one point, she had to use her hands to feel along the wall. Finally, she arrived at a door with nothing on it. The dog barked and the door opened. Inside was a neat and tidy apartment with what looked like family photos on the walls. She stepped in and took a close look at the photos and saw herself, her former husband, Lewis, and their daughters and son. She moved from picture to picture, and memories and visions of her former life swam into her mind. She looked up and noticed the bedroom door was ajar. Dreamlike, she floated like a ghost toward it and looked in. There was Lewis, her former husband, lying on the bed, still, and not moving. He was fully dressed in a dark suit with a red tie. The expression on his face was serene. She knelt down and stroked his face. He opened his eyes and smiled at her.

    She awoke with a jolt. That was it! Lewis Weeks was really her deceased husband. Yes, I know that doesn't sound right, she told herself. But she was sure of it. She felt it. He had come back for some reason. Did she believe in reincarnation? If so, didn't people come back as animals instead of people? He had always taken care of her, and now . . .

    Wait a minute. Was she losing her mind? Did she really believe that? She got up and went to the bathroom. She turned on the water and threw cold water on her face. It was just a dream. Just a dream . . . . Getting older was starting to make her think about what would happen to her when it was her time. Did she believe in Heaven? Would she see Lewis there? She had frankly never given it much thought until now.

    She decided to put her red Nike sneakers on, grabbed her coat, and headed down to the lobby. She was taking the stairs every time now rather than the elevator. Using the stairs had helped her hip pain. She noticed almost no one took the stairs in this building. Funny how we all just end up stiffer with age and stop doing all the activities we used to do, she thought. Even simple things like walking and taking the stairs. It's easy to stop when no one else does it, either.

Outside, the air was crisp. Red and yellow leaves covered the sidewalk. Mary Jean looked up at the sky and saw her familiar white clouds set against a cerulean-blue backdrop. She smelled the sweet scent of honeysuckle as she walked down the sidewalk. Her step bounced along more than usual. She sidestepped some wet leaves and was astonished at her quickness.

"They should clean these up or someone's going to slip and fall," she said out loud.

She thought of her son, her daughters. They had such busy lives. She was so fortunate that they often thought of her, taking her out to lunch or helping her with her finances. She seemed to be looking outward these days, feeling grateful for things she normally would have taken for granted.

She continued down the walkway until she could see the elementary school across the road. She'd never walked this far before but felt a fresh burst of energy as the wind blew in her face and mussed up her hair. The kids were all outside playing various games—games even she remembered playing when she was little, like hopscotch and dodgeball. There were squeals of laughter and a general buzz of activity coming from the schoolyard. She noticed a scrawny, little black-haired boy off to the side, sitting all by himself. He was watching the other kids, looking hopeful that someone might invite him to play. The boy looked up and noticed Mary Jean on the street. He waved, and, surprised, she waved back. Not many people ever waved at Mary Jean. But then, she guessed, she usually wasn't very quick to greet people she did not know. Mary Jean smiled and turned around to head back to the facility. It's too bad when kids are left out, she thought. Growing up is hard. Sometimes she felt left out herself when eating dinner at the dining hall. She felt she just didn't have any friends these days, but then again, she had always felt kind of alone at Kingsley, busy with her family with not much time for making friends anyway.

The school bell rang behind her, signaling the end of recess. She heard the sounds of doors slamming and frantic shouts from teachers. She wondered when they would meet with the children who were going to help with the garden. Would that little lone boy be one of them? She would like it if he was.

In the cars around them, adults were staring down at their phones as they waited for their kids to be dismissed from school. People were driving too fast, and one even honked at her as she stepped off onto a gravel path. A car stopped in the road to allow Mary Jean to cross.

Everyone is in such a hurry these days, she mused. No courtesy out there on the road.

Her thoughts went back to her dream. What did it mean? Some people believed that dreams were a way for them to work through their problems or inspire their futures. Maybe she just missed Lewis so much and this was a way for her to process her grief. Good grief, indeed! It had been ten years since he'd died, for Pete's sake. But still . . .

She walked into the retirement home, mumbling about the leaves on the sidewalk and not saying hello to the lady working at the front desk. She slowly climbed the stairs one at a time and noticed Charlotte coming her way.

"HI, MARY JEAN. I SEE YOU ARE TAKING THE STAIRS THESE DAYS. GOOD FOR YOU!"

Charlotte was hard of hearing and often talked

too loudly. Several residents looked up from what they were doing to stare at her.

"Oh, I thought I'd give it a try since my hip pain and bunion have been getting better. I think it's the walking that is helping it."

"WALKING HELPS ME, TOO," Charlotte yelled.

It was getting close to dinnertime, so Mary Jean hurried into her room to get ready. Perhaps she'd sit at a different table and meet new people. Maybe the conversation would be more stimulating for once.

6

The days seemed to pass by quickly. September was over and they were already into mid-October. The days were starting to get shorter. Mary Jean could no longer go out in the evening after dinner for a short stroll. She missed those after-dinner walks with Lewis, which they had been taking regularly. She was getting stronger and wanted to keep looking for opportunities to challenge herself outside her comfort zone.

That morning, the sun streamed into her living room, and the day looked promising. Today, she thought she'd join the group outing to the coast on the bus that left at 9 a.m. Some children from the school were also going to go, and they were all to meet and have lunch together at a beach hotel. Now, how had this come about? We've never done anything like this before, thought Mary Jean.

She packed a bag with an extra sweater and a windbreaker. You never know how cold it is going to be on the coast, she thought, especially in October. An idea came to her. She walked into the bedroom and opened her top desk drawer and removed a new digital camera she had received from her middle daughter, Nora, for her birthday a couple of years ago. It was still in its box. She hadn't even opened it. What a silly gift this was, she had thought back then. Why would I need a camera? Now she carefully opened the box and took it out. She placed it in her bag, as well as a water bottle.

Mary Jean glanced at the clock on the living room wall and knew she had to hurry to make the bus downstairs in front of the lobby. She closed the door and walked down the hallway. She decided to take the elevator this time since she had such a load. When the doors opened, there stood Lewis! What a shock that was. He was the only one in the elevator, so when the doors closed, he took her hand and squeezed it.

"Have a wonderful time on the coast," he said. "I'll see you when you get back."

"Why aren't you going?

"I have work to do."

"You truly are the mystery man, aren't you?"

"Well, I make it a habit to never tell anyone I care about what I'm really up to as it might scare them."

"Well, now you are really scaring me."

"Please don't worry. Just have a good time, and remember: things all work out for the best."

With that, the doors opened and Mary Jean stepped out with her bag packed with provisions. She joined the line to get on the bus. She looked over her shoulder and saw Lewis watching her.

The residents were all decked out in their beach clothes, which consisted of long light-colored pants, long-sleeve tops to keep the sun off their papery arms, white socks and SAS shoes, floppy white hats, and bags full of sweaters, jackets, or windbreakers to keep the cold at bay. Most sported the fit-over sunglasses that wrap around over regular glasses. Some residents needed help climbing up into the bus. Many who were already seated were quietly looking out the windows. Others had walkers and wheelchairs, which were packed in a special place beneath the bus. Mary Jean was proud of herself. She hadn't needed to use a walker since that first walk with Lewis.

Their journey was uneventful. There were many stops along the way to use the restroom. Mary Jean thought about all the trips her family used to take to their beach house when her children were grown. She and Lewis would meet one of the kids there with their children, and they would all stay together in that tiny two-bedroom house. Dinners would be simple: spaghetti with meatballs and a salad. They might have apple pie and ice cream for dessert, her signature dish. They'd all walk down to the beach in the evening after dinner, the little ones scampering ahead to play in the sand or chase the waves as they came in. So much work, though, maintaining that house. They eventually had to sell it. The house was long gone, but the memories hadn't faded, thank goodness.

The bus sped along at a pretty good clip, passing farmland and making its way through the coastal mountain forests. They were headed to Cannon Beach and a small hotel that they had reserved for the day that opened on to the beachfront. The air was still heavy with fog as they got closer to the beach, as it often was in the mornings. The bus pulled up to the hotel, and residents woke up from their naps and busied themselves with collecting their things. It took such a long time, it seemed, to unload everyone.

"Mary Jean, will you please move your bag so I can make my way down through the aisle?" said Claire, who was standing behind her and waiting patiently as Mary Jean scooted her bag out of the way.

Mary Jean watched as several people passed her and made their way off the bus. Finally, it was her turn to get off. She carefully stepped down with the help of the driver and headed to the hotel lobby.

The lobby was simple. It was painted blue with white trim. The floor was a gray linoleum. There were some fake flowers at the lobby desk and a painting of a lighthouse on the wall. The room was a decent size for a hotel lobby, and the residents queued up slowly with walkers or on their own. A middle-aged lady with blond hair and brunette streaks smiled at Mary Jean as she approached the desk. They had been asked to check in before going anywhere. The lady wore a tight, low-cut white T-shirt and a flowing purple cotton skirt. She wore silver hoop earrings and a beaded stone necklace, as well as two turquoise rings, one on each hand. She's too old to be wearing that outfit, thought Mary Jean.

"Write your name down here, honey."

Why did some people have to call her honey? Mary Jean didn't smile as she wrote her name down on the list.

She walked outside and placed her bag down on a chair. The ocean breeze felt good on her skin, and she breathed in the moist air and sighed. She noticed that all the residents who had checked in were sitting down on the chairs provided on the patio. The space was cemented and had nine tables with chairs neatly pushed in around them. The tables were covered with lime-green plastic tablecloths that were held down by river rocks.

"Lunch in a half hour," mumbled Claire, who was sitting next to her.

"How do you know that?" said Mary Jean.

"There's a sign on the lobby desk that says lunch at 11:30 a.m.," said Claire.

Mary Jean thought, Well, I guess some of us are more observant than others.

The waves pounded the shore and the clouds filled the sky. It was quite a bit cooler here. She reached for her sweater and put it on. Well, I ought to get up and walk along the beach, she thought. I didn't come here just to sit in a chair. So she walked out on the gravel path that led to the beach with her camera. She turned around and noticed that no one was joining her. She searched the patio for Charlotte, her neighbor friend whom she'd often see walking around the building. Surely, she would walk to the beach. Not finding her anywhere, she reluctantly turned toward the beach to get a little exercise. She looked down and saw broken sea anemones by her feet, as well as a partial starfish. There were lots of empty clam and oyster shells. She stopped to take in the long sweep of the beachfront, the large rocks that jutted up out of the green-blue water. Waves crashed against them, sending up white foam around the rocks.

"Now is as good a time as any for a photo shoot," she said to herself. She took several photos of the landscape, then put her camera back in her bag. She looked down and saw a very red rock. She began to stoop over to try and pick it up when a little boy shot in front of her and grabbed it.

"Here, let me get this for you!" he shouted over the sound of the waves crashing on the beach. The boy was barefoot, had black hair, was thin, and wore a red T-shirt and denim shorts. His smile revealed a couple of missing front teeth and a face that had seen a lot of sun lately. Mary Jean looked more closely and realized she knew this boy. He had been the one standing by himself on the playground at the elementary school. Other children from the school were playing on the beach with residents from the home.

"I recognize you. You waved at me when I was walking past your playground the other day. Do you remember?"

"Yes, I saw you walking. You were by yourself. Like me. I was hoping someone would pick me to play dodgeball. But no one did."

"Well, I'm sorry about that. Let's see if we can find any shells that are worthy of taking back as souvenirs."

They walked into the wind, stopping every now and again to sift through all the debris on the beach for a shiny shell or interesting rock.

"What's your name?" asked Mary Jean.

"Derek," said the little boy.

"I used to know a boy named Derek when I was in elementary school. He used to throw rocks at us and tease us and I was always telling the teachers on him and he was put in detention and then we didn't see him for a long time and I guess he got expelled . . . I really don't know, maybe his family moved away or maybe he was homeless. I remember another boy called Rufus. Isn't that a funny name, Rufus? Well, he . . ."

"You need to stop talking."

"What?"

"Ask me another question, please?"

"Well, okay. What grade are you in?"

"I'm in third grade. Do you like the beach?"

"Oh, I love the beach. We used to come here all the time when my husband was still alive. He loved the beach, too, and we would have our kids and grandkids over and make dinner then walk down to the beach in the evening and watch the sun go down . . ."

Derek looked at her with wide eyes and gulped once.

"What's wrong, Derek?"

"I can't keep track of what you're saying. You talk fast and a lot."

"What?"

"Can you ask me something again?"

Mary Jean looked at Derek. She took a breath and let it out slowly. Why was she always so nervous when she was talking? This sure was an uppity little boy. Who did he think he was? She'd play along.

"What's your favorite color?"

"Red," said Derek. "And yours?"

"Blue, but look here, I'm wearing my mystery red shoes today. Your favorite color."

"Why do you say 'mystery shoes?'" Derek looked down at her shoes.

"Because I don't know who gave them to me, for one. And two, a mystery man showed up at my door also wearing red Nike shoes."

He smiled and they continued to walk down the beach, glancing down every now and again for treasures. Derek talked about his parents and his younger sister, their trips to the beach, and how he hated being the oldest.

"I'm the one who always gets in trouble, and it's never my fault."

Yes, that was what her oldest son would always say, too. He often teased his sisters incessantly and then swore it was never his fault when they came crying to Mary Jean. That time seemed so far away.

When it was time for lunch, Mary Jean and Derek

turned around and headed back to the hotel. When they arrived, there were about fifteen other children paired up with residents at the tables. Derek followed Mary Jean and sat down at the table nearest the buffet spread, which was laden with salads of all kinds, as well as two different types of desserts. There were also two kinds of soups and some crackers on a plate with cheese. Derek was hungry and scooted up to the line as soon as their table was signaled to go help themselves. Many residents needed help, so it took some time getting food for everyone. When they were all seated, a short prayer was said and they all began to eat.

7

The bus pulled up around 5 p.m. Soon it would be suppertime. Mary Jean was tired after the walking, talking with Derek, and the long ride home. What a pleasant day it had been, though. It was so refreshing to talk to a youngster. He was smart as a whip and helpful, too. I guess there is hope for the younger generation after all, she thought. She said hello to the lady at the desk and headed up the stairs to her apartment. When she got to her door, she noticed it was ajar.

That's odd, thought Mary Jean. The house cleaners should be done by now. When she opened the door, she heard the bedroom door close with a thump. Who could that be?

She called out, "Who is that?" No one answered. She put her bag down on the floor and walked slowly toward the door. No sound could be heard except for her own labored breathing as she slowly turned the handle on the door . . .

She pushed the door open. There from under the bed poked out the head of the little black-and-white dog, Spot.

"Well, what are you doing in here? You sure gave me a start!"

She coaxed the dog out from under the bed, and he willingly followed her to the living room. How the heck had he got in here? Another mystery unfolding right here in her apartment.... She tied a thin, long scarf of hers around Spot's collar as a leash. The dog took the scarf in his mouth and tried to play tug of war with her.

"Now, stop that. You'll ruin my scarf! We are going to have to find Lewis and get you back home." She walked out the door and down the hall with the little dog at her side. They passed several residents heading to the dining hall. Most were stooped over and shuffling.

"Are people getting older or am I just in better shape than most?" she said to herself. She turned the corner and practically ran smack into Lewis.

"Oh, I was looking all over for him," said Lewis.

"How did he get into my apartment?" asked Mary Jean.

"He was in your apartment?" replied Lewis.

"Yes. He was under my bed."

Lewis looked perplexed and took Spot from Mary Jean. He squatted down and looked in the rat terrier's eyes as if the dog could tell him what had happened. The dog whined and licked his cheek. Lewis stood up.

"I think I know how this happened."

"What are you talking about?" said Mary Jean.

"This will all become clearer in time," said Lewis. He quickly turned and walked away toward his apartment, tugging the dog after him. Mary Jean shrugged her shoulders and headed toward the dining hall. Then, she remembered that she had meant to ask Lewis what number his apartment was. She turned and headed back in the direction he had gone, hoping to follow him. When she turned the corner, he was gone. The row of doors along the hallway were closed. She had not heard the sound of a door opening or closing.

Disappeared into thin air, thought Mary Jean. Why would someone steal Lewis's dog and put him in my apartment? There were many unanswered questions yet to be resolved. Maybe Spot had escaped on purpose and was trying to tell her something. After all, hadn't he been in her dream leading her to her husband, Lewis? She pondered this thought for a while as she turned and walked to the dining hall for supper.

She chose a table in front of the window that looked down into the gardens, joining Mr. Leffel and his wife. She hadn't sat with them in quite some time. Maybe they were better conversationalists than others.

"How was the beach, Mary Jean?" asked Mr. Leffel.

"It was very pleasant. We had the elementary school kids there with us. I walked on the beach with a dark-haired boy named Derek. He's nine years old and quite smart. He told me all about his family."

She stopped there, remembering the boy's remarks when they were on the beach. She took several deep breaths and felt herself start to relax. There, that was better. She paused, waiting for Mr. Leffel to respond.

"What a jolly good idea to invite the youngsters from the school to participate with the elders. I understand they are also going to help us with a garden project this summer," he said.

"Yes. Miss Harriet, the activities director, said they plan on coming to meet with us tomorrow so we can talk about what we'd like to do together. Find out what we both like to plant."

"Well, I think I'd choose some fresh greens, like kale and spring lettuce. Nothing's better than fresh greens from the garden in your salad. It would be quite an improvement to what we are served here."

As if on cue, the servers brought out a green salad. The wilted greens looked pathetic alongside the canned beet, which looked too red to be real.

"Yes, fresh greens would be something to look forward to," said Mary Jean as she took a bite of the salad.

Next came the chicken stew on egg noodles, overcooked peas, and a little paper cup of applesauce on the side.

"I remember when we made our own homemade applesauce from the apples on our tree," said Mary Jean. "How sweet the apples tasted!"

She remembered Lewis tending his tomatoes and other vegetables in their backyard. She would can all the tomatoes and use the sauce she made throughout the winter, too. Abby, her oldest daughter, did that now. Luckily, she always shared whatever she canned with the rest of the family.

When the dessert came, Mary Jean asked if Mrs. Leffel had enjoyed gardening in her early years. She said she had, that she loved making rhubarb pies and soups from the endless winter squash they harvested every fall. She talked about the different dishes she used to love to make, the home-cooked meals. Do all of us continue to live in the past, rich in memories, full of the senses of smell, of taste, and of toiling hard outside? Mary Jean wondered. She thought of the food she missed, the pleasures of being outside, the experiences of family and loved ones.

Mary Jean started on her dessert. She glanced out of the window down at the garden and noticed that there were two men there, digging. What were they doing? It was the wrong time of year to be doing anything in the garden. They were partially obscured by a large bush, so she could not make out what was happening. Her suspicion grew.

"Do you see those men down in the garden? What do you think they are doing?" said Mary Jean.

"Perhaps they are working on the drainage ditch," said Mr. Leffel. "I heard there was a problem with water accumulating near the fountain."

"Oh?" said Mary Jean. My mind must be overactive, she thought to herself. Why do I always think morbid thoughts?

She excused herself, thanked the Leffels for a good conversation, and left hurriedly. She walked down the stairs slowly and headed for the garden. She had to check this out for herself. She stepped out into the cold air and semidarkness. There were two tall lamps that lit up the gravel path toward the fountain. The gravel crunched under her feet and the bats swooped randomly through the air, catching insects in the dark. The night was calm. No stars were out, and the clouds covered the moon, making it darker than usual. She could hear rustling and some digging sounds around the corner behind the big bush that she had seen from the upstairs dining hall. As she rounded the corner, two men were dusting off their hands and gathering their shovels up, getting ready to leave. Mary Jean startled them as she stepped around the bush on the path.

"Whoa!" said the taller of the two men. There was

a large mound of dirt next to the fountain alongside the path. Both men appeared surprised to see Mary Jean.

The taller man had on a brown Carhartt coat and denim jeans. His tousled brown hair was long over his ears, and he wore black-rimmed glasses. He was young, in his mid twenties.

The other man grunted loudly as he picked up the shovels. He was older, perhaps mid-thirties, with short blond hair and a white baseball hat.

"What are you doing out here?" he said angrily.

Mary Jean said, "I thought I'd step out for some fresh air after supper." She knew she had a worried look on her face.

"Well, you'd better get inside. It's cold out here," said the younger one. They started to walk away.

Mary Jean asked, "What were you doing out here?"

"Why do you ask?" the tall one replied.

"I was just curious," she said.

"Well, we are just fixing a drain line to the fountain. Nothing for you to worry about."

They stood staring at her, waiting for her to leave. She reluctantly turned around and headed back to the building. She could feel their eyes boring into her back. She let herself into the building and looked out again at the garden. They were gone. She stayed there for a full ten minutes before she let herself back out onto the path that led to the fountain. She had to see for herself. She stepped carefully along the path and turned the corner again around the large bush. She could tell that the fresh mound of dirt did not look like a line that had been dug up to the fountain. It was only about two feet long. Interesting . . .

The next morning, Mary Jean headed to breakfast in the dining hall and sat at the same spot as she had the night before. She gazed out at the fountain. Nothing spectacular or out of place. Maybe a walk down there again was in order. As soon as she received her coffee, Lewis showed up and sat at her table.

"Good morning," he said.

"Good morning. I am glad you are here. What are your plans today?"

"I plan to go to the resident library to do some research. Would you care to come with me?" he asked.

"I'd love to, but I am meeting with the school children this morning. They are coming to talk with us about next summer's garden plans. Are you sure you want to miss that?"

"I'd like to, but I have to find out some information very soon. It's very important."

"What could be so important for an old man in a retirement center?" Mary Jean said jokingly.

"I plan on filling you in soon."

Their breakfast arrived, and he changed the topic to her beach excursion. He listened with rapt attention, and his twinkling blue eyes showed that he was sharing in her adventure as if he had actually been there with her. He laughed when she explained how Derek interrupted her long diatribes and got her to ask him more questions. She had learned to take deep breaths before she spoke. She knew this helped her to relax, and when she was relaxed, she realized that she paused more and would let the other person speak.

"What a smart young lad this Derek is," remarked Lewis. "I am glad you and he shared an adventure together. You are making new memories and have something new and exciting to talk about."

Yes, that was it. She had struck out and done something new that made her life and *herself* more exciting. I need to keep challenging myself even if it does seem harder, she thought. It's easy to say I am too old or too stiff or in too much pain to do something different or new. But it helps to have people support me. She was glad Lewis was here, and she hoped that she would see Derek again at the garden meeting.

They finished their breakfast and walked downstairs. Lewis said goodbye, and she turned to go out to the garden for a walk. She was intercepted by Mrs. Lemon, the manager of Kingsley Retirement Home for Seniors.

"Well hello, Mary Jean. Where are you headed this fine morning?" she said.

"I am stepping out to make my rounds around the facility for my morning walk. Then I am going to the meeting with the school children at ten," said Mary Jean.

"I heard you were out in the garden last night. Please steer clear of the fountain area. They are doing work on the drainage ditch to the fountain and I don't want anyone getting hurt until they are done. We are cementing the area around the fountain, and until that is done, that area is off limits. We will be putting up barriers so people know to stay away."

"Thank you for that information, Mrs. Lemon. I will be sure to avoid it on my walk."

"Have a good day, Mary Jean." And Mrs. Lemon walked toward the kitchen at a brisk pace.

Mary Jean walked outside and looked both ways to make sure no one was watching her. She then turned to the right and headed around the building on the path toward the back and the inner courtyard and garden. The sky was dark, and the wind picked up. Mounds of wet green fir needles covered the path.

As she made her way to the back, she noticed the two men she had seen earlier. They were heading out of the garden. She quickly put her hood on and, with her head down, walked swiftly along the path past them. They did not recognize her. Soon, she arrived at the courtyard. The mound was flattened and barriers had been put up, slightly obscuring the site. She pushed past them and looked more closely at the mound. With great effort, she kneeled down and pushed the soil around with her hand. Luckily, the ground was soft so it did not hurt her knees. As she dug down with her fingers, she felt a metal lid. Before she could go further, she heard a sound further down the path. She quickly pushed the dirt back on the mound, patted it down, and left.

As she walked back the other way, she wondered what was in the metal box, if that was what it was. She hurried to the meeting room to meet the children and their teacher.

8

The eighteen third graders were seated in front of the room. Their teacher, Mrs. Lacy, was a tall woman of about thirty with long blond hair swept up away from her face and clipped at the back of her head. She wore modern black glasses and a blue flowered blouse that was open at the neck. She had on tan slacks and low heels. Mrs. Lacy kept nervously glancing at her watch as Mary Jean walked in and took a seat. There were only about ten residents in the room. More than I expected, thought Mary Jean. They probably have nothing better to do; that's why they're here.

Miss Harriet, the activities director, cleared her throat. "It looks like this is it. Let me introduce Mrs. Lacy and her third grade class from Lafayette Elementary School. They have come to talk about the garden project for this summer. Mrs. Lacy, I'll let you tell us what the project is all about." She took a seat in the front row.

"Thank you for coming today to greet the kids and learn more about the garden project. This is a joint venture to design and plant a vegetable garden next year during the spring. At first, we thought about planting the garden in Kingsley Retirement Home's courtyard, but the space is too small for a group of kids and residents, and so we have decided to relocate the site to a nearby public park. The park has donated a site big enough for a community garden so that there will be room for all." She paused, then continued. "I understand many of you had gardens for much of your lives. I understand, though, that the years have made it challenging for many of you to tend a garden yourselves. Perhaps this is where the children could help. This experience would be priceless for the children. Together, we could produce fresh vegetables and fruits to supplement our menus both in the school and in the retirement home. I suggest we meet one more time to plan and design the garden next spring, and then once a week to tend it over the summer. We already have donations of seeds and small plants from local nurseries. How many of you would be willing to participate in this project?"

Mary Jean raised her hand, and slowly, others also raised theirs. About three-quarters of the hands were raised. Surprising, thought Mary Jean.

"The more volunteers we have, the easier it will be. Please spread the word and bring your friends to the next meeting." Next, she asked each child to stand and state their name and what they wanted to plant. Several of the residents smiled, and Mary Jean could see their eyes light up, as if they were remembering the times when they had been that age and what they had done in their gardens or on their farms as children. Mary Jean finally spied Derek among the children, the dark-haired boy she had walked with on the beach.

Afterward, the cafeteria staff brought in cookies

and milk for the children and residents. The children went back for seconds. Mary Jean walked up to Derek.

"Miss Mary Jean, you are here! I saw you raise your hand to say you wanted to help plant the garden. I want to plant tomatoes. What do you want to plant?"

Together, they talked about what they would plant and how soon it would take to grow and eat. By the time they finished off the cookies on their plates, it was time for the children to go back to school.

"I'll see you at the next meeting when we choose our seeds, Miss Mary Jean," he said and smiled with an impish grin before running to catch up with his classmates down the hall. Mary Jean smiled and sighed.

Like a breath of fresh air, these young faces are, she thought. She looked around the room and noticed lots of talk among the residents in the room. They had looks of anticipation on their faces. Of that feeling that there was something to look forward to.

Something is often missing in our daily lives here, she thought.

Mary Jean decided to get some fresh air, something she had started doing at least twice a day. She drew her coat around her and stepped outside. The sun was shining through gray clouds. It was cool but not cold.

It was warm for October. She saw Larry, the cook, hurrying around the corner toward where the cars were parked.

"That man always looks like he is afraid of the horrors that may be lurking in the shadows," she muttered to herself. "He's always looking over his shoulder like someone is following him. Or maybe it's the actions of a guilty man . . . hmmm."

He glanced back at her as he turned the corner

and was out of sight. Mary Jean headed around the building, walking slowly. Her hip was hurting more than usual today. Her motto these days, though, was "keep moving," and the pain usually resolved itself.

As she made her way toward the entry of the retirement home and through the glass door, she saw Lewis walking down the stairs. Nice timing. He greeted her.

"Hi, Mary Jean. Just the lady I was hoping to see. Have you been staying away from the lunches in the dining hall?"

"Yes, I am stocked up for a couple of weeks of lunches. I've been cooking some really good food for once. It's been a long time since I did that for myself."

"That makes me feel much more comfortable. Come with me. I want to show you something."

He took her by the arm and steered her back toward the dining hall. Since it was an odd hour, no one was in the kitchen. Lewis looked up and down the room and, finding no one around, entered the kitchen with Mary Jean in tow. They maneuvered carefully through the kitchen. He led her to the pantry to where the spices were stored. On the shelves was a little tin with the word mints on it. He opened it swiftly and took out a little square package of powder.

"What are you doing?" said Mary Jean.

He deftly slipped it into his pocket, put the lid back on, and steered Mary Jean out of the pantry.

"Let's head to your room," said Lewis.

There were a few residents having tea in the dining room. A couple talked quietly between themselves and did not look up as Lewis and Mary Jean emerged from the kitchen. A waltz was playing in the background through the speakers. House cleaners were out cleaning the apartments with their carts in the hallways. Mary Jean wondered if they would run into Mrs. Lemon, the manager, or Larry, the cook. Finally, the pair arrived at Mary Jean's apartment. She unlocked the door and they scurried in, hoping they had not been noticed. They seated themselves on her blue couch with a crocheted orange throw laid over the back and two cushions in the shape of quilted cats—one a tabby and the other a calico with orange, black, and white colors, a gift from one of her daughters.

"Now are you going to tell me what you've got in your pocket?"

"I'm pretty sure it's the drug they call Special K, also known as ketamine. It's one of those date-rape drugs."

"What? Why is this drug in the kitchen? And how in the world did you know where it was hidden?"

"I have my sources. And one of them is a new one who has a good nose."

"What? You mean Spot?"

"The very one." Lewis smiled and shook his head. "I never would've found it without him. In his previous life, he must have been a sniffer dog. I was snooping in the kitchen one afternoon when everyone seemed to be asleep, and he led me to the pantry. I picked him up and he got very excited around the third shelf up."

Mary Jean shifted on the couch. What did all this mean?

"What are they doing with that drug?"

"It is a dissociative general anesthetic used as a horse tranquilizer. It has hypnotic, stimulant, and hallucinogenic properties. It's very fast acting and can cause unconsciousness within thirty minutes, about the time most of us finish our lunch. It can cause dizziness, dissociation, impaired motor skills, and potentially fatal respiratory failure. People who are given this drug can feel detached from their body and surroundings, a state referred to as conscious sedation. You may be aware of what's happening to you but unable to move or talk. This drug can also produce a one-to-two-hour period of amnesia. It's especially dangerous when mixed with alcohol or other drugs. It can be slipped into a beverage without a person's knowledge, such as water, tea, coffee, or other drinks served here in the cafeteria. It could even be put into a resident's Jell-O." Mary Jean thought about the tea she had drunk a while back when she last had lunch in the dining room.

Mary Jean felt very violated. Why would anyone want to do such a thing?

"So, are you saying what I think you are saying? That the residents I've been seeing wheeled into Memory Care are disabled because of a drug?"

"Yes, I'm afraid so. Kingsley Retirement Home has been losing money hand over fist this whole past year. I think someone is fooling with the books and funneling the money out to an offshore account. They need more money, so they are drugging residents and making it look like they need the more expensive Memory Care facilities so they can cover themselves. Memory Care patients are charged quite a bit more for their specialized care. This way, the retirement home can make much more money."

"That is a despicable thing to do to helpless elders," Mary Jean said. Money sure corrupts people, she thought. "Why do you suspect they only put the drug in the lunch food?"

Lewis smiled. "I've been researching Kingsley's

financial situation for a while. I knew they were in the hole a long time ago and were getting desperate to save their business. I had my suspicions about the cooks drugging the food, but I could never prove it. Luckily, you introduced me to Spot. You may not have known that I've been going to the dining hall with Spot. He whines when he can smell it in the food. I've discreetly let him smell the Jell-O, beverages, and other food items at every meal and narrowed it down to various lunch items, confirming my theory. Almost everyone comes to lunch, but often they will skip breakfast. Targeting one meal is less conspicuous."

"So, what are we going to do about this? Shall we contact the police?"

"No, not yet. We may scare the true culprit away. I want to do a little more investigating and get to the bottom of this. The important thing now is that you are safe eating lunch in your apartment. I want to protect the other residents as well, but I have to go about this carefully or we both could be exposed."

"I hope you know what you are doing." She looked carefully at Lewis. He looked as if he hadn't slept for several days. But he had a determined look on his face. Her frown softened and she took hold of his hand.

"Thank you for alerting me to this. We must do something very soon to protect the others." He smiled and squeezed her hand.

"Oh, I have something to tell you," she added. "I saw some men digging down in the garden by the fountain. When they left, I went down to investigate and found what I think is a metal box buried down there. We need to check it out. It could be related to the ketamine scandal."

"Yes, it could. I will see what I can find out."

Lewis got up and said a hurried goodbye. Mary Jean looked longingly after him as he made his way down the hallway. His broad shoulders and long gait were just like Lewis's, her late husband.

As she shut the door behind him, memories flooded her mind. The grief was still there. She remembered walking up to the open casket of her husband and thinking how peaceful he looked, as if he were still sleeping on the living room couch with the cat curled up next to him. That was where he had spent his last moments of life, right there on the couch. That day, he had been wearing a green L. L. Bean shirt and his brown cotton work pants. She remembered trying to wake him, calling, "Lewis, Lewis, can't you hear me? Wake up, wake up!" When the ambulance came to take his body away, she couldn't believe he was leaving her. Tears ran down her cheeks. The pain was as if someone had ripped her arm off her body. How would she manage, all alone . . . ?

Mary Jean walked to the kitchen to make some tea. She decided she would eat dinner in her apartment tonight. She didn't feel like being around anyone else. She got out some tomato soup and heated it up. "Maybe just a few crackers and cheese with it, and I'll have some leftover salad."

Mystery Lewis. Who was he? Mary Jean was becoming convinced he was her husband from a different realm.

9

The next morning, Mary Jean awoke with a headache. She slowly got out of bed, went into the bathroom, and drank some water from the small Dixie cup on the counter. That was better. Maybe she was just dehydrated. She could hear the house cleaners vacuuming next door and hurriedly walked into the kitchen to see what time it was. Nine o'clock! How had she slept in so late? She got dressed and made herself some instant oatmeal and poured a small glass of cranberry juice.

There was a knock at the door. Mary Jean finished up the last of her breakfast and put the dishes in the sink. She wiped her mouth and quickly checked her reflection in the mirror in the hallway. She saw an old woman looking back at her. "How did I get so old?"she said to herself.

She opened the door to reveal Sarah, the black-haired house cleaner.

"May I clean your apartment now?" she asked.

"Well, I guess so," said Mary Jean, reluctantly glancing back at the disarray of her living room. "I'll just grab my book and be out of your way."

"Before you go, I was wondering if you've eaten

lunch in the dining hall lately?" asked Sarah. "I haven't seen you around."

"No. I've decided I enjoy a little more cooking in my life, and lunches are easy to make."

"Well, I would continue to eat lunch in your apartment, if I were you," said Sarah. "The menu doesn't seem too interesting, anyway." I think she must know about this, thought Mary Jean. I wonder if she is warning me?

Mary Jean walked into the living room and straightened the pillows on the couch, then grabbed her book from the coffee table. Sarah let herself in, dragging her vacuum cleaner behind her, leaving her cleaning cart in the doorway.

"Shouldn't be long," murmured Sarah as Mary Jean slipped out the door around the cart.

How would Sarah know about the lunches? Mary Jean thought as she headed down to the resident library. She recalled her last encounter with Sarah. Sarah wouldn't have warned me if she was in on it, Mary Jean concluded. I should tell Lewis about her.

Some of the residents were milling about the hallway, making their way to various activities, but there weren't many of them around. Out of the corner of her eye, Mary Jean noticed two residents were being wheeled down the hall, looking out of sorts.

There goes more of them, she thought. No wonder there aren't very many people walking around; they're all being taken to the Memory Care Unit. Lewis had better hurry up and figure out what's going on so we can save these poor people. Half the residents, it seemed, didn't have families advocating for them. Most were lucky to have visitors once every few months. Anything could happen within these walls, and no one would ever know. A relative might just show up one day to visit and be told their loved one had slipped downhill and was now residing in the Memory Care Unit; nothing they could do about it.

Mary Jean let herself into the library and chose a green chair next to the window to sit and read her book. Only one other person was in the library. She recognized the woman and called out to her.

"Hi, Mable. How are you?"

"I'm doing all right, Mary Jean. What are you reading today?" she asked.

"I'm reading a book by Barbara Kingsolver. It's about food. I think I'd rather read a good mystery instead. How about you? What are you reading?"

"Oh, it's just another book of short stories my daughter brought by. I like that I don't have to stick with one long story. I can finish one before my eyes give out."

"I know what you mean," said Mary Jean as she wiped her eyes with a tissue. Her eyes had been bothering her lately, and she was having more trouble reading.

Something was happening outside in the garden below that caught Mary Jean's attention. She looked past the elm trees and onto the grass way and saw a little black-and-white dog. It was Spot! He was running around like a Tasmanian devil with his nose to the ground. Lewis was nowhere to be seen—again. The sky threatened rain and the wind was blowing. The boughs of the trees swayed slowly as the wind lifted them to and fro, as if to a lullaby.

Mary Jean gathered her things and headed back to her apartment for a sweater. She wanted to see if Spot was in trouble and where the heck Lewis was. She murmured goodbye to Mable and walked quickly down to her apartment. When she arrived, she found the door locked and the cleaning cart was abandoned in the hallway. What was this? She found her key and inserted it unsteadily into the lock.

As the door swung open, Mary Jean saw Sarah on the floor, unconscious. She knelt down and felt for a pulse. There wasn't one; Sarah was dead. Frantically, Mary Jean called the front desk and told the operator what she had found. Almost immediately, a group of people filed into her small apartment. Men picked up the house cleaner and put her on a rolling cart. They headed out the door while the manager remained behind to question Mary Jean as to what had happened. She told her what she knew and how she had just stopped by her apartment to pick up a sweater so she could go outside when she found the house cleaner on the floor. It was all quite shocking. Everyone was in and out of the apartment before she knew it. Strangely, it seemed like they hadn't needed any sort of prolonged investigation. Thoughts whirled about Mary Jean's head, and she was so confused that she couldn't figure out what had happened—and why it had happened—at all.

Mary Jean composed herself and remembered why she had come to her apartment in the first place. She grabbed a sweater and headed down the stairs in search for Spot—and hopefully Lewis. Spot was nowhere to be seen. She walked quickly across the grass way, calling his name.

"Spot! Spot! Come here!" yelled Mary Jean as she anxiously scanned the field, paying attention to areas around the bushes and trees where dogs liked to mark their territory.

Out of the corner of her eye, Mary Jean saw a man rounding the building toward the inside courtyard where the garden was. She quickened her pace and was on a mission to follow that man. She watched her step as she crossed the parking lot and stepped up onto the sidewalk. It was wet from the rain that day, and she felt a little wobbly walking so fast. When she rounded the corner, there was Lewis and Spot. They were standing at the freshly dug area where Mary Jean had discovered the metal box. Spot was digging and Lewis seemed to be working on something. Mary Jean approached them.

"Well, what do we have here?" Before Mary Jean could speak, the manager, Mrs. Lemon, walked up toward them on the gravel walkway. Lewis stood back.

"Oh, my dog must have found a bone or something he thinks would be good to eat." Lewis backed away and seemed to be holding something in his hand behind his back. Mrs. Lemon didn't seem to notice. She seemed to only be addressing Mary Jean.

"You know, dogs must be kept on their leashes at all times while on the grounds."

"Oh yes, I will put him on his leash right away." Lewis hesitated. Mrs. Lemon continued to look at Mary Jean as if she had not heard Lewis speak. Mary Jean grabbed the leash from his hand and snapped it onto Spot's collar.

Mrs. Lemon stood there, staring at her for some time. Finally satisfied, she said, "It's getting cold out here. You ought to go in."

With that, she turned and slowly walked back to the building, glancing once behind her.

Lewis waited until Mrs. Lemon had entered the building before he exposed the small shovel he was holding behind his back.

"Thanks for saving me," he said.

"You're quite welcome," replied Mary Jean. She looked at him strangely and said, "I guessed you probably had your hands full."

"Spot and I found the area you were talking about. You're right—those men were not working on the fountain drainage line. They were burying something."

They both looked around to make sure they were alone, and Mary Jean even walked ten yards down toward the building to make sure no one was about. She quickly walked back to Lewis and saw that he had already exposed the metal box. He was down on his hands and knees with Spot who was helping to dig the rest of the dirt away. Lewis lifted the box out from its grave and brushed it off. It was an ordinary metal box, similar to the small security deposit boxes that banks used to hold important documents. He covered up the hole and randomly spread a few leaves over the spot to make it look more natural. He then placed the box, which wasn't very large, under his coat. Together, they swiftly made their way back to the building. They decided to go to his apartment since Mary Jean was nervous about going back to hers since the unexpected death of Sarah.

Once inside Lewis's apartment, they removed their coats and let Spot off his leash. Mary Jean let out a great sigh of relief. She felt safe here with Lewis. She studied his face while he made tea in the kitchenette. He had a broad, angular face with a pronounced brow. His eyes always made her heart skip a beat. His demeanor was confident. His skin was a weathered brown, probably because he spent so much time outside. He had been a very good influence on her, getting her outside more, and with that had come a spark of motivation to do more with these last few years of her life. Before meeting Lewis, she had thought her life was over and was just letting the days pass by with no plans, no desires, no thoughts of doing anything but sitting on her couch reading and walking into the dining hall for meals. Her world had become very small, consumed with the minutiae of food and gossip, and the walls of the building were the perimeter of her world.

The tea was hot and strong. They sat at his small kitchen table across from each other with the box in the center between them.

"Well, let's open it," said Lewis as he reached for it. He studied the lock on the front. It was open. He raised the lid, and there lay about thirty little clear plastic bags of a crystalline-like powder, though it was more shard-like than powder.

"It's what I thought," murmured Lewis.

Spot was getting excited and jumped up on Lewis's knee.

"He smells it. He helped me find the stuff in the kitchen pantry in the dining hall. Now we've found their big stash. They'll be looking around for it once they find it gone."

Mary Jean felt anxious and wished they hadn't dug the thing up. She wondered if the death of Sarah was at all connected to this.

"I forgot to tell you that Sarah, my house cleaner, was just found dead in my apartment. Earlier, she tried to warn me not to eat lunch in the dining room. Do you think she knew about the ketamine, like us? And was she killed because someone found out she knew about it?"

"That's terrible. Poor woman. That makes sense.

These guys will do anything to cover up their scheme." Lewis looked thoughtful as he pondered this new information.

"What should we do now?' asked Mary Jean. "I thought it was strange that Kingsley did not call the police. They just took the body away, and there was no mention of an ongoing investigation at all. We must go to the police with this information!"

Lewis furrowed his brow and looked like he was thinking deeply about something.

"What is it?" said Mary Jean.

"We can't go to the police just yet. We don't know if they are involved."

"What? Why do you think that?

"Because I know the chief of police. He is Mrs. Lemon's brother-in-law, and he is a crooked guy."

10

Lewis closed the box and sat back in his chair. He rubbed his eyes and looked straight into Mary Jean's eyes.

"We need to document this and then put it back before anyone suspects anything."

He got up and went into his bedroom. Mary Jean heard him rummaging around, opening and closing his bureau, walking to and fro, until he finally exclaimed, "I found it!" He hurried back over to the table with his cell phone in hand.

"These are handy little things when it comes to taking a good photo," he said. He set up the shot with the metal box open, showing the little plastic bags lined up in rows.

"That ought to do it," he said. Lewis then shut the box and shoved it into a brown paper sack he had taken from under the kitchen sink.

"How will we get it back without being noticed?" said Mary Jean.

"The same way we uncovered it." Lewis shifted in his chair.

"I wonder how many people are involved and why?" said Mary Jean. "Those men who were digging probably knew. Mrs. Lemon seems suspicious, always appearing when we are in the courtyard. And what about the cook, Larry, who is often seen with Mrs. Lemon whispering in the hallways or the kitchen? And now Sarah has mysteriously died in my apartment! Did she know too much? Am I next?"

Mary Jean felt herself becoming hysterical. She took some deep breaths to slow her rapidly beating heart. All of this was getting too complicated, and she felt she couldn't trust anyone anymore. She wondered if she should call her children and have them take her away from this place. And if the chief of police was involved, they were really doomed.

"I have an investigator friend from the outside who will help," said Lewis. "We will be all right if we stay undercover until we have made all the connections and have all the information we need."

Mary Jean felt doubtful. She also felt sad that if she did end up leaving this place, she would not see Lewis anymore or get to grow the garden with Derek and the other kids. She had things to look forward to now, and she was excited about the future. That hadn't happened for a very long time, this excitement or motivation to do something different with her life.

"You know, I've thought about leaving. About calling my family and having them take me away from here."

"That might look suspicious, like you know something," Lewis said. "I promise I will keep you safe. I think we need to act like nothing is happening until I can wrap things up with my investigator friend."

Mary Jean looked down at her shoes and continued.

"As soon as I thought about it, I put it out of my mind. Because, you see, I would miss the things that you have introduced to me since I met you. I would miss the long walks we now take—and then there are the children and the garden project. I feel like my life is brighter, and though the future is short, it can be rich and full to the end."

Lewis smiled. He reached across the table and took her hand. Mary Jean felt a tingling sensation, and again, memories floated through her mind. She closed her eyes and thought of barbecues in the park by the covered bridge in Scio; Lewis's parents' farm in Crabtree where fluffy white ewes and their lambs dotted the green pastures; fall days walking along the rows of maple trees by the river trail together; the feel of the first hints of snow in the foothills from their home. Mary Jean was overwhelmed with emotion, and tears ran down her cheeks as joy washed over her.

When she opened her eyes, Lewis was smiling at her. It was as if he could read her mind.

He stood up and said, "I need to get this back in the ground before anyone notices."

"All right. But be careful. I'll head back to my room." Together, they left the apartment, and at the intersection of the hallways, Lewis gave her a confident salute and headed downstairs to the courtyard.

Mary Jean hoped they would come out of this safely and be able to spend more time together soon without the burden of this crisis over their heads.

The halls were vacant, as expected at this time of night. As she passed each resident's door, she looked at the decorations from family members that they had put up, such as handcrafted note cards, teddy bears, and family photographs. Some doors had nothing on them. A pang of sadness filled Mary Jean's heart.

When she got to her room, it looked like no one had ever been there, milling about and removing a dead body. I guess they have done whatever they needed to do, she thought to herself. However, she couldn't get out of her head how strange it was that the room wasn't cordoned off, that an investigation had not been started, and that there were no police called in. But it was late. She felt exhausted with all they had found and the overwhelming emotions she had experienced over the course of one day. She had felt reluctant to return to her apartment, but Lewis had assured her that he would keep her safe even if she did not know how. She got herself ready for bed. As she slipped into the smooth sheets, she was there in her memories again, smelling and even tasting the foods she used to cook, feeling the small little hands of her firstborn infant son and the embrace of her ever-present husband.

The next morning, Mary Jean was up at the crack of dawn. She had slept through the night without waking. Another first. When she stepped out of bed, she felt lighter and more agile. Her head was clear. Apparently, she had worked through all her negative emotions from yesterday. It's amazing what a good night's sleep can do to you, she thought. She opened the drapes and witnessed the sun coming up and filtering through the giant oak trees that lined the driveway in front of the retirement home. Birds were lined up in a row of about twenty on an electric wire, singing their hearts out. She dressed with care, choosing a newer blue skirt and jacket with a white blouse. She wanted to look her best for church. Yes, she was going to church, another thing she had stopped doing over the last year. She wanted to go this morning. She wanted to see friends she hadn't seen in a long while—the few that were left.

Breakfast was different, too. She chose a different

table than the one she usually sat at and smiled when she sat down. She said good morning to each person and waited to hear how they were doing rather than jump in and fill the air with her usual babble. It was interesting hearing about other people's families, their upcoming trips, and their hobbies. She felt renewed and actually enjoyed the breakfast served to her. She looked around, hoping to see Lewis. He was seldom at breakfast; she just never knew when he'd pop up.

Once again, she decided to take the stairs instead of the elevator. Usually, her knees hurt too much, but now that she was walking more, the pain had subsided. She simply did not notice it as much.

She climbed into the bus that would bring her to church, waiting while residents slowly made their way in wheelchairs or walkers or on their own two feet. She took her seat and glanced out the window to watch the morning unfold. As she contemplated the upcoming sermon, Lewis bounced on to the bus and approached her seat, saying, "May I sit with you?"

"Of course. I'm glad you made it. Did you get the deed done?" she whispered.

"Indeed, I did," he said.

The bus started up and soon they were headed to the Presbyterian church just outside of Maple Grove. Trees filled with white and pink blossoms lined the road as the bus turned out of the driveway of the retirement home. Bits of conversation started up here and there, with bouts of coughing piercing the lulls. Mary Jean looked at her fellow passengers. Some were hunched over snoring, while others were staring vacantly out the window. She felt like she was in a different place than the others. These last few weeks, she was feeling a transformation taking place.

They arrived in the church parking lot and filed out slowly, many needing a helping hand as they navigated the steps. Once inside the church, Lewis and Mary Jean took seats up front. The altar was filled with flowers of pinks, blues, and violets. White carnations and baby's-breath contrasted with the colors as if an artist had chosen the palette. Sunlight streamed in through the tall, angular stained-glass windows, setting the stage for a spiritual awakening.

The pastor began with greeting his congregation. People were encouraged to turn toward their neighbors all around them and shake hands in greeting. Mary Jean did this to her left and in front of her, and when she turned behind her, there was Mrs. Lemon!

"Why, it is surprising to see you here, Mary Jean," she said. "You always were too tired to come to church." She smiled crookedly.

"Now that you mention it, Mrs. Lemon, I am feeling remarkably energetic and youthful lately. I think it is all the walking I've been doing this past month."

"Yes. I've seen you in the courtyard a few times, and sometimes with that black-and-white dog."

Mary Jean couldn't help but wonder. Mrs. Lemon seemed to know a whole lot about her comings and goings and had even noticed Spot. Had she noticed Lewis as well? Didn't she speak to him just yesterday in the garden? Surely she knew who he was. He had an apartment at Kingsley. I've been in his room, haven't I? thought Mary Jean. Her heart was racing. She looked at Lewis next to her. Didn't Mrs. Lemon see him? Why hadn't she said anything about him being there next to her? Did he fade in and out of her reality? "Am I imagining him?" she whispered to herself. There was so much to ponder.

The next hour was a blur, conjuring up new feelings of renewal. Words of grace and thankfulness hung in the air as Mary Jean looked forward to the many things that would keep her engaged in her life, like the garden project and Derek. She also struggled with how she and Lewis were going to resolve the sinister acts of Mrs. Lemon. Surely, Mrs. Lemon was involved in all of this. Was it true she was hurting the home's residents for financial gain? How was the house cleaner involved, and how had she died?

But most of all . . . who was Lewis?

11

A few months had passed, and the halls were rather quiet at Kingsley. Since the death of the house cleaner last October, Mary Jean had seen less people being wheeled off to Memory Care. She wondered why; perhaps whoever had killed Sarah had decided to lay low for a while. Lewis was continuing with his investigations behind the scenes to get proof of the people who were involved in the scandal, but with no recent developments. In the meantime, Mary Jean continued to eat in her apartment for lunch just to be safe.

It was early spring. Today, the kids from Lafayette Elementary School and the residents were meeting in the activity room at Kingsley to plan out the design of their summer vegetable garden in the public park near them. Each resident was going to pair up with a student and pick out their seeds. Mary Jean used to love spending the winter months dreaming about garden design. She would pore over gardening catalogs and pick out heirloom vegetable seeds, as well as plenty of flowers.

When Mary Jean entered the activities room, a small group of students was sitting together on one side of the room talking loudly with each other. Their teacher, Mrs. Lacy, asked for everyone to sit down.

"I'd like all the residents to pair up with a student please. Make your way to the table in front to pick your seeds and let the park officials know what you've chosen and who your partner is."

Mary Jean looked at the group of students and found Derek sitting in the far corner. She walked over to him and said, "Would you like to come with me and decide what we are going to grow in this garden?"

Derek looked up at her and smiled. He took her hand, and together, they walked over to the long table. While they waited in line, they discussed what they wanted to plant. Derek wanted some herbs, like basil and oregano, as well as some sweet cherry tomatoes.

"Sweet 100s and some Italian Plum. Should be delicious," said Mary Jean.

When they got to the front of the line, there were dozens of seed packets arranged neatly and in alphabetical order in wooden boxes. Derek picked up the seeds they had decided on, and a park official wrote down his name in a notebook and entered his seeds on the next line.

"And who is helping you?" she asked.

"Mary Jean. Right here." He pointed to Mary Jean, who was standing next to him.

"Okay," she said and put his seeds in a small paper bag with his name on it. "We will hold these for you when we meet in the summer to do the planting."

Derek and Mary Jean went back to sit down and talked about their plan for their little patch in the garden. They decided to group the tomatoes together and put the herbs in a group next to them. Mary Jean wanted to find some marigolds to plant in borders around their patch. She told him they helped to repel insects.

"What would you cook with tomatoes and these herbs?" asked Derek.

"Why, these are perfect for making an Italian spaghetti sauce, Derek. I've made plenty from my gardens over the years. My children loved spaghetti and meatballs with lots of tomato sauce. One of my daughters still grows her own tomatoes, makes lots of sauce, and puts it in jars so she and her husband can eat it year-round."

"How do you make it?"

"You cook the tomatoes down and add freshly chopped garlic, basil, and oregano. You let it simmer for a long time so all the flavors blend together."

Derek listened carefully and then asked, "Can you make me some from our plants?"

"Well, I can ask my daughter, Abby, if she would."

At the end of the meeting, Mary Jean got up from her seat and took hold of Derek's little hand, and they walked out to the bus that was waiting for the students to board. There was another bus parked out front, waiting to take some residents to the park and cemetery.

"Are you coming to the park with us?" asked Mary Jean.

"No. My mom told me to come straight home. We have chores to do."

"Well, chores will teach you to work hard and to take satisfaction in a job well done."

Derek gave her a half smile as she released his hand and he boarded the bus that would take the students back to the school.

I sure hope everything is okay at home, thought

Mary Jean. He looks so thin. And his hair looks as if it hasn't been washed in weeks. Next time, I need to ask him more questions about his home life. Mary Jean waited as the other students got on the bus. She watched it drive off, and then the resident bus moved into its place.

The resident bus was almost full when the driver stepped out to see if anyone was left outside. Once he was satisfied that they were all on board, he took the driver's seat and closed the bus doors. They were on their way to their next adventure—a walk in the park. There was also the cemetery next door for visits to loved ones who had passed. Mary Jean thought about Lewis's gravesite and knew she had been avoiding it for some time. It brought back such longing that always made her feel sad instead of happy whenever she visited. But today felt different. Today, she would pick some wild flowers in the garden and put them on his grave. She wanted to talk to him and tell him how renewed in spirit she was feeling today.

The beautiful spring day was turning a bit showery. Mary Jean was glad she had brought her umbrella. She quickly unpacked it from her large bag and put it on the seat next to her so she'd have it ready when she got off the bus. Bright yellow daffodils and white crocus lined the driveway into the park. Luscious, pink cherry blossoms covered the trees that dotted the park, which had two ponds that were filled with geese and resident ducks. Some of the ladies had brought bread to feed the birds. She always thought that was wrong—that you weren't supposed to feed the wildlife. But today she could see the smiles all around and thought that if such a simple thing brought so much happiness, how could it be wrong?

The clouds were getting darker and it felt cool.

Mary Jean's Red Shoes

Spring showers were probably around the corner. She wrapped her sweater a little more closely around her as she stepped off the bus with her umbrella. She eyed a bench and sat down. She'd brought her red sneakers in a cloth bag so she could navigate the paths more safely. She quickly changed and put her nice shoes in the bag and slung it over her shoulder. She headed over to the wilder part of the garden where the path wove up a little hill. Up there, you were allowed to pick the wild flowers.

    She breathed heavily as she made her way up the little knoll and found another bench to rest on. Several chickadees were chattering away in the bush next to her. Butterflies were feeding on the nectar of flowers in tall bushes a few feet away. It felt peaceful here. She looked down from where she had come, the large public grounds where ladies were milling about in pairs and in threes, stopping every now and again to sit on benches or to bend down to look more closely at some flower or to feed the ducks. Why didn't she come here more often? Getting outdoors, being surrounded by trees with swaying branches with the wind on your face, and seeing grasses so tall that they brushed your fingertips . . . had she just forgotten how healing this was? Mary Jean sighed. Being outdoors in nature should be a prescription for one's health.

    She stood up and walked farther into the woods, bending down every so often to pick some purple, then blue, and lastly white wild flowers until she had a handsome bouquet for Lewis's grave. She turned around and walked carefully down the hill, marveling at her agility compared to just a few months ago.

    Lewis's gravesite was on the south side of the cemetery. She walked slowly, observing which gravesites had fresh flowers and which ones had not been visited in quite some time. When she finally came to Lewis's, she saw red fake flowers in a vase. She'd forgotten that she'd left those the last time she visited. She'd thought at the time that at least they wouldn't wilt—that they would look good from a distance and make it seem like the gravesite was well attended. But now she thought it looked cheap. She picked them up and put them in her bag. She then placed the bouquet of wildflowers on top of the grave.

"There. Now you have something fresh and beautiful." She stood looking down on his grave and closed her eyes. "I know you have been with me. Isn't that right? You are protecting me. I don't understand it, but I know it is you. Thank you for looking after me."

With that, she turned around and headed back to the park. She wasn't one to mince words. But something stirred in the leaves on the ground. Birds started their chatter more loudly, and she thought about the church services she had started attending every Sunday and how much the music always moved her.

She hurried toward the group of residents who were lining up to board the bus. The rain had stopped, and the sun was peeking out through the clouds. It almost felt warm now. Soon, they would be having lunch at the restaurant along the river. She actually felt hungry. She really hadn't felt hungry for quite a while until she started exercising more. She thought about how she had been eating differently, too, in the last few months. She ate more meat at dinner and had an egg for breakfast more often than not. She ate fresh fruits for snacks and usually had a salad with dinner or lunch. *No wonder I feel better* and have more energy; I'm eating more, she thought. Her strength and balance were changing, too. It made sense. More exercise, better appetite—she was getting stronger.

She took a seat near the window and was soon joined by Hattie.

"How was your walk up to the woods, Mary Jean?" she asked.

Mary Jean replied with a distant look in her eyes, "Very peaceful."

12

The next morning, Mary Jean woke up early. It was very quiet, and the light was just peeking in between her curtains. She slowly got out of bed and went to the bathroom. After some tea, toast, and avocado slices, she dressed warmly and put on her red shoes.

She carefully opened her door and looked down the hall. She saw no one as she stepped out and headed toward the library. She quietly descended the stairs. To her left, down the hallway, was an aide wheeling a resident in a wheelchair toward the elevator. The resident seemed to be hallucinating—she was talking about clowns in the hallway giving away balloons. Her voice was shaky as she called out to several clowns to follow her to make sure she was safe. The elevator dinged and the door opened. The aide spoke sharply to her, telling her to be quiet, as he looked in each direction to see if anyone was watching.

Mary Jean sucked in a breath. It's starting again, she thought. Where was Lewis? She needed to find him. It had been a few weeks since she had last seen him. She wondered if he was making any progress on the scam that was going on. She went outside and proceeded along the perimeter walkway that skirted the building. Her arms swung at her sides as she pushed herself to pick up the pace. Lewis always seemed to know where she was, and so she suspected that he would soon show up. She rounded the corner and headed to the courtyard.

She saw him sitting on the bench near the center of the courtyard with Spot on his leash. He wore a wool beret and navy-blue wool sweater. His back was to her as she approached.

"Well, fancy meeting you here, Lewis," she said. He turned around and smiled. His eyes always startled her when she saw him, as if it were the first time she was meeting him. Spot wagged his tail and smelled her legs. He was too polite to jump up on her.

"It's always a good day when I see you, Mary Jean." He moved over on the bench and made room for her. As she sat down, he took her hand in his and gave it a squeeze.

"I know you have questions," he said. He looked into her eyes with a deep understanding, and she felt her heart speed up.

She blushed and looked down and said, "I saw another person being taken to the Memory Care Unit. It was frightening. She was seeing things and calling out to imaginary clowns. I wanted to help her, but I was afraid." She kept looking down, avoiding his eyes.

"Don't worry, Mary Jean. I've gotten someone else to help. His name is Jack Holden. He's a private investigator. I don't trust the police; they are in on it. So, I decided to hire him to help me. It seems things are starting to ramp back up, and I'm very concerned for your welfare. I think it's now gotten to a point where you should ask your kids to take you away for a little while."

"Oh Lewis, I couldn't do that. That would be way too much of an imposition on them with their busy lives. They wouldn't believe me if I told them why, either. They would probably get *me* hauled off to Memory Care!"

"Well, you might be right about that." He smiled, which took the tension away a bit. "Are you still taking your lunch in your apartment rather than in the dining hall?" She looked up to meet his gaze and saw the concern in his eyes.

"Yes. I stay in my apartment and only go in for dinner."

"Good." He got up from the bench, still holding her hand. He helped her up and wrapped his arms around her. His embrace felt so reassuring. She felt so very loved at that moment. They stayed there, holding each other for several minutes. Mary Jean couldn't help but wonder when they would have to finally say goodbye.

"Let's continue your walk," he said, and hand in hand, they followed the pathway out of the courtyard and headed toward the street sidewalk outside of the retirement home.

"Lewis, have you figured out if Sarah, the housekeeper, was really killed?" Mary Jean asked. "I haven't heard any update from management the last few months. Maybe she wasn't dead after all; maybe she was whisked away to the Memory Care Unit and that is why no one made a big deal about it?" The morning was brisk, but she could tell it was going to warm up fast. As soon as they stepped out of the shadows of the trees, the sun warmed their backs.

"I don't have proof yet, but I'm pretty sure the

management is behind it. She very well may be in the Memory Care Unit. That would explain why there wasn't a murder investigation. I think she must have stumbled upon the scam unintentionally, and they decided to remove her."

Lewis continued, "As I mentioned before, Kingsley Retirement Home has been losing money this whole past year. Someone is funneling the money out to an offshore account, and they are putting residents in Memory Care to cover themselves. Do you remember when I said I knew the chief of police and that he was a crooked guy who is Mrs. Lemon's brother-in-law?"

"I do!"

"Well, he never fully investigated what happened with Sarah. According to my sources, he said she suffered a heart attack and did not die but was moved to a rehabilitation center. But Sarah was only thirty-four years old! I'm not sure I entirely believe him. My theory is that Sarah was an innocent bystander who became too curious and was taken out because she knew too much or had seen something. I hope Jack Holden can shed a little more light on all of this sooner rather than later."

They passed the McMenamins Inn and decided to go inside for a cup of coffee. Lewis tied Spot up to a small tree on the lawn and told him to stay. Inside, the dining room was buzzing with frenetic activity. The walls were covered in fanciful artwork and the hanging light fixtures were whimsical and fun. Groups of families were having breakfast. Lewis chose a corner seat that looked out at the spa pool. The waitress was young and wore her hair up high in a ponytail. She had tattoos up and down her arms. She even had a small ring in her nose.

How could these kids show up to work looking like that? Mary Jean thought. But I guess times are changing, and I am being left behind. The waitress was polite and very nice, and Mary Jean thought she should not judge her by her looks alone.

"What have you been up to since I last saw you?" asked Lewis.

"We finally had our garden meeting. I met with Derek, and we picked some seeds out to plant in the garden for next season. He asked me if I could make some marinara sauce once the tomatoes are ripe and the herbs are up. I'm looking forward to seeing the garden full of vegetables and the residents out enjoying the weather with the children. Lewis, these children keep us young. I feel like I have a purpose and I am not just stuck in my own small world at the home."

"I agree with you. When we can share what we know with a child, it helps us feel connected and cared for. Some of these kids don't have their parents around very much to teach them these things. These parents are working all the time, and they have no energy to spend with their kids. That's why they say it takes a village to raise a child."

"I'm worried about Derek. He looked thin the last time I saw him, and his hair looked dirty. I don't want to pry or make him feel uncomfortable, but I wish there was something I could do. I thought about visiting his parents to tell them about the garden project. Maybe then I could get a better understanding of what's going on in his home life."

"Be careful with that, Mary Jean. You never know what you will find, and you may not like it. You'd better check with his teacher to make sure that is okay to do. The school may not like the residents contacting the kids' families."

"You're right. I should probably just be a good role model for him and leave it at that." She looked at her watch and said, "Oh my goodness, it's 10 a.m. already!" Where had the time gone? Time flew by when she was with Lewis. All her worries melted away. She could say anything to him, and she knew he would always treat her with love and support. That's what she could do for Derek.

"I need to get back for my 11 a.m. morning yoga class," said Mary Jean.

"You're taking a yoga class?" Lewis's eyes were wide with surprise.

"Yes. My hips have been hurting and I've been pretty stiff, so when I saw the class was being offered, I thought I should try it. It's especially suited for us old folks so they don't push you too hard." She laughed, and Lewis grinned. She never in a million years would have thought she'd be taking a yoga class. They paid their bill and walked outside to get Spot. He was sleeping under the tree right where they had left him. He was so happy to see them that he forgot his manners and jumped up on Lewis. Lewis caught his paws gently, and they did a little jig together. Together, they walked back to the home, singing the same tune that Mary Jean used to sing with her late husband. The words came easily to both of them, just like old times.

Once they said their goodbyes, Mary Jean walked back to her little apartment. She quickly changed into her stretch pants and a loose top for the yoga class. She sipped a glass of water before she headed out. The class did not have very many participants;

she counted eight. Most of them were women, but there was one man. "Hey," she said to herself, "that's Lewis!"

She quickly walked over and tapped him on the shoulder. He turned around and said, "I thought I should join you." He grinned from ear to ear as they laid their mats out together. The teacher put on soft mediation music, greeted the class, and encouraged everyone to greet each other before they started. Mary Jean felt like she was ten years younger, standing next to her beau amid all these "young" women.

13

Spring was halfway gone, and the planting for the garden project would soon be in full swing. Mary Jean looked at her calendar and realized they would be planting in a few weeks' time. She hadn't seen Derek for a few weeks and wondered how he was getting along. She packed the pasta salad with chicken that she had made and some fruit and threw a towel into her bag as an afterthought. She and Lewis were going down to the river for a picnic lunch with some other residents, and maybe she would even wade in the water.

He was waiting in the lobby for her. He had a concerned look on his face when she approached.

"Is everything all right?" she asked.

"Well, I've found out some information from Jack."

"You mean the detective guy you hired?"

"Yes. The very one. He's found a connection between Mrs. Lemon and Larry, the cook."

"Well?"

"They appear to be working together, tainting the food with the ketamine we found in the box buried in the garden. Jack found some emails in which they referred to it by its common name, Special K, and they have restocked their stash in cereal boxes in the pantry. Jack's been on the trail this past week. He thinks the chief of police, Mr. Schultz, is supplying it for a cut in the profits from the increase of residents in the Memory Care Unit."

"This is terrible! What are we going to do?" This recent information had really put a damper on their picnic outing for her.

"Well, we need to find out where their offshore accounts are and how much money laundering we are talking about—and we need proof of that. So we still need to lay low and let Jack do his work. He might bring in international professionals to investigate the offshore accounts. For now, we'll just have to take it one day at a time. I'll keep you posted, so don't worry. I think you are safe because they are only tainting the lunches. If anything changes, I'll let you know. Spot and I will keep checking the food served at dinner."

This did not make Mary Jean feel any better. But she was going to try and put this out of her mind so she could enjoy the day with Lewis.

The bus pulled up in front of the lobby, and a number of residents boarded, each carrying lunches and towels. Lewis and Mary Jean took a seat in the back and settled in for the hour-long ride. The traffic was heavy at first as they crawled through the city's stoplights. Bulbs like red tulips, purple gladiolas, and white hyacinths were blooming in drifts of color in the parks and gardens. Just out of town, fields of green grass were tall and uniform, stretching for miles.

They stopped briefly at a rest stop for a bathroom break. Cars filled the parking lot, which was full of commuters and truckers resting from their long hauls up and down the freeway. Mary Jean sighed and reflected on the spring break family vacations she and her late husband would take with the kids over to the coast. The kids were usually fighting in the back and anxious to "get there." They often stopped for milkshakes at Larry's, but Larry's was no longer around. The countryside was filled with more developments now and more people traveling than ever before. Back then, you could always count on finding a hotel room easily, and you did not have to drive around the block seventeen times to find a parking place.

People shifted in their seats, talking about the latest great-grandchild to arrive or their last visit from family. Soon, there was a steady lull of voices and people shuffled about to get comfortable.

"A penny for your thoughts?" said Lewis.

"Oh, I've been thinking about how things have changed. Not at Kingsley, but how there are more people and more houses in general, and the familiar places seem to be all gone. My family used to stop at this milkshake place, and it isn't even here anymore. We used to travel to the coast all the time. Now every place is so crowded. The last time I went to the coast when Derek was with me, I was so surprised by how crowded it was."

"Yes. What will be left for our great-grandkids? Too many people are killing our planet, but I don't see that changing very soon."

The bus slowed to a halt. They had reached the park by the river. It was a beautiful day. Mary Jean let the problems that were clouding her head slip away. They stepped off the bus and walked along the river on a well-worn path, getting away from the other residents. They were searching for just the right spot to settle down for lunch. Lewis saw a picnic table under a fir tree and made a beeline for it before someone else could take it. The benches were sprinkled with pine needles and they were a little dusty, but it would do. The sounds of the river were soothing, and a few orange California poppies dotted the trail.

They unpacked their lunch of pasta salad and fruit. Their appetites weren't as big as when they were younger. Mary Jean imagined the strawberry pie, roast beef sandwiches, and potato salad they used to bring on family picnics. The kids, especially her oldest son, had big appetites.

"What a gorgeous place to share a lunch together," said Lewis.

"I am so glad you asked me to do this. It is something I just haven't felt like doing in a long time. Having you here makes me feel more open to getting out of my apartment. I see that it is so easy to just stay inside. I forgot what I was missing."

Mary Jean smiled and touched Lewis's hand. What was she going to do without him? She wanted to ask him how long he was going to stay. Somehow, she knew he wasn't real in the sense that, well, real people were.

"Lewis, can I ask you something?"

"Of course. What is it?" Lewis stopped chewing his pasta salad and looked into her eyes. He saw sadness and was briefly taken aback.

"Lewis, how long are you staying?" she asked timidly.

"How long am I staying where? Do you mean here, right now?"

"I mean here, with me, at Kingsley, in this life." Mary Jean was frightened of his answer.

"Well, that all depends." His eyes twinkled, lightening up the seriousness of her question.

"What do you mean?" she asked.

"I'm here to protect you, first and foremost. But I am also here to show you the way to happiness for the rest of your life."

"Well, that is all fine and good, and I am deeply touched. But you haven't answered my question. It frightens me that you would disappear out of my life. I am not sure I would want to go on living. My life has changed so much since you showed up. Bringing me those silly, old red shoes . . . who would have thought they would be the beginning of a new life for me?"

Lewis smiled and closed his eyes. When he opened them, she saw a brilliance that made her feel elated.

"I will be with you always, in one way or another."

"You are truly a man of mystery, and you have a way with words, too," she said with a laugh.

They finished up their lunch, then followed the path a bit further down the river. It was warm, so Mary Jean took her sweater off. The wind felt soft against her skin, and there was a gentle sound of rushing water rippling over the rocks. Large, tall fir and cedar gave them shade as they continued down the river, stopping to admire the blue heron or to catch a glimpse of a fish jumping out of the water. They came to a small sandy beach where the water lapped up against a shallow bench.

"Let's get our feet wet!" Mary Jean said excitedly.

They removed their shoes, and Lewis was the first to step into the water. He held out his hand to her. She took it and carefully dipped one foot in.

"Oh, that is cold! But it feels nice." The sand was smooth and a little muddy. But there were no big or sharp rocks around to hurt her feet.

"Okay, that's enough. My feet are going numb," said Lewis. They stepped onto their towel that was laid on the grass just below the bench. They each sat down, dried their feet, and put their socks and shoes back on.

"My son, Marcus, likes to fly-fish. Have you done it?"

"No, I never made the time to do those kinds of things. I was brought up to value working, and working only. I worked on the weekends in the Coast Guard on top of a full-time teaching job."

Mary Jean pondered this for a while before she spoke.

"That sure sounds like my late husband's life. You two seem very similar in your upbringing and in your choices of how to spend your time. But that was our generation, wasn't it? I didn't have many hobbies or interests besides reading. I was too busy raising four kids, cooking, cleaning, canning, baking, and what have you. At least I did some work for an artist co-op maintaining the books. I used to play the piano but never picked it back up when I was older."

"Looking back, I think I would have changed a few things," Lewis said. "I would have spent more time with my kids and gone fishing once a month."

They decided it was time to turn around and return to the bus. They had heard a horn earlier, signaling people to pack up their things and head back.

It had been a beautiful day, thought Mary Jean. The best I've had in a long, long time. She realized that sharing life's wonders was one of the keys to happiness. And to stay in the moment, not to start thinking and worrying about what could happen in the future. She made a mental note to practice this one habit more often each day. She had always been a worrier, always anxious. Here was one more thing that Lewis had helped her to see about herself. And what had he meant when he had said, "I will be with you always, in one way or another"? She guessed she would have to find out, but for now, she was boarding the bus with a man she loved.

14

It was finally summer and time to plant the garden. Mary Jean hurriedly made her bed and dressed quickly. She had slept in and was going to be late. When she made her way down to the lobby, the group was already boarding the activities bus, and she was the last one on. She found a seat next to Hattie whom she hadn't seen for a while even though she lived just down the hall from her.

"I can't believe how late I slept in! I didn't even have time to have breakfast," said Mary Jean.

"I always set my alarm or I would sleep in, too," said Hattie.

"Are you excited to be planting with the kids today?" asked Mary Jean.

"Not especially. The girl I am paired with always complains and isn't very interested in the garden."

"Maybe there is trouble at home? Have you tried talking about what interests her? Or ask her what she has been doing this summer?" said Mary Jean.

"No, I haven't. I am not a child psychologist, so I think that is a waste of time." She turned her head toward the window and sighed.

Mary Jean reached into her bag and brought out

the seeds that Derek had picked out. Tomatoes, basil, and oregano. She wondered if the tomato plants would grow up tall and strong or end up taking forever to bear fruit. She remembered her summers waiting for the fruit to turn a deep red before picking them. That made the best marinara sauce. She would add lots of fresh garlic and basil from the garden, along with some olive oil and a dash of red wine.

Summer had started with a bang, and it seemed a little on the late side to plant the seeds. But at least it had started, and several residents had decided to join. The kids needed something to do during their summer break, too, so it was a win-win situation. The bus rounded a bend, and there was the garden site. It looked like someone had worked the soil up and added some smelly compost. She noticed parents dropping their kids off. The kids looked anxiously for their elderly partners. Mary Jean saw Derek standing by himself with his head down. His hair was mussed, and his clothes were soiled. She walked quickly over to him.

"Derek, how are you?" she said.

"Hi. I'm okay," he replied.

"I have our seeds. Let's go see where our plot is." She smiled at him and offered her hand. He slowly took it and let himself be led toward the table of ladies who had their plot number and seeds.

"Mary Jean and Derek Meyers," stated Mary Jean.

"Here you go. You have plot number three. It's right over there, close to the faucet. And here are your seeds." The lady, who had big glasses and a big smile, pointed to the area that would become theirs to fill with all the good stuff to make spaghetti. Mary Jean and Derek made their way over to their plot. The sky was a clear blue without a whisper of a cloud in it. Butterflies were flitting about here and there, and Derek even saw a hummingbird checking out some flowers nearby. Its tiny wings beat so fast that a buzzing sound could be heard.

"These birds are so tiny but very, very fast," he said. He watched the hummingbird fly from one mass of flowers to the next. Its bright green color shone in the sunlight. Another one darted toward it, acting as though it was protecting its territory.

"Maybe I can get some seeds for flowers that hummingbirds like so we can attract more to our garden. Would you like that?' said Mary Jean.

"Sure," he said. He stared at the birds, following their frenetic flight with an intense concentration. He finally looked away and stared into nowhere in particular as though he were thinking about something troubling.

Mary Jean asked, "Where would you like to plant the tomatoes?" Derek snapped out of his trance and picked up a trowel that Mary Jean had brought.

Together, they planted their garden following the plan they had put together in the spring. They planted way more tomatoes than they needed and lots of oregano and basil. They figured they could share their harvest with the other residents or trade some of their produce for different vegetables. Mary Jean showed Derek how to make a furrow and how deep to plant the seeds. She used little stakes and string provided by the activities director to make straight rows. They watered each row, with Mary Jean helping Derek hold the hose carefully so they wouldn't flood the little seeds. Derek seemed to enjoy the work, and so Mary Jean took the opportunity to ask him about what else he was doing this summer.

"I'm at home by myself because both my parents

work. The neighbor comes over a couple of times a day to check on me and my sister, though. It's pretty boring." Derek talked with a rasp in his voice as if he were getting over a cold.

"Have you been sick? Your nose sounds stuffy."

"Yes. A little. The house gets pretty smoky when my dad is smoking inside. It irritates my throat and makes my eyes water."

"Doesn't he go outside to smoke?" Mary Jean was concerned.

"No. Sometimes he opens a window a little."

They had finished planting. Mary Jean took Derek over to a bench, and they sat down to catch their breath and drink some water. It was getting pretty hot.

"What did you have for breakfast this morning, Derek?"

"I had some Pop-Tarts and a glass of Kool-Aid."

"That's not very healthy. Have you ever had oatmeal?" That was what she used to prepare for her kids most mornings, along with eggs and orange juice, while Lewis would make French toast and pancakes on the weekends.

"No. Only when I go over to the neighbor's house." Mary Jean shook her head. It was sad to think some families fed their kids this way.

Just then, the bus honked its horn to signal it was time for the residents to return to Kingsley.

"Well, I'll see you in a week to check on our garden," said Mary Jean.

Parents were arriving to pick up their kids. Mary Jean overheard the kids talking excitedly about their experience. Some kids were dragging their parents over to show them their handiwork. Derek waited by himself on the bench where they had been sitting. No car had showed up yet to pick him up. Mary

Jean watched as parents drove away and volunteers cleaned up the site, packed up their chairs, and left. It was almost time for her bus to leave, and she reluctantly boarded. Finally, a dirty, gray Ford truck pulled up just as the bus was leaving. Mary Jean stood up and strained to see what Derek's parents looked like. A large man with long black hair, a red flannel shirt, and soiled jeans stepped out of the truck. He whistled to catch Derek's attention.

I guess their washing machine must have broken, thought Mary Jean as the bus rumbled down the dirt road toward the highway.

The next morning was even hotter than the previous day. Mary Jean splashed cold water on her face and looked into the mirror. Sometimes she did not recognize herself. Where had all the time gone? How had she gotten so old? When had she started getting those hairs on her lip? No one ever talked about what it was like to get old. She quickly dressed in her lightest clothing and made herself some coffee. She didn't feel like going to the dining hall for breakfast this morning. Her hip ached, and she couldn't bend two of her fingers. It seemed all that planting had made her arthritis flare up. All she could think about were her aches and pains and then how unkempt Derek had looked. She felt helpless about so many things. She couldn't ease her pains, and she couldn't help Derek have a better life.

Sometimes, life was just unforgiving. So many of her friends had passed away. She often wondered what was the purpose of going on when she didn't know anyone anymore.

Mary Jean felt like she was spiraling downward into negative thoughts. A knock on her door seemed like uncanny timing. She slowly got up, and when she opened the door, Mrs. Lemon almost fell into her.

"Well, excuse me, Mary Jean. I must have lost my balance." She straightened her skirt and pulled herself together.

"What is it, Mrs. Lemon? Can I help you with something?" asked Mary Jean.

"I was checking why you haven't come in for breakfast," said Mrs. Lemon.

"Well, I just didn't feel like it," said Mary Jean.

"I think you should come. We are having some special French toast and pancakes with fresh blueberries and syrup." Mary Jean thought this was unusual. Mrs. Lemon never cared whether or not she came to a meal. This seemed fishy.

"Well, thank you for the invitation, but I think I will take a rain check this time," said Mary Jean, smiling broadly. Mrs. Lemon's pencil eyebrows slid down into a frown. Her nervous tic on the side of her mouth started acting up. She seemed perturbed and agitated. She stared at Mary Jean for some time. This was really getting awkward.

"Well, all right. I am concerned about how you are eating. I will send someone with a 10 a.m. snack for you, okay? Something high in protein." She gave Mary Jean a pained smile and left abruptly. What was that about anyway?

"I need to talk with Lewis and tell him what's happening," said Mary Jean to herself.

With that, she tiptoed out of her room and headed to Lewis's apartment. Just as she turned around the corner, she saw Hattie being wheeled to the elevator. Hattie! she thought. There was nothing wrong with Hattie. She had just sat next to her yesterday on the bus to the garden! This was terrible. Mary Jean had to do something, and fast. She walked quickly to the elevator, but it closed just as she arrived. Drat! She needed Lewis's help. She turned around and headed to his apartment. When she got there, she knocked loudly on his door. No one answered. Where was he?

15

She heard a dog bark. She knocked again, harder this time. Still no answer. She looked up and down the hallway, searching for a house cleaner who could open the door. There was no one about, just one resident hobbling on her cane toward the media room. Spot's bark became frantic, and just as she turned around, she saw Mrs. Lemon again coming toward her from around the corner. Mary Jean wasn't sure what to do next, so she just stood there, waiting for her to arrive.

"Well, Mary Jean, what are you doing on this side of the facility?" Mrs. Lemon looked her up and down with a look of steel on her face.

"I thought I'd get a little exercise," Mary Jean said.

"Yes, I noticed you've been out and about more than usual. Don't forget I am bringing you a 10 a.m. snack. Be sure to be in your room. On second thought, I'd like you to come with me. I have something to show you."

Mrs. Lemon quickly grabbed Mary Jean's hand and began leading her toward the media room where Mary Jean had seen that last resident enter. Mary Jean felt afraid. She stiffened as Mrs. Lemon pulled at her hand. As she meekly followed Mrs. Lemon, she thought she heard Lewis's door open.

Someone said, "Hey, Mary Jean, come back here."

Mary Jean stopped, withdrew her hand from Mrs. Lemon, and turned around. The door was ajar. She walked briskly toward the door, ignoring Mrs. Lemon's calls to come back. When she got there, Lewis grabbed her arm and pulled her into the apartment and slammed the door.

"Lewis! I thought you weren't in. I knocked several times and Spot was barking . . ."

"I know. But I had to wait until I thought the coast was clear. Spot wasn't helping much with his barking and all. I'm just glad I caught you. I'm not sure what Mrs. Lemon is up to, but I knew I had to get you back here. She's been lurking around the hallways, and I think she was looking for you. I saw her outside your door the other day when you were away planting the garden."

"Well, that makes sense. This morning I think she was eavesdropping at my door. She almost fell through the doorway when I opened it! But what I came to tell you is that they have taken Hattie away in a wheelchair toward the elevator! Probably to the Memory Care Unit! We must do something, and quickly!"

"Try and stay calm, Mary Jean. I know this is unsettling and frightening. Jack Holden, the PI I told you about, has someone planted up there to keep an eye out for suspicious activity. They will probably stop them, and we will be closer to cracking this case!"

Lewis took her hand and led her to the couch. He motioned her to sit down and went to the kitchen to get her a glass of water. The water was cool and refreshing, and she drank it all.

"You'd better stay here for a while until Mrs. Lemon has cleared out. I have some papers to share with you from Jack."

With that, Lewis walked over to a small desk and pulled open the top drawer. He picked up a small stack of papers. He shuffled through them and picked out two. He walked over to the couch and sat down next to Mary Jean. The clock said it was 9:35 a.m. Mary Jean thought about what would happen if she was not home to receive the snack that Mrs. Lemon had said she was sending over. Would they open her door? Would they search her apartment? Well, she had nothing to hide, so what was she afraid of? What if they bugged her apartment?

"These are copies of emails that Mrs. Lemon and Mr. Schultz, the police chief, have sent to each other in the last few months. I picked the most incriminating ones to show you."

He handed them to Mary Jean, and she read them carefully. It was as Lewis had suspected. It looked like the two were colluding together and skimming money from all the new Memory Care residents. They also talked about money laundering schemes that would cover up their illegal activities that were in offshore accounts. Jack had done some good work!

"Jack is a sharp guy, isn't he?" said Lewis. "He is quite the young hacker who can do wonders on the internet."

Lewis returned the two pages to the desk drawer. He wiped some sweat from his forehead and drew a handkerchief from his pocket and blew his nose. He looked intently at her.

"You are going to have to leave, Mary Jean. It is no longer safe for you here."

Mary Jean looked down at her feet. Kingsley has

been her home for the last six years. She had no other place to go. Her children would think she was losing it. They might send *her* off to Memory Care. Perhaps that was Mrs. Lemon's back-up plan.

"I have nowhere else to go, Lewis," she said quietly.

"Certainly one of your children will think of something. Marcus is sharp and will listen to you. He'll come up with some alternatives."

"You can't be serious. Even he will think I am getting dementia. And I'll end up in Memory Care where Mrs. Lemon wants me." Mary Jean shrunk even more into the couch. A few tears slid down her cheek.

"Well, if they catch the person wheeling Hattie, knocked out by ketamine, then most of our worries are over and you may not have to move."

He put his arm around her, and they sat like that for quite a while, thinking about their dilemma. "Don't worry," Lewis said. "Something big is happening—and real soon. I can't tell you what, but get ready, because it's coming." Mary Jean sat up and looked at Lewis with wide eyes. Before she could process what he said, she remembered she had to be back in her apartment. Mary Jean looked up at the clock—it was 10 a.m.

"I have to go! Mrs. Lemon is having a snack brought to my apartment. If I'm not there, they may snoop around and, I don't know, place a bug in my apartment or something. I'll catch up with you at dinner tonight and we can talk more."

With that, she got up and headed out the door.

16

When Mary Jean got to her apartment, the door was open. She stepped in and found two house cleaners tidying up her apartment.

"I didn't know you were scheduled to clean today," she said.

"We weren't. Mrs. Lemon sent us to do it today, and she wanted us to bring you a snack." The other maid stepped forward and added, "She also said you were going to be gone next—"

"Shhh . . . Maggie. You weren't supposed to tell her," whispered the other house cleaner.

"Gone? I'm not going to be gone. Why would she tell you that?" Mary Jean's eyes widened and her heart thumped in her chest.

"We just follow directions, Mary Jean."

They bustled around the apartment, dusting and wiping surfaces. Mary Jean went into her bedroom and closed the door. She searched carefully, looking for anything conspicuous. She checked her lamps and even looked behind the mirror. She found nothing. She got her red Nike sneakers out and put them on. She grabbed a light sweater because it could still get cool under the shaded trees.

One of the house cleaners looked up, concerned that Mary Jean was leaving.

"Don't forget your protein drink. Mrs. Lemon said you weren't getting enough protein, so you be sure to drink it." The house cleaner pointed to the kitchen counter where a glass of pink liquid stood.

"Well, ladies, I am going out for a walk. I'll have that when I get back," she said and headed out the door. No way was she going to drink anything Mrs. Lemon fixed for her!

It was warm outside, so she headed to the park where it was mostly shaded. There were too many unknowns. Money laundering? The police chief involved? And how would they save Hattie? Mary Jean walked along the cement sidewalk under the sprawling oak trees. Being outdoors made her feel more alive and took her to places of solace and memories. Her hip felt better when she moved, as did most of her daily aches and pains. If only there was someone she could tell about her suspicions and report that Hattie had been drugged . . . but the police chief was a crook! Who would help them? Perhaps Jack Holden knew the FBI . . .

Mary Jean turned left and headed to the fountain. She liked to throw a penny into it and make a wish whenever she was there. She opened her purse and found some pocket change in the bottom. She selected a nickel this time. "This calls for something bigger," she said to herself. She wished for the safety of her friend and for Lewis to be real.

It was noon, and Mary Jean decided to do the short walk to McMenamins for lunch. She recalled how Marcus and his wife would often encourage her to walk there whenever they spoke. She always complained and told them that she was weak and had poor balance. That she needed her walker. Now here she was, doing the walk without a thought and all by herself, as well.

She made her way slowly up the steps, holding the handrail carefully. She entered the wide hallway that led to the restaurant. She stopped to study the whimsical paintings on the wall. She never used to notice the artwork. She was led to a window that looked out to the outdoor hot tub. A couple was soaking in their bathing suits. They were sitting close together, talking and looking into each other's eyes with interest. You could tell they were very attracted to each other. "I remember when Lewis and I used to look at each other like that," she murmured to herself.

The waitress came and handed her a menu. She brought a glass and skillfully poured water into it.

"Can I get you anything to drink?" she asked.

"No, thank you. I'll just have water." Mary Jean looked over the menu. She had worked up quite an appetite after her walk in the park and the trip over here to the restaurant. She looked over the specials for seniors and decided the mini spinach and tomato pizza looked good. It came with a small side salad, so she'd get plenty of veggies. She prided herself on having eaten well most of her life. She had to, especially when Lewis had his two open-heart surgeries. Low fat, low cholesterol, lots of veggies and fruit, and smaller meat portions. She was careful with his diet. His job as a high school teacher had been stressful. He didn't believe in exercise, except for the occasional game of golf with his buddies. He had died at seventy-nine years old, just shy of his eightieth birthday. He had fallen asleep on the couch with the cat curled up with him and never woken up. It had been such a shock.

That had happened almost eleven years ago. It seemed like just yesterday. That was the trouble with aging; everything went by in a blink of an eye.

The waitress came and took her order. Mary Jean wished Lewis or one of her kids were here. This was where they usually came for lunch when one of them was visiting.

Her cell phone rang. She picked it up and recognized her grandson's voice on the phone.

"Hi Grandma, how are you?" Finley asked.

"I'm okay. I'm having lunch by myself at McMenamins right now. I wish someone were here to eat with me." The couple outside in the hot tub was kissing. Mary Jean looked away.

"Grandma, I have some really good news! Lisa and I have a son! He was born yesterday morning by C-section. Lisa and the baby are doing fine. We are tired but are heading home in a couple of days depending on how Lisa feels."

"Oh, that's amazing news! I am so excited for both of you. I have something for him that I'd like to give to you. Maybe your father can bring it down sometime. It's nothing much; just a little baby throw I knitted."

"That would be great, Grandma. I'll look forward to seeing it! I have to go now but just wanted to give you the news myself. Talk to you later."

"Okay, Finley. Good to hear from you." Mary Jean hung up. She couldn't believe her ears. She had known the date was getting close, but she had momentarily lost track of time. How exciting! She was a great-grandma now.

Her pizza and salad arrived, and Mary Jean ate

while contemplating the news. She would have to wait before she could hold the little baby. Finley and Lisa would need time to get settled at home and in their new routine, which could take a while. She paid her bill. The couple outside was getting out of the tub. The man draped a towel around his sweetheart and took her hand, leading her back to their room. Mary Jean thought of Lewis Weeks again and wondered who he was. She knew she had feelings for him. She looked forward to having dinner with him that night.

Outside, the sun was brilliant and the sky was a deep blue. The air was so dry. They were in a record drought, and the foothills were usually blanketed in a smoky haze this time of the year. There were some days when she stayed inside because it was hard to breathe. That was why she liked going to the coast because it seemed the smoke did not make its way there.

When she was back at Kingsley, she looked around expectantly for Lewis as she walked through the main entrance. At times, it seemed like he would show up just when she was looking for him. He was nowhere in sight, so she decided to go to the library and find a new book to read.

The library was empty, which seemed odd for the afternoon. Mary Jean was thirsty and looked around for the pitcher of water that was usually sitting on the table next to the fireplace. She poured herself a glass and picked up one of the cookies from the tray on the table. She browsed the shelves, looking for a book that might appeal to her. She enjoyed light mystery stories without too much violence and picked one from the shelves. A green love seat in the back of the library looked inviting, so she headed that way, finishing up her cookie and being careful not to drop crumbs everywhere. As soon as she got comfortable, she felt a wave of fatigue hit her. She became very drowsy and felt herself melt into the pillows on the couch. Her book dropped with a mild thump onto the carpet. She drifted as if in another world, and as always, Lewis came to mind . . .

17

Mary Jean felt someone shaking her gently, waking her up. She opened her eyes.

"Lewis, what are you doing here in the library?"

Her eyes adjusted, and she saw that they had company. Lewis chuckled and said, "Jack, this is Mary Jean, the friend I was telling you about."

Jack was a short and stout man with a graying beard and short black hair. He had a strong brow, an angular nose, and dark brown eyes. He wore blue jeans, a sports jacket, and comfortable-looking shoes. He had a warm smile, and Mary Jean immediately liked him.

"It's nice to meet you, Mary Jean. Too bad it is under these dark circumstances." He shook her hand carefully and gave her a nod.

"Oh, you are Jack Holden, the PI that Lewis has been telling me about! Why are you two talking right here where everyone can see you?" she whispered.

"Mary Jean, I have good news," said Lewis. "It's over. We have brought the FBI in to arrest Mrs. Lemon, Mr. Schultz and the cook. I didn't tell you earlier when we were in my apartment because we were still collecting information to incriminate them. But it's all out in the open now. People are shocked. They are bringing in new management next week." Jack Holden looked relaxed as Lewis explained what had just happened.

Lewis continued, "The FBI got involved because of the offshore laundering, and Jack intercepted the people who were taking Hattie to the Memory Care Unit this morning. She's going to be all right. I can't say as much for a few of the other residents, I'm afraid."

Mary Jean felt a wave of relief for her friend but sadness for the others whose fate she knew was not as promising. As she listened to the two men, she felt a headache coming on and massaged her temples.

"The FBI is sending in an additional team to collect the books and compile more evidence to make sure it is an airtight case. They are trying to keep everything here at Kingsley running smoothly so residents don't start moving out in a rush. We also found Sarah in the Memory Care Unit. She hadn't died after all. She was sedated but is awake now, though she doesn't remember a thing."

Jack Holden looked down at his wristwatch and said, "I've got to get going. I am meeting the FBI at the police station to arrest Mr. Schultz." He tipped his hat at Mary Jean and went on his way.

Lewis and Mary Jean left the library and walked up the stairs to her apartment. She felt like she was being dragged along on wheels. She was so relieved that Mrs. Lemon and her cohorts had been caught and arrested. She could finally get some much-needed rest. Mary Jean slowly unlocked her door, and they stepped inside.

"I think I am going to lie down for a while. Go

ahead and make yourself a cup of coffee and relax in the living room. All of this has been so draining."

"Go right ahead, Mary Jean. I'll catch up on the news in the paper and have a little sit-down myself."

Mary Jean closed the door to her bedroom and lay down on her bed. She closed her eyes and tried not to think about what could have happened if Mrs. Lemon had led her to the media room. Had they been waiting for her there, ready to drug or sedate her and haul her off to the Memory Care Unit like all the others? But she needn't worry anymore since Mrs. Lemon was being arrested. Thoughts swirled in her mind, and a fog descended.

When she opened her eyes, she could not move. All around her, nurses moved with brisk efficiency. There were other residents, too, crammed into what looked like an ICU room in a hospital. People were hooked up to machines with IVs, and many of them looked up at the ceiling with blank stares. Where was she? How had she gotten here? She tried to cry out, but nothing came out of her mouth. She began to panic but steeled herself to quell her anxiety. She had to stay focused. She had to figure out how to make contact with one of the nurses.

As if reading her mind, a young nurse in her thirties with a curly bob came over to check on her. Mary Jean stared at her with frantic eyes. The nurse would not look at her. Mary Jean tried to move her arm, but nothing happened. Finally, with all her strength, she managed to move her head just a little, and this caught the nurse's attention.

"Oh, Mary Jean, I think you are waking up!" she said. Mary Jean stared at her with a questioning look in her eyes.

"Yes, in about a half hour or so, you should be

able to move your arms and maybe even speak." Mary Jean felt the briefest sense of relief before falling back asleep.

Someone brushed her arm, and Mary Jean woke with a start. She was in the same bed in the ICU. The last thing Mary Jean remembered was entering the building and deciding to go to the library to find a book. Or, wait, did she also remember seeing Lewis and Jack Holden in the library? When had reality ended and when had her dream started? She thought she had run into Lewis and Jack and that they had told her the case had been cracked. They had saved Hattie and arrested Mrs. Lemon. Then, didn't she go up to her apartment with Lewis? She had laid down for a nap . . . or had she?

Mary Jean lay motionless while machines whirred around her. Her mind was fuzzy, and she could not make sense of what was real and what wasn't . . . . She feebly lifted her hand. The patient next to her was sitting up, drinking from a sippy cup. She looked very tired and had a vacant look in her eyes. Mary Jean heard nurses whispering to each other before leaving the room. Another patient started yelling, and a nurse came through the door to attend to him. He was flailing his arms and moaning as if he were fighting off demons in a faraway place. Mary Jean recognized a woman on the other side of the room. It was Hattie! She seemed like she was in a coma or a deep sleep.

Just then, a tall, lanky man in a white coat came into the room. He had a stethoscope around his neck, so he was probably the doctor. Mary Jean was afraid. He was heading toward her bed.

"Hello, Mary Jean. I see you are awake. How

are you feeling?" He had kind blue eyes and thick blondish-red hair.

"Where am I? Who are you?" asked Mary Jean.

"I know you must feel very disoriented. You and many of the residents were brought to St. Vincent's Hospital from Kingsley Retirement Home a few days ago. You were drugged with ketamine by one of Mrs. Lemon's cohorts. Someone reported a demented woman hallucinating in the library, and so you were taken to the Memory Care Unit. An unknown person caught you being wheeled in, and you were rushed to this hospital to recover. You were one of the lucky ones."

Mary Jean couldn't believe her ears. How had they managed to drug her? She thought she had been safe by not eating lunch in the dining room and avoiding the protein drink brought to her room. She thought back to her last memories. Had she eaten cookies in the library? Also, she must have dreamed that she had made it safely back to her apartment with Lewis. That all the bad players in the case had been caught. Had she also dreamed up the FBI? Where was Lewis when she needed him?

"You should be feeling much better by the evening," continued the doctor. "We will probably move you to a private room tomorrow just so we can monitor your progress for a day or two." He patted her hand and turned to examine the patient next to her.

18

That evening, Mary Jean was moved to a private room. It had a large window looking out onto a green field with a row of birch trees. There were also mounds of yellow lilies that looked pretty against the white bark. The lovely scenery made her stay here more bearable. It was late June, and Mary Jean had spent the past few days in the hospital recovering. She needed to get better so she could care for the garden with Derek. She wondered how he was doing and was anxious to see him.

There was a knock on the door.

"Come in," Mary Jean said in a hoarse voice.

In walked Marcus, Nora, Abby, and Shiela. All her children were here in the same room. I guess it takes being near death for this to happen, Mary Jean thought.

"Hi, Mom. How are you feeling?" asked Marcus.

"Not bad now that I know where I am." Her daughters crowded around her and Shiela showed her some flowers she had picked from her garden. Nora searched in a cupboard, found a vase, filled it with water, and handed it to Shiela. Shiela arranged the flowers evenly in the vase and set them on the table near the bed.

"Mom, why didn't you tell us there was something fishy going on at Kingsley?" asked Shiela.

"I don't know. I thought you would think I was losing it. Then I'd end up in the Memory Care Unit anyway," she said.

"Well, it *is* really hard to believe that crooked people would do such a thing to old, vulnerable people."

"Welcome to the real world." Mary Jean looked out the window.

The sky was blue, without a cloud in sight. Mary Jean longed for the drought to be over. She actually missed the rain. She never thought she would be thinking such a thing living in Oregon where you could expect rain all but two months out of the year.

"Mom, we would like to move you to a different facility," said Marcus.

"I suppose that might be a good idea. But where? Kingsley is affordable and close to Shiela and Nora. And did I dream this as well: did they arrest everyone in management at Kingsley?"

Marcus replied, "I read in the newspaper that someone had made an anonymous call to the media a few months ago to report the apparent death of a house cleaner at Kingsley, the use of ketamine in the lunch meals, and the involvement of the chief of police. The media investigated and eventually uncovered the story, leading to the arrests. So yes—Mrs. Lemon, Mr. Schultz, and the cook are all in custody."

I sure had a whopper of a dream, thought Mary Jean to herself. Mary Jean frowned as if deep in thought. Marcus could see his mother was upset and tried to console her by saying, "New management is underway at Kingsley now. I just don't know how soon that will take place. Look, this has been a huge scandal, and many of the residents are leaving."

Abby stepped up closer to the bed and said, "We have a new place scoped out. It's the new one they were building last year just west of Kingsley on the other side of town. It's called Springfield Acres."

"I don't know. I need to think about it. And talk with some of the other residents," said Mary Jean.

She looked out the window again. Here it came again. Change. She wasn't very good at change.

Mary Jean was discharged the next morning. Nora picked her up and took her to her house. Mary Jean was to stay there until a decision was made about where she was going to live permanently. Nora lived in Hillsboro with her husband, Nick. They didn't have children, and Nick was retired now. It would be different having him around the house all the time, thought Mary Jean. Not just for me but also for Nora. Nora was used to having the house to herself all day. She worked at home as a freelance writer and was very good at her work. She was in demand for her articles on how to attract birds to your garden and was an expert on alternative energy sources. She was an avid gardener and filled their tiny lot with a myriad of plants. Luckily, Nick liked to be outdoors, too, and he helped with the composting and weeding.

What was going to happen with the garden project? What about Derek? She knew he was looking forward to seeing his plants grow and to learn about making marinara sauce. The tomatoes would probably not be ready to harvest until a couple of months. It always seemed like they were ready for picking in late September just after her birthday. Luckily, the last week or so, volunteers had been coming to the garden to water the garden bed for the residents who could not make it. She hoped Derek had been there, too, to water their vulnerable seeds.

"Nora, can you take me to the resident's garden plot in the park tomorrow?" asked Mary Jean. "I want to check on our plants to make sure everything is all right."

"Sure, Mom. We can go out tomorrow morning after I water *my* plants." Nora finished her coffee and hurried outside to tend to her garden. Mary Jean sat back in the kitchen chair and sighed. This was not going to work out for very long. She needed her own place. Maybe Marcus could come over and take her to the new retirement home to see what it was like. She also needed to get back to Kingsley to see if any of the residents she knew were still there. She wanted to talk with them about what they were going to do.

The next morning was brisk, and the wind was whipping up a breeze. Nora drove carefully, always keeping to the speed limit when Mary Jean was with her. Mary Jean relaxed in her seat and watched the scenery go by. The traffic was heavy as they made their way west toward Maple Grove on the freeway. As they drove up the driveway into Kingsley, Mary Jean shouted out, "Stop here!" The driveway was filled with cars. People were loading boxes into the trunks. A couple of U-Haul trailers were parked side by side in the parking lot. Nora turned into the Kingsley parking lot and stopped the car.

"Why do you want to stop here?" Nora asked.

"I want to see who is leaving and who is staying," she said briskly. "Help me out of the car, please."

Nora reluctantly opened her door and went around to help Mary Jean out of the car. Together, they walked up to the nearest resident who was sitting in a U-Haul truck.

"Is that you, Hattie?"

Mary Jean looked through the window. She was happy to see the familiar look back in Hattie's eyes. Hattie rolled down the window.

"What are you doing here, Mary Jean?" Hattie asked.

"I wanted to see who was leaving Kingsley. Is anybody staying?" she asked.

"I think they ordered everyone out. There is a massive investigation going on, and they said they are closing down the facility for quite some time. Many of the residents are moving to the new Springfield Acres. It's a little more expensive, but they have a therapy pool and an actual restaurant there."

"I'm going to try and get over there to check it out soon," said Mary Jean. "Right now, I am going over to the garden plot to check out our vegetables and herbs. It's good to see you, Hattie. I am so glad you are alright."

"I just got out of the hospital yesterday," Hattie said. "I am staying at my son's house in Portland until next Monday. Hopefully I will see you over at Springfield Acres."

Mary Jean nodded, and she and Nora walked back to the car.

"I've seen enough," Mary Jean said. "I think I've made up my mind."

With that, they got into the car and proceeded to the garden plot. When they arrived, several residents and their students were milling about, weeding and watering their seeds. Mary Jean found her plot and saw that it was well tended. She smiled to herself and hoped that Derek had been the one keeping the little plot looking so well. Satisfied, she turned to her daughter and said, "Nora, it looks like everything is doing well here. Let's go get a milkshake!"

They headed back to the car and proceeded to their favorite restaurant for milkshakes. During the drive, Mary Jean thought about the big change that was soon to happen. Moving again. At her age, any little change seemed huge. She was less inclined to take chances, of course, and she always chose the safest path. And why not? She was in her nineties, and everything was more challenging compared to when she was young. She tried to think of a time when adventure was fun, something she looked forward to. Lewis and she had done lots of traveling, from Africa to Asia and many other countries in between. But now? She didn't even like going to Abby's house two hours away. She just hoped there were lots of beautiful places to walk at in the new home.

As she pondered those things, Nora asked, "So, what are you thinking, Mom? Isn't it exciting to imagine moving to a place that has so much to offer?"

Mary Jean smiled and said, "I'm trying to be positive about that. Maybe when I see it it, I'll be more excited. And I'm hoping that I'll know someone there."

"Oh, I bet you will. And you will meet new friends, too. You're never too old to make new friends."

Mary Jean smiled and thought about Lewis Weeks. Had he been the unknown person who had saved her from being wheeled into Memory Care? She wondered if she would ever see him again.

They parked the car and ventured into the restaurant. They found a seat by a window and went back and forth on what flavor they wanted. After ordering, Mary Jean said to her daughter, "We have a long summer ahead of us. What would you like to do while I stay at your house? It might be a little while before I get moved to the new place—if I go there, that is."

"How about we visit the Oregon Garden in Silverton?" said Nora.

"I would love that." Mary Jean was starting to see the possibilities after all.

19

The summer months passed quickly with Mary Jean visiting the garden plot and meeting up with Derek once a week or so. Lately, she had skipped a couple of weeks so Nora and she could plan some outings together. Nora and Mary Jean made their trip to Silverton and explored the Oregon Gardens. There were art galleries and wineries on the agenda, as well, and Mary Jean felt the newness rubbing off on her. It was fun to mix up the days, to try new things.

It was late September and another birthday loomed ahead. This morning, Mary Jean was going back to the garden plot after some time away to harvest tomatoes with Nora. There were several people there, a mix of middle-aged volunteers, young children, and a few residents. They were bending over weeding, wrestling with hoses, and harvesting their vegetables. Mary Jean looked earnestly for Derek, hoping he might be here. Then she saw a boy sitting on an old wooden bench under a maple tree. That sure looks like Derek, she thought. Nora stopped to talk with one of the volunteers as Mary Jean hurried over to the boy on the bench. He was looking down and swinging his legs.

"Derek! How are you?" Mary Jean stood over him. He raised his head, and she noticed a large bruise on the side of his face.

"What happened to your face?" Mary Jean looked in horror at the darkening bruise. His cheekbone was swollen, and it was turning a dark purple color.

"I fell," he said and looked away at the volunteers working on their gardens.

"When did this happen?" she asked.

"About three days ago," he said.

"Would you like to talk about it?"

Mary Jean sat next to him on the bench. They watched as people scurried around their gardens. Derek brushed a bee from his arm. His black hair was combed, she noticed, and his clothes actually looked clean.

"Not really. You know, you never told me what happened at Kingsley," he said. "Did they save all the residents?" He admitted that he was not sure if he should bring it up and that he had been worried about her. The scandal had been reported in all the papers, and he had heard his mom talk about it.

"We had some problems at the resident home, and many of us ended up in the hospital for a few days. But we are all right now. Many of us are moving to a new facility. When I'm there, I'm still hoping I'll get to participate in the garden project." She smiled and patted his hand. "You look good . . . except for your bruise, of course. Let's go check on our garden."

He jumped up, and together, they walked over to their plot to examine their plants. There were several plump tomatoes on the vines, and the basil and oregano were bushy and healthy looking.

"Someone's been working very hard," said Mary Jean. "There are hardly any weeds."

"My dad and I have been coming over a few times the past few weeks you've been gone. We weeded and watered, and as you can see, everything has gotten so big. I've been thinking about what you said about making the marinara sauce. Can you write down the recipe for us?" Derek seemed to perk up and then quickly walked over to his backpack. He brought over a pencil and a notepad for Mary Jean.

"I'd be glad to," she said. She wrote down her recipe, which included lots of garlic and caramelized onions, which she had forgotten to mention when she first told him about making marinara sauce. "Then add a little red wine, if you have it, and fresh basil and oregano." She also wrote her phone number and name down. "You can call me if you have any questions. Maybe we could make this together when I move into my new apartment at Springfield Acres."

"That would be fun," he said.

Nora showed up with a big plastic bowl, and they all got to work harvesting the fruits of their labor. The smells were intoxicating—red, ripe tomatoes and the fragrant leaves of the basil and sweet oregano. Mary Jean could almost taste the thick marinara sauce. Other volunteers showed up to say hello and offer help. Kids were raking and picking up weeds. The compost pile in the corner was growing with debris. The sun warmed their backs, and orange butterflies danced around them. Mary Jean breathed deeply and held on to this moment. Wasn't this what life was all about? Short but spectacular moments that ignited all the senses.

When they were done, the three of them headed to Nora's car. It was lunchtime.

"Derek, is your father coming to pick you up today?" It was Saturday, so the parents usually transported their kids to and from the garden.

"Yeah, he should be here soon. We're going to have a picnic at the park. He's bringing my mom and sister. After that, we are going to drive down to Albany to see the big carousel!"

Derek's eyes lit up and he launched into a speech about all the different kinds of animals that he could ride on. Mary Jean had heard all about the new carousel. It had been a huge community effort that had taken more than a decade to come to fruition. Wood craftsmen and artists worked together to design, carve, and paint those magnificent creatures. Community members donated money to support the creation of different animals and got to have their family names engraved on the sculpture. Maybe Springfield Acres residents would like to visit the carousel sometime as a field trip, thought Mary Jean .

"That sounds wonderful, Derek," she said. "I'll see you next week. Let me know how your spaghetti sauce turns out." She gave him the bowl of produce. The wind had picked up, and Mary Jean watched as the colorful leaves swirled around, making mini-dust-devils around the garden. The sun was high in the cloudy sky. Sometimes, things changed for the better, she thought.

Mary Jean and Nora said their goodbyes to the group that was still there and headed down the gravel road toward the car.

"You two sure seem to have developed a special bond," said Nora.

"Yes. I think we have." Mary Jean felt happy. Happier than she had been in a long time. Maybe, somehow, she was making a difference. But something else was happening in that family. Derek looked cleaner, but what about that bruise? Had he really fallen? Or had someone hit him? Mary Jean knew she had to find out. It could have happened at school.

"Do you know what happened to Derek's face?" asked Nora. "I noticed that big purple bruise. I hope someone didn't hit him." Mary Jean detected the concern in her voice.

"He said he fell. But I've been wondering about that myself. He did look neater, and his clothes were cleaner than usual. So it looks like someone is taking better care of him." But she knew she didn't sound confident about that. "I'll have to find out more the next time I see him." Mary Jean thought to herself that the usually chipper Derek had been much less talkative today.

On the way home, the traffic was bad. Mary Jean hated being stuck in the car when other cars whizzed by around her. People drove faster now, it seemed, compared to when she was driving. She was glad she had stopped about two years ago. No one had told her that she needed to stop driving; she just knew it was time. Just like when she knew it was time to move out of the family home into a small condo after Lewis died. After five years there, she was also the one to decide to move to Kingsley. She didn't want to worry about keeping up the place and doing repairs—and, well, she was lonely. The neighbors never invited her over, and she was tired of eating alone all the time. Each time she moved, she put things that she didn't need anymore in boxes and had Marcus cart them over to Goodwill. Each move pared down her belongings into more manageable quantities.

Nora turned right, then left, and headed for the vegetarian café she liked so much. She and her husband had been vegetarian for over ten years now. Mary Jean enjoyed vegetarian meals and would eat almost anything as long as it wasn't too greasy. Well, she'd take that back. The last time her son took her out for lunch at McMenamins, she'd ordered fish and chips. But she'd also thought it wasn't that greasy. She reflected on that moment. Good food sure was one thing she still enjoyed. She knew some of the residents on the assisted side were on a diet of pureed foods. Boy, she was grateful she could still chew and swallow. Those foods looked so unappetizing. The cooks tried to make them look like the real thing, but brown puree made thick like a hamburger patty still made her stomach churn.

 As they headed to the cafe, Mary Jean thought about what she would order. A veggie burger sounds pretty good right about now, she thought.

20

Mary Jean sat in Nora's living room, drinking some coffee. It was 9 a.m. Today was the day Marcus was coming over to move her into Springfield Acres. Marcus had hired some guys to load up her belongings in a U-Haul truck, and they were going to meet them at Springfield Acres in about an hour so she could tell them where she wanted everything. She was both sad and excited. She wondered what had happened to Lewis. Surely he would be there, wouldn't he? Mary Jean had been so distracted, caught up in the corruption and fallout at Kingsley, what with being in the hospital, that she hadn't had time to think about where Lewis was.

Nora answered a knock on the door. Marcus stood there in a baseball cap and jeans.

"Hi, Mom. Are you ready to go? It's the big day; you're moving into your new place! Are you excited?" Marcus looked like a kid in a candy shop. He was more excited than she was.

"I think my mind is preoccupied at the moment. I'm still processing everything that went on at Kingsley. And it's a little sad to be leaving, but the new place looks like it may have a little more to offer."

She sighed, grabbed her bag and coat, and stepped out the door.

Marcus helped his mother into the truck and closed the door. They got on the freeway and headed west. It wasn't far; just five miles outside of town.

"Your new apartment is a little bit bigger, and you have a nice view of the garden and courtyard, as well as some beautiful birch trees." Marcus was watching his mother carefully to see how she was taking the new move.

"That's nice, honey," she said. She stared out the window and noticed the fields were all tilled up. The rains hadn't come yet, so there was still a lot of dust in the air. Little whirlwinds or dust devils skipped through the fields. Her eyes felt heavy, and she felt displaced as they headed north out of Maple Grove and toward her new home.

Marcus opened the truck door for Mary Jean, and she carefully stepped down from the tall truck seat. At least there was a step and a handle to help her reach the ground. Marcus held her one hand as she lowered herself to the ground unsteadily.

Springfield Acres was set on twenty acres of good farmland. How they had managed to get permission to build here, Mary Jean did not know. I guess there were a lot of us getting older and needing a place to live, she thought. It did look luxurious, with paved hiking trails, lots of green space with trees, and even an indoor pool. There were two restaurants on campus, both built in a Pacific Northwest style. The walls were painted with deep, rich browns and greens accented with mustard yellow. There was a community hall where exercise classes took place. Another building housed the art programs. The director, Mrs. Laymon, gave them a tour of the grounds. As they rode in a golf cart, she pointed out to various buildings, describing what went on there. They stopped and got out from time to time, poking their heads into buildings to look at what was inside.

When they were brought to the ceramics center, which was equipped with a kiln, Mary Jean said, "My daughter-in-law would sure like this place!"

They watched as residents sat at tables working on their clay projects. An instructor walked from table to table, giving encouragement and direction when needed. The room was open and airy, with big windows reaching to the ceiling. One resident was struggling to roll out her clay, and the instructor hurried to her side to help. Another was staring out the windows, just sitting there. A group of four women were chatting together on high stools with their clay projects at various stages before them. Mary Jean could actually discern what the shapes were: one was a dog with a very long body and floppy ears; there was also a bird, a mug, and a bowl.

That group of women look like they know what they are doing, Mary Jean thought. I wonder if I could make a bowl. She watched as the women talked and worked on their projects and thought what a wonderful way it was to spend the time—being creative and visiting with friends. She could enjoy that kind of thing.

"We'd better get you back to your room so you can instruct the movers where to put your things," said Mrs. Laymon.

They returned to the cart and drove off toward the main facility. Springfield Acres was built in a modern design, with plenty of warm wood arches and painted blocks of cantaloupe, cream, and green. The landscaping outside was all sustainable with native plants, so little mowing was needed. The building had solar panels on the roof facing southwest. Water was collected in large barrels from the gutters and used to water the garden. The main courtyard was the gem of the facility. It was like having a park right at your doorstep. Glass windows were abundantly placed all along the building so residents inside could look down into the gardens from all levels.

Mary Jean and Marcus took the elevator up to the second floor and walked down the hallway looking for her room number. The hallway was brightly painted, and artwork from local artists hung all along the walls. The floor was a light bamboo. The feeling of light and energy flowed everywhere you walked, unlike at the old facility, which had been largely painted in an institutional green. They finally arrived at #226. A man from the U-Haul was waiting, and Marcus spoke to him while Mary Jean unlocked the door and went inside.

A wall of windows looked down on the garden below. There was a balcony, just like her old apartment. But this balcony was bigger, and it already contained four turquoise pots of blooming orange begonias. A wooden bench with two plump yellow cushions was pushed up against the wall. What a lovely place to sit and enjoy the view, thought Mary Jean. She went back inside and looked at the light, open space, which contained a small modern kitchen with a white quartz countertop and knotty alder cabinets. The apartment had a kitchen, bathroom, spacious living room, and large bedroom. It was kind of the same format as her old apartment, but more spacious and lighter and, of course, newer. Her old bathroom had only a shower, but this new one had a modern, safe, soaking tub with a European handheld showerhead.

"Mom, this place is amazing!'" said Marcus.

There was a knock on the open door. Two men were standing outside, carrying some small pieces of furniture.

"The movers are here. You should tell them where you'd like to put everything."

Mary Jean just stared at this beautiful space. She turned to the man and said, "Just bring it all up. There's so much room in here, I'm sure we'll have no trouble setting it all in the living room for now." She smiled and turned to take another look at her new home.

The workers brought one piece after another, and Mary Jean instructed them on where to put the furniture. When everything was brought up and the U-Haul drove off, Mary Jean sat down on her couch and looked around. Her new kitchen had ample room for a few new things, if she wanted them. There was space in the center of the living room for her new great-grandson to play in. Her bedroom was also spacious. She no longer tripped over her extra chair, which she used to drape her yoga clothes on in the evening to air out.

"Marcus, how am I going to afford this place? It must be so expensive!"

"Mom, it is more expensive, but you and Dad saved lots of money, and you can afford this. We all decided you should have more opportunities, and this place seems to have it all."

Mary Jean thought about some of the residents back at Kingsley who would not be able to afford such luxury. She immediately felt guilty that she had this great opportunity for better living than some of her old friends. Where would they end up? There was only one other retirement center nearby, and it was very old and much smaller. She felt privileged and thought, once again, how unfair life could be.

But what was foremost on her mind was Lewis. Now that she was moved in, she needed to see if he was here, too. He said he would never leave her, that he would be with her in one way or another. Still, what had he meant by that? Mary Jean suddenly felt panicked. What if she never saw him again?

21

Her first night at Springfield Acres was mixed. She felt a bit disoriented and slept fitfully. She wondered how many Kingsley residents had moved here. She was again feeling guilty for being here at all. Adjustments were harder to make as you got older. Change was almost life-threatening.

The next morning, she was having her morning coffee when a hummingbird on her balcony caught her eye. She slowly walked over to the sliding glass door and looked out. The hummingbird darted over and hovered right in front of her.

What a dazzling sight, thought Mary Jean.

The bird was an iridescent green with dark blue and metallic spots that shimmered in the light. Its wings beat so fast that they were blurred almost from sight. So adept at hovering, the bird was a marvel. It seemed immensely curious, and when Mary Jean moved to the right, so did the little bird.

"What a courageous little hummingbird you are. You don't seem at all afraid of me," Mary Jean said.

She studied the bird and realized that if the glass door was not between them, it would be inches from her face. She had never been this close to a hummingbird before, or any bird for that matter. She held her breath for a moment and stood motionless in hopes of making it last as long as possible. The tiny bird took one last look at her and darted away in a blink of an eye. Did that really happen? Mary Jean wondered. She realized that such brief moments of wonder produced a heightened sense of happiness, and that most people did not dwell on these fleeting experiences because they were too busy getting somewhere else or "staring at their phones," she added under her breath.

Mary Jean stood there awhile, the awe slowly fading away. How many tiny moments of pleasure had she missed in her life? Too busy getting meals on the table, picking up after her kids in the house, running errands, or rushing to work, with little time to just be. No time to let ideas come to her because her brain was usually too full. No time to stop and wonder, to feel grateful and enjoy life, or to sit with herself and meditate on what she really loved, what brought her pleasure, and who she was.

She stood staring out the glass door, thinking. What did she really want to do? She went into her new bedroom, threw open the closet, and grabbed her red sneakers.

"It all started with you," she said. She sat down in the living room and put her shoes on. She grabbed her sweater and headed out to explore her new world. She felt stiff and sore and tired, but she forced herself to move one foot in front of the other and hurried out the door.

There were residents walking in the halls and young people with jeans and starched shirts pushing carts of artwork. The young men and women were talking together, deciding which pieces to display and where. Mary Jean did not recognize the residents in the hallway and didn't feel especially talkative, so she quickly brushed by them.

One of the young people smiled and said hello, and Mary Jean nodded her head and smiled as she passed. She continued to walk down the hall until she came to the cafeteria. In the corner by the tall windows, she recognized someone. It was Hattie! At least she would know one person here.

"Hattie! Hi! How are you doing?" said Mary Jean. Hattie looked up, and there were dark circles under her eyes. She smiled as she recognized Mary Jean.

"I'm doing okay. How do you like the new place? Pretty fancy, isn't it?" Hattie invited Mary Jean to sit with her.

As Mary Jean sat down, she looked through the windows at the large, open garden space below them.

"Kingsley had a courtyard, too. Only this one is so much bigger, with a soaring glassed-in roof, and trees even," said Mary Jean. "I love the walkways, too. I can't wait to go outside and explore the place. There are golf carts that will take you to the various buildings if you don't want to walk." Mary Jean stopped talking and looked at Hattie. Hattie seemed barely there. It seemed she was reliving the nightmare in the ICU.

"Hattie, it was really awful, wasn't it? I was scared, too. You almost died. Those terrible people. So greedy and no shame in taking advantage of us older people. I don't know if I can trust anyone anymore." Mary Jean took her hand and squeezed it.

Hattie looked down, and a tear rolled down her cheek. She was remembering her harrowing experience of being whisked away to Memory Care under the influence of ketamine.

"I was terrified when I woke up," said Hattie. "I

didn't know if I was alive or dead. I couldn't move my arms or legs. I couldn't even talk."

"I can't imagine how that must have felt." But Mary Jean could imagine it because she had been through it, too. However, she didn't want to tell Hattie. Hattie stared out the windows and sighed.

"Why don't you come outside with me? We can explore the grounds and facilities together and see what they have to offer." Mary Jean waited expectantly while Hattie sat in silence.

"I'm taking baby steps," said Hattie. "You go along, and maybe tomorrow I'll venture out." She forced a smile and took a sip of her coffee.

"All right. I'll check in with you tomorrow. There is someone I am looking for, so I should get going." Mary Jean stood up and waved goodbye to Hattie before she made her way toward the entryway downstairs.

Fall was in full swing. The maple leaves had left a watercolor of reds and yellows on the sidewalks. The yellow leaves of the birch trees contrasted brightly against the white of the tree trunks. Mary Jean followed the path that led down to the ceramics center. She thought she'd check that out first so she could tell her daughter-in-law all about it when she and Marcus visited next. The sun was hot on her back, and the sky was a brilliant cerulean blue. Great care had been taken in the landscaping. There wasn't a lot of lawn, so there was probably no wasted fuel on mowing. Shrubs of rust and gold dotted the grounds with tufts of blue-green grasses in between.

The color of the buildings echoed the interior palette of the apartments—fern green and subtle melon orange with creams and mustard yellow. The large door to the ceramics center had been swung open, revealing potting wheels lined up in tidy rows. Large canvas-colored tables with sturdy stools were grouped on one side of the room. Not many people were there, but a small group was working on sculptures. As she got closer to the building, she felt a tap on her shoulder. The wind had picked up, and fallen leaves swirled up around her. She looked behind her, and there was Lewis!

22

"Lewis! I never thought I'd see you again! Are you living here?" Mary Jean was wide-eyed as she looked at her dear friend.

"Well, you could say that, I guess. I told you I'd never leave you. So here I am." He was meticulously dressed as usual.

Lewis embraced her, and they stood like that for some time. Mary Jean knew that this was another one of those special moments. She tried to savor it so it would last. She breathed in the scent of him: old leather, a faint tobacco smell, and Old Spice shaving cream. The wind continued to move the leaves around and above them as they stood holding each other closely.

"It's so good to see you out and about, walking in your red sneakers," he said.

"You taught me to put one foot in front of the other, even if I don't feel like it." She smiled and held his large hand in hers.

She studied his face and saw the shine in his bright blue eyes and felt the energy he exuded. The lines around his eyes and wrinkles in his face were a map of his past, giving him character in his old age.

His face and body may have aged, but his energy for life still shone, and that was what had always helped her face another day when she was feeling down.

Together, they walked past the ceramics center and continued following the winding path lined with pine and fir trees, bushes, and flowers, still hanging on to the beauty from summer. A couple was approaching on the path and Mary Jean recognized the Leffels from Kingsley! They stopped and chatted, mainly to Mary Jean, not seeming to notice Lewis. When they continued on, Mary Jean wondered again if she was the only one who could see Lewis.

"Why didn't those people see you?" Mary Jean asked.

"Oh, I think they were just more interested in talking with you," said Lewis.

"Now, come on, what's really going on here? What should I know that you are not telling me? Are you . . . a figment of my imagination? Or am I just going crazy?" Mary Jean stopped walking and looked straight into Lewis's eyes.

"You worry too much. Enjoy these moments. Isn't that what life is all about? Do we need answers to everything?" Lewis looked at her innocently.

"That's easy for you to say. You're not the one who feels like she is going crazy. Am I going to get any answers out of you?"

"What would be the fun of that?" He looked down and studied his red sneakers. "I honestly don't have all the answers. I am really only like a messenger. I just do what I am told. I don't ask questions. I follow my heart."

"But what does that *mean*?" asked Mary Jean.

Lewis took her hand and walked her over to a nearby bench. They sat down. Mary Jean saw more residents being driven around in carts to the pool or to the yoga room.

"One day, you will understand who I am and what I represent. The most important thing to me is that you are safe, and I can rest now. Just remember: I will always be in here."

He tapped his chest where his heart was and held her hand over it. She sighed and rested her head on his shoulder. They watched a flock of geese fly above them in V formation, honking randomly. Then, several quail scampered across the walkway to hide in the bushes along the path. Robins were pulling up juicy worms from the moist soil by some rocks nearby. And in the distance, she heard a woodpecker drilling the wood. These were all the sights and sounds of the outdoors, away from the hustle and bustle of the suburbs.

Mary Jean thought about what Lewis had said. She decided to let the topic rest. Maybe he was right. Sometimes you never get answers. I guess that's what faith is, she thought. She recalled all the Sundays when she had gone to church. They never really talked about miracles like this, but they did talk about faith. And that was good enough for her.

"Well, let's get one of those carts and have a look around, shall we?" said Lewis. "I like to walk, but this place is pretty big, and I don't know if it would be wise to tackle it all in one day on foot."

"Sounds like a plan," said Mary Jean.

They waved down a cart and the attendant drove them to the pool, the yoga room, and the two restaurants. They took a break and had some lunch at the Thai restaurant that overlooked a pond with water lilies and a real blue heron. They sipped on green tea and talked about the corruption at Kingsley and what a close call it had been for Mary Jean. Mary Jean told Lewis about what Marcus had told her—that an anonymous person had called the media, which eventually led to an investigation and the arrests. Then she also told him about her strange dream involving the FBI and the rest of it. Maybe, in her own way, with all the bits and pieces of information she had had, that was how she resolved it. It was good to get all that straightened out in her mind.

The afternoon went by quickly, and soon Mary Jean felt like she needed to return to her apartment for a nap. They caught another cart and headed back to the main building.

"I hope this isn't goodbye." Mary Jean almost whispered the word.

"No, I told you I'd be around for a while longer." He bent down and kissed her lightly on the lips. She hadn't been kissed like that in years. She looked up into his eyes and knew everything was going to be okay. He gave her a quick hug, and she left him standing there, watching her, as she went inside.

She took the elevator up to her floor, tired from the day's activities. She liked the way the light streamed in to all corners of the building. She was looking forward to settling in for a rest. "One thing at a time," she said to herself. "First I'll rest, and then I'll decide what's next." So many choices here. She wondered about the garden project and if she would see Derek again. She had so much to ask him. How did he get that bruise on his face? Was his family treating him well? She hoped he was all right.

She opened her door and walked over to the couch. She removed her sneakers and went to use the bathroom. The beautiful cream and soft turquoise interior colors were making her feel relaxed and a bit sleepy. She lay down on the couch and threw the blue-patterned quilt over her body. Her head rested on the down pillow her youngest daughter had given her for her last birthday. With that memory, she nodded off to sleep.

23

Music filtered into the room. A beautiful acoustic guitar, some strings, and a man's low voice filled the air. She moved the blanket aside and sat up. That was such lovely music. Where was it coming from? She got up, walked to the sliding glass door, and looked down into the courtyard. A man was surrounded by a dozen residents. There was a trio of musicians: a guitarist, a violinist, and a harpist all set up in the garden.

This is amazing, thought Mary Jean. We never had live music at Kingsley.

She hurried to grab her windbreaker and headed out of the apartment and down the hall to the elevator.

I should take the stairs, she told herself, but I feel a little unsteady. Thoughts tumbled around in her head as she rode the elevator down. When it opened, she looked for the exit and headed in that direction. The music was being piped into the dining hall. She opened the door to the courtyard and walked toward the group of residents and musicians. The day had become overcast, and it was cool but still warm for October.

She paused, taking in the scene. The days had tumbled by so quickly. She reflected on her ninety-second birthday at the end of September. They had rented a gazebo in the park where the garden plots were. All her kids were there, as well as her grandson, Finley, and his wife, Lisa, who brought their new great-grandson, Ivan; and she got to hold him for the first time. Abby made a homemade carrot cake, and everyone brought something to share. It was always a surprise to see what everyone would bring. The weather was warm, and they sat around and ate, talking of their past summer adventures and what plans they had for the future. She felt the warmth of family around her. It had been a wonderful day.

In the courtyard in front of the musicians, refreshments were being served: lemonade and hot tea with some marionberry scones. They looked delicious. Temporary folding chairs were set in rows before the ensemble. Mary Jean took an empty seat by an elderly man with a cane. She didn't recognize him. He wore glasses and was tall, thin, and meticulously dressed. His pants looked to be wool and tailored to fit his slim build. He wore a rust-colored shirt under a herringbone gray blazer. He had a few wisps of white hair that curled out from under his navy fedora cap.

He turned to her and said, "Hello. I am Arman. I don't think we have met."

"Hello, I'm Mary Jean. Nice to meet you." They shook hands, and he held her hand a moment longer and looked into her eyes. His blue eyes were warm and inviting.

"Were you at Kingsley?" asked Mary Jean.

He shook his head no and answered, "I am new to these retirement homes. I have lived by myself for the past twenty years. My family decided to move me here because I have just given up driving. And because there is a ceramics center here. I have taken classes at the community college for the past five years."

"What do you like to make?"

"I make statues of animals. The last one I finished was a polar bear. Oh, I'm not very good, but I enjoy working with the clay. You ought to join me." His smile was infectious, and Mary Jean replied, "I might just do that."

Mary Jean turned back to look at the musicians. They were playing a classical piece. She recognized it as she used to play classical music on the piano years ago. They listened in silence, and she noticed she did not know the others either who sat in this small group. She wondered how many of the other Kingsley residents had moved over here—and how many others had been injured or had even died on account of the crookedness of Mrs. Lemon.

She sat for another hour, listening to the music. She loved the garden with its informal setting of native plants and flowers, as well as a water feature that seemed to draw the birds. There were birch trees with white, crackly bark, a few maples that had lost their leaves, and bunches of various species of grasses dotted the landscape. The paths were a combination of pavement and gravel, probably to accommodate the people in wheelchairs.

Mary Jean wanted to find the activities director to ask if Springfield was involved in the garden project that Kingsley had started. She wanted to meet up with Derek again to see how he was doing. She wondered how he was getting on with his family. Clouds were starting to form, and temperatures seemed to be dropping, so Mary Jean made her way back into the building. She went over to the information office and asked where she could find the activities director. The lady directed her to an office down the hall and to the right. Outside the door, she saw a name plate that said MRS. LESLIE DRAKE, ACTIVITES DIRECTOR. She wondered what this woman would be like. After her experience at Kingsley, she was a bit nervous about meeting Springfield Acres's activities director. She timidly knocked on the door.

The door opened, and there stood an average-sized woman with a big bust. She was wearing a navy-blue dress that was fitted around her torso and that draped nicely in an A-line down to just above her knee. A beautiful multicolored scarf was wrapped expertly around her neck. She wore flats, and her hair was a mousey brown streaked with gray, falling thick and wavy down to her shoulders. She had hazel eyes and a welcoming smile.

"Oh, please come in! I'm Leslie. Please sit down. Can I get you some coffee or tea?"

"No thank you. I just had a few questions. I guess almost everyone is new here? Are there many residents here from Kingsley?" Mary Jean looked the woman up and down, assessing what kind of person she was. The woman made her feel comfortable right off the bat. Maybe this wouldn't be so bad after all.

"Oh yes, we have quite a few from Kingsley, but most of them are in the High Assistance Care Unit. We don't like to use the name *Memory Care* because of the experience everyone had at Kingsley. Many of the more independent residents went elsewhere, but we have many new residents from other parts of Oregon. I don't think they can make these kinds of retirement homes fast enough to keep up with the demand."

Leslie reached into a box on her desk. "Would

you care for a cookie? I made them myself. I like to dabble in the kitchen. Springfield has the most beautiful baking area. They will have baking classes there as well, so be sure to check it out. Some of the residents like to make their own cookies during Christmastime to give to family and friends."

Mary Jean took a cookie. It was a fancy one, decorated with artistry in a beautiful fox shape, and the icing had been applied like a watercolor brush to paint the details of the fox's fur and eyes. Nothing ordinary about this woman, thought Mary Jean.

"I wondered if Springfield Acres is part of the garden project we were involved in at Kingsley," said Mary Jean. "Are we going to be able to plan next year's garden with the same kids as we did last summer? There is a boy, Derek, whom I want to see again, if possible. I was hoping there would be continuity in the relationships we formed while doing the project." Mary Jean leaned in toward the director, and her concern showed in her knitted brow as it did in her strained voice.

"We haven't worked out all those details yet, but I think it would be very important to continue that project and keep the kids and residents connected. We strive to involve our residents in the community, and so this directly follows our long-term philosophy."

Mary Jean was hopeful. She stood up and said goodbye, deciding that Leslie was going to be a good, honest leader for the garden project.

24

The next day was stormy, so Mary Jean decided she would check out Springfield's library. She wandered down the hallway, turned left, walked down another hallway, then turned right. She wanted to see what kind of selection they had. She had something on her mind and hoped they would have a section of books that addressed what she had been thinking about for some time.

The library doors were double glassed and encased in a rich, dark wood. As she stepped into the space, the ceiling loomed high above her. Massive, exposed wood beams stretched across the space, giving the room an airy, open feeling. There were rows and rows of books on an array of mahogany-colored shelves. The reading area was cozy, with a tall river-rock fireplace and plush, green velvet chairs. She stopped by the desk where an assistant was studying the computer. The assistant looked up from her work.

"May I help you?" She was young, in her late twenties, with a dove-gray turtleneck sweater. A short string of pearls hung from her neck. Her earrings were droplets of turquoise encased in silver. She was dark skinned with wavy black hair streaked with blond highlights and tied in a ponytail. Her complexion was clear, and youth shone from her perfect oval face.

Mary Jean thought, I remember when I was young and my complexion was as clear as that. Oh, youth . . . it fades so quickly.

She tried not to stare at the petite woman with the big brown eyes and long lashes. Her lips were full, and she wore a faint shade of lipstick that had been all but worn off from her drinking a cup of coffee. Mary Jean noticed the red smudges of color on the edge of her coffee mug.

"Maybe you can help me. I am looking for books on the afterlife. You know, where we go when we die. Reincarnation, heaven—anything like that."

The girl's eyes widened, and she looked taken aback. Then she quickly recovered and said, "Well, let me see. I think we do have a section on that subject. Let me show you where they are located."

She walked Mary Jean over to the far end of the library to a corner where religious books of all kinds were organized. Mary Jean still wasn't entirely sure what she was looking for, but this was a good start.

"Thank you very much. I'll just browse through these."

The young woman smiled and walked back to her computer station. Mary Jean looked tentatively at the rows of books. She read the various titles and moved methodically through the rows, searching for something that might provide the answers to the question she had secretly kept hidden away in her mind.

Proof of Heaven, by Eben Alexander, MD
Life after Life, by Raymond A. Moody, Jr., MD

Many Lives, Many Masters, by Brian Weiss, MD
Only Love Is Real, by Brian Weiss, MD

What was it about all these doctors feeling the need to write books about the afterlife? It looked like this Brian Weiss sure had a lot of books on the subject. Mary Jean picked up a book and read the summary on the back cover. The book was about two people who had known each other in their past lives. She took the book out from the shelf and checked it out.

Mary Jean returned to her apartment. She sat down on the couch and started reading. This sounded so much like what she was experiencing with Lewis! Perhaps there was some truth to this. She continued reading and was startled by the phone's shrill ring. She put the book down and answered. It was Finley.

"Hi Grandma, how are you?"

"I'm fine. I've been taking in the new facility, and there is a lot more going on here. They have a ceramics center, a pool, a large indoor garden, a place to do yoga . . . but I'm not sure if I know very many people here anymore. It seems many of the Kingsley residents went somewhere else or are housed in the High Assistance Care Unit. That means Memory Care, but they don't want to use that word anymore, and . . ."

"Grandma. Slow down. You sound a bit overwhelmed, which is to be ex—"

"And I met the new activities director and she seems really nice. It seems they will be continuing the garden project, so I am thankful for that. But I don't know if I'll ever see Derek again and I'm worried there is something wrong in his family and I don't know if I can afford this place . . ."

"Grandma. Just relax. I called to ask if Lisa and

I can bring baby Ivan up to visit you this weekend."

Mary Jean fell silent. She realized she was slipping back into her old habit of running on and on and not stopping to let the other person say a word—talking only about herself and not asking the other person anything about them.

What's happening to me? she thought. Maybe I am overwhelmed. Overwhelmed with these new ideas of what comes after life and what is happening now: starting all over in a new home and always feeling older and less able every day . . .

"Grandma, are you still there? Are you all right?" Finley waited awhile and was about to ask again when Mary Jean said, "Yes. I'm all right. Just a little scattered today. There are a lot of new things to take in. I would love a visit from the three of you." She paused to let him answer.

"Okay then. How about 11 a.m. this Saturday? We will take you out to lunch."

"That will be fine. Okay, I'll see you then."

She hung up the phone and took a deep breath. Getting older just seemed to be getting harder. She needed to see Lewis again. She wanted to talk to him about the ideas she was exploring and also what she had been experiencing since moving here. She noticed that many of the new residents were much younger than she was. She was beginning to feel more isolated and left out.

They still have lots of energy, but I am just declining with each day, she thought. She felt a cloud of depression start to float over her. She needed to focus on the upcoming visit. It would be so nice to see Ivan again. She was so happy that Lisa and Finley were so thoughtful, coming up to visit her almost once a month.

Mary Jean also knew that just moving her body toward anything, sometimes just one step at a time, would help her feel better, both physically and mentally. She got up and decided to pay a visit to the ceramics center. She didn't feel like it, but if she could just walk to the door, open it, and start walking slowly down the hall, pretty soon one thing would lead to another. Perhaps the day would look a little brighter.

Outside, she noticed Hattie walking with the Leffels. I guess we stick together, thought Mary Jean. At least she had made one new friend, Arman. She hoped she would see him in the ceramics center. He was even older than she was but seemed sharp and engaged with life. It's always nice to have someone older pave the way for you, thought Mary Jean. It's inspiring and makes me reach for the opportunities that are out there.

These thoughts lightened her step, and she proceeded outside to the shuttle area.

25

Rain pelted the sidewalks, and the trees swayed as the wind gusts picked up. Mary Jean was standing in the facility's entryway looking out at the weather. She had her raincoat on and was feeling more and more like retreating back to her apartment and sipping hot tea. But she was determined to keep moving to change the way she was feeling.

The minibus pulled up to the covered archway in front of the entrance to the building. These little buses came at regular intervals to pick residents up and deliver them to the various buildings on the campus. May Jean and two others boarded the little van. Her stop at the ceramics center was first. When they arrived, she slowly got up and was helped down by the driver to the covered walkway that led to the building. She could see residents inside through the large glass windows.

When she opened the door, a middle-aged African American woman, heavyset with a deeply lined face, walked up to greet her.

"Hi, I'm Kia Rhoades. Welcome to the ceramics center! Please come take a seat at this table. We are just beginning the sculpture class. I will seat you . . ."

"Oh, I am not here to work with the clay or take a class. I just want to watch." Mary Jean glanced around the room.

"Oh, no worries. I'll just put this piece of clay here, and if you change your mind, you can play around with it." She smiled and introduced her to the other residents in the room. Mary Jean sat down at the table with her mound of clay in front of her. Sitting next to her was Arman, the man she met yesterday.

"Good morning, Mary Jean. I don't know if you remember, but we met yesterday in the garden while the music was playing. My name is Arman."

He was just as well dressed as when she had first met him. Dark tailored trousers, a light blue shirt with a collar, and a tan sport coat. He also wore two hearing aids, so Mary Jean was careful to speak up.

"Good morning, Arman. It's really nice to see you. I'm just watching. I know nothing about working with clay."

"That's one of the best ways to learn. Observation. A very keen strategy. But eventually, it is good to experiment. If you don't fail, you are not learning." He smiled as he said this and picked up his wad of clay.

She watched as he worked, kneading his clay like bread. One by one, he made coils and placed them on a little platform that swiveled. He carefully wet and attached the coils, working upward, until he had a type of vessel. He pushed the clay together along each rim of the coils, sealing it as he worked his way around the form. Then he used a large wooden spoon to pat the clay to make it uniform. He added more coils, some smaller than the others, then stretched and manipulated the walls into a shape that looked more and more like a polar bear.

"That's amazing! It's taking on a shape," Mary Jean said. He got up and went to a cubby along the wall. He brought back two sculptures he had previously made: a raven and a bighorn sheep.

"These are marvelous!" Mary Jean exclaimed. "May I pick them up?"

"Yes," he said.

She picked the raven up ever so carefully and turned it around in her hands. It had a calm expression on its face. It was jet black, with wonderful detailing on its back to depict feathers, and it had yellow claws. Its head was cocked to the right, and its beak was open and holding a seed pod of some sort.

"Ravens are very smart birds. They can trick other animals out of their food. They are great little thieves."

Mary Jean put the raven down and picked up the bighorn sheep. The sculpture was about seven inches high and five inches long. The animal was striking with its large grooved horns, deep chest, and a coat of hair so lifelike that you just wanted to touch it. The hooves were also detailed, and the glaze was a matte white with some dark accents in certain areas.

"How long did it take you to learn to do this?' asked Mary Jean.

"Well, I don't know. I just kept at it. I come mainly for the people. They are so interesting and friendly here. They were encouraging and helpful, flattering and funny. I gradually improved without really knowing it. I find this is a very relaxing and challenging way to spend my time." He winked at her, and Mary Jean blushed.

Noticing the two were talking, Kia walked over and commented on Arman's sculpture.

"Arman, that is fantastic!" She smiled and looked

over at Mary Jean. "Better watch out for this one. He's a charmer."

Mary Jean watched as Kia made the rounds to the other tables, giving encouragement and telling jokes. The residents were laughing and seemed to be having a good time. Mary Jean noticed there were just as many men as woman. One woman was a resident whom Mary Jean recognized from Kingsley. She was younger than Mary Jean and had always kept to herself and stayed in her room. Mary Jean didn't know her well, but she knew her family did not come visit very often. She often sat in silence in the dining hall and rarely spoke to anyone. Who would have thought that working with clay would open her up? Maybe this was a hobby she had done when she was younger, Mary Jean thought, or maybe it was something she had done in another life. She thought about the book she was reading about reincarnation and living multiple lives, and things started taking on a different perspective.

I wish Lewis were here, she thought. I have so many questions to ask him. Did he have a room in the new facility? Or did he just show up when it was convenient for him? How many of the people here had lived a previous life as someone else? Were they bringing old hobbies to their new lives, as well as developing new skills? Did their previous lives influence what they chose to do in this life?

The rain had stopped outside, but the wind still blew, rattling the windows. It was dark outside but the lights were bright in the room. The laughter and easy-going nature of the people here filled Mary Jean with a warm glow.

She picked up her clay and tried to knead it like she had seen Arman doing. He ignored her and worked quietly beside her, whistling a little tune. She pushed it to and fro, and gradually, it became more pliable. Her hands became tired, and she stopped.

"That's good. Now make a little hollow bowl shape, like this." He pulled off a small piece of clay and stuck his thumb in the center of it. He turned it upside down and started working around it in a circle, pulling the edges down and hollowing it like a bowl. He handed it to Mary Jean, and she gave it a try. It was fun pushing the clay around, but she wasn't sure what she was making.

"Okay, now turn it over, and you have a bowl, right? Now make another one, and I'll show you how to glue them together with water and a little roughening up."

Soon, she had a shape that looked like an egg. He showed her which tools to use to make it smooth or to give it texture, whatever she wanted.

"All right. You're done. Now it needs to dry on the shelf over there for a few days, then they will do the first firing called a bisque fire. After that, you get to put on the glaze. Then it gets fired again in the high fire."

Mary Jean was thrilled that she had completed something. She was excited to see what it would look like after the bisque firing. She realized this was something she needed more in her life—something to look forward to. A small challenge. New friends.

"Thank you for your help. It was a lot of fun, and I am looking forward to returning and finishing my project. With your help, of course." She got up, and Arman walked her to the door. He tipped his hat and said, "See you next time."

26

Music filtered into the apartment. Mary Jean stirred slightly and opened her eyes. She felt a bit too warm and slowly removed the top cover. She closed her eyes again and drifted in and out of sleep for a while. It was classical music, maybe Bach. She was remembering a session with her teacher when she was in high school—sitting at the piano in her living room. The right notes came easily. She loved the cadence of the song and how calming it made her feel.

She heard a rustling sound. It sounded like somebody was pushing something underneath the door. She glanced at the clock beside her bed and saw that it was still early, just 6 a.m. It's probably just the activities director giving us the schedule for today, she thought. She lay there now, wide awake and thinking of music, of mastering all the songs as a young person, of playing in church, of how proud she'd felt. It was good to master things in life.

She got up and shuffled to the bathroom. When she looked in the mirror, she saw an aging lady with white flyaway hair, pale wrinkled skin, and sagging blue eyes. My life has flown by, and now here I am, still kicking, still living life, she thought. I've been given yet another day to learn something new. I have aches and pains, but nothing so bad that I can't persevere and walk outside or down the hall. I can chew my own food; I can remember my children's names. I can even remember dates of important things that have happened in the past. My eyes are still good, and I can read books that transport me elsewhere. I can think critically and do my own taxes. I have so much to be thankful for.

She smiled at the lady in the mirror. It was going to be a good day.

The cafeteria was one of Mary Jean's favorite places to go in the new facility. It had huge floor-to-ceiling windows that looked down on a glassed-in garden that was full of plants and a large water feature. All the colors used in the room reminded her of nature: warm browns, bright greens, and blues. A pop of color like pumpkin showed up here and there. She sat down at a table in the corner next to the big window. A carafe of coffee was already on the table, and she poured herself a cup. There was even a small stainless steel pitcher of steamed milk. That reminded her of a previous trip to Switzerland with her husband, Lewis. Every hostel had strong coffee served with steamed milk.

The waitress came by and asked her what she would like from the options available. She chose the French toast with strawberries. She sipped her coffee and wondered if someone would come sit with her. Residents ambled in, some with walkers and some assisted in wheelchairs. Others came in small groups, looking robust for their ages.

There were quite a mix of ages here in this new facility. She thought of Arman, who was older than she was but still very sharp. This group looked younger, maybe mid-eighties. "They look like they still play tennis," she said out loud to herself.

One of the men in the young group eyed Mary Jean all alone in the corner and steered his threesome over to her table.

"Good morning. I'm George, and these are my two friends, Ann and Lucy. May we join you for breakfast?"

George was a tall, lean man still with a good head of salt-and-pepper hair. He had deep brown eyes and a boyish grin. He looked like a lady's man: tall, dark, and handsome. Ann was plump, of average height, and with blue eyes and little makeup. Her short gray hair was tucked behind her ears. She looked a little shy but smiled at Mary Jean as she held out her hand. Mary Jean shook her hand and motioned for them to sit. Lucy was tall and a bit heavy, with dyed black hair and olive skin. She had tastefully applied makeup, which accented her beautiful hazel eyes and prominent cheekbones.

Lucy was the first to speak. "Are you from Kingsley?" she asked.

"Yes, I am."

"That was awful what happened there. You must have been so frightened. I assume you got away unharmed."

"Well, I was drugged. I was lucky that someone found me in time and got me to the hospital where they took care of me. I recovered quickly. Some of the others were less fortunate."

They all helped themselves to coffee. The waitress came and took their orders. Mary Jean learned that the three friends were from out of state. They had come to Oregon because Springfield Acres was a state-of-the-art facility for seniors. There was now a waiting list as more people heard about the new retirement center. Mary Jean was lucky to have gotten in. Many of the residents from her old facility had been given first choice by the managers because of what had happened at Kingsley. The management was very involved with the community and worked with other organizations to benefit their residents and help the community as a whole.

Their breakfasts were served, and they all sat around enjoying the conversation and delicious food. A relaxing mix of piano and guitar music played softly in the background. Light filtered in from the large windows as the sun broke through the clouds.

"I understand there is a garden project underway that includes some of the school children nearby," said Lucy.

"Yes," said Mary Jean. "It was started at my old facility. I am glad they decided to continue it here. I saw it announced in the activities director's schedule of events this morning. Did you receive one under the door?"

"Yes, I saw that. But I haven't taken the time to read the details yet," said Lucy.

George and Ann nodded their heads. They had read about it, too.

"I think it is a wonderful idea to involve the children," said George. "I used to garden with my grandchildren, but they later moved far away, so that was that." He looked down, his brow furrowing while he reflected briefly on that time. He seemed to be momentarily saddened by the thought.

"What happened to your family? Why did they move away?" asked Mary Jean.

"Oh, my son got a job offer he couldn't refuse.

I could have moved with them, but the only places I could stay over there were unacceptable. I felt I needed a change and heard about this facility. I wasn't done living yet!" But his eyes told a different story to Mary Jean. She could read loss, then resignation, and finally acceptance. Family meant so much. She knew there must be more to the story.

Ann jumped in to change the subject.

"I never had an interest in gardening. I was always too busy volunteering to have time to learn. My family grew up in the city, and we couldn't grow a thing in our apartment. So it will be a new experience for me." She looked down into the garden below them and said, "I think I will enjoy trying something new."

Mary Jean couldn't believe someone could get through life without growing anything. Didn't most women love flowers? She guessed not everyone liked the responsibility of growing things.

They finished their meal and said their goodbyes. The three were off to check out the barn, which had a few therapy horses. Ann was excited because her friend who would soon be moving to Springfield suffered from depression, and she hoped she would benefit from the program. They also had therapy dogs, which she had seen in the rooms with some residents. Mary Jean thought about Spot. What had happened to him? Was he also like Lewis, a spirit from some other realm?

Mary Jean decided to head back to the ceramics center to glaze her egg. She was excited to see what that entailed. She hoped Arman would be there to give her a hand. He was so interesting, and she wanted to learn more about him.

The day became warmer and the sun was staying put, so Mary Jean took only her sweater and walked to the shuttle area. She could see several residents out on the walking paths, enjoying the clear day. As the shuttle approached, a few more residents got in line. A dog barked behind her, and she turned to see what it was. She couldn't believe her eyes. Off on one of the walking paths was Spot! The last time she had seen Spot was at Kingsley. She thought Lewis had him, but Spot appeared to be out here alone. She took off in a fast walk in his direction.

"Here, Spot! Come! Spot! Come here!" He looked in her direction toward the frantic sound of her voice and immediately ran to her, wagging his tail all the way. Within seconds, Spot was jumping on her, trying to lick her face, but he had to be satisfied with licking her hand as she could not stoop to greet him. She noticed he was not wearing his collar. What had happened to Lewis? Why was Spot loose? She was unsure of what to do next. The shuttle bus had taken off, so she would have to wait another fifteen minutes for the next one. But first she would have to find something to put on Spot to control him. Luckily, he obediently followed her as she walked back to the lobby.

"Hello," she said to the lady at the front desk. "I live in apartment #226. I found this dog loose and wondered if you could locate his owner for me. I think he lives here. His name is Lewis Weeks. He's about five-foot-nine and has wispy gray hair and blue eyes."

Before the lady at the front desk could check her records, Mary Jean heard someone calling her name. She turned around—and there was Lewis, coming down the stairs.

27

"Where are your red shoes?" asked Lewis.

"What?" Mary Jean was wide-eyed. All she wanted to do was give him a hug. How could he stand there and ask such a question?

"Your red shoes. You should have them on when you're out walking. You'll be more comfortable." He smiled, and his blue eyes twinkled like she remembered when she'd first met him. He had brought Spot's collar and leash with him. He walked over, smiling, and thanked her for "finding" Spot. He clipped Spot's collar and leash on him.

"I don't know how he got loose. He's a smart one. He sees the door ajar and wants to go out exploring. He's made friends with everyone here already and knows how to get outside without me." He took Mary Jean by the hand, and together, the three of them walked outside.

"Where have you been? So, you do live here? What apartment are you in? You aren't getting away before you answer some of my questions."

Before Lewis could reply, Mary Jean suddenly heard a loud voice speaking. "Mary Jean, are you all right?" Mary Jean blinked hard twice. Arman was standing beside her. Several of the residents were looking at her. Was she losing her mind? Had she been talking to herself? She tried to think about what had just happened. I thought I was talking with Lewis, she thought. I thought I had rescued Spot and returned him to Lewis. He lives here—or so I thought.

"Mary Jean! Do you want me to take you to the infirmary?" Arman continued. "You were looking blank for several minutes and not answering my questions. I'm worried about you. Please talk to me." Arman had his arm on her shoulder. He was very gently shaking her, as if to wake her up from a trance.

"No, Arman. I think I'm all right. I . . . I . . . I had a momentary lapse in my memory. I thought I was somewhere else and talking with another person. It's all very disturbing. Give me a minute to collect my thoughts."

Mary Jean was sitting at her table in the ceramics center. She was shocked because she thought she had run into Lewis and Spot in the lobby of the main building. Now here she was, back with Arman, working on her clay project. Her clay egg was sitting on the table. It had a glaze on it. It appeared finished. When had she done that? It appeared she'd had a slip in her memory.

"Arman, how long have I been here?" Mary Jean's voice was quiet, barely audible.

"Why, you've been here for half an hour, at least. Maybe forty-five minutes. We went through the glazing process, and you chose two very beautiful blue glazes. Your egg now needs to go on the shelves over there so it can get into the final firing."

Mary Jean got up slowly and carefully placed her little egg on the shelves that Arman had pointed out.

She looked at the other pieces there: a swan with a long, winding neck, an intricately decorated wide bowl, two mugs that looked exactly alike, and a large horse with an arching neck and flowing mane. She headed back to Arman's table and sat down.

"I think I will go back to my room," she said.

"That's probably a good idea. You just need a little rest. Don't worry. Everything will be fine."

He squeezed her hand and walked her to the door. Then Kia came over and walked her the rest of the way to the shuttle station. When the shuttle arrived, Kia gave her a big hug before she boarded the bus. Mary Jean looked out the window and watched a resident ride a therapy horse in an outside arena. This place was too perfect to be real. Therapy horses? Therapy dogs? Ceramics center? Glassed-in gardens? Perfect food? Was she dreaming or what?

She walked up the stairs and down the hall to apartment #226. Her name was on the plaque next to the door. She felt for her key in the pocket of her sweater. It was there. She was not dreaming . . . right? She opened her door and walked into the kitchen. All she needed was a cup of tea. As she heated up the water, she listened to her messages on her phone. Her son was coming over to help her with her cell phone—would she be available next Saturday? There was another message from her youngest daughter, Shiela—would she like a ride to Fred Meyer to go shopping tomorrow? These messages seemed real. How did she know what was real and what was not?

The edges of her reality were getting blurred, and things just were not black and white. Sometimes, she thought she was in another world and would just get glimpses of her old world. It was hard to delineate between the old and new. Was this what it felt like to die? Was there an adaptation that had to happen as you merged into the next world or life?

The tea kettle was whistling, so she poured herself some hot water and dunked a tea bag in it as these thoughts whirled through her mind. Making sense of things was getting harder and harder. How old was she? When had her last birthday been? She had always had an excellent memory for facts and dates. Were things changing?

She sipped her tea and picked up the phone.

"I'll see if I am crazy or not," she said to herself. She dialed her son's phone number, which was on a piece of paper on the wall. It rung about six times before an answering machine came on: "This is Marcus, and I can't come to the phone right now. If you leave your name and phone number, I'll get back to you right away. Thanks for calling."

Mary Jean wasn't convinced. She dialed Shiela's number.

". . . If you leave your name and phone number, I'll get back to you as soon as possible."

Mary Jean sat there for a few minutes. They could just both be away from their phones. That was possible. With her tea gone, she went to the kitchen to rinse the cup and put it away. Maybe she should talk to the resident shrink. Maybe he could help her sort out her thoughts. She drifted back into the living room and flipped through some magazines. She had laundry to do, so she gathered up her dirty clothes and towels and headed to the laundry room. When befuddled, get into action, she thought. Just put one foot in front of the other, as Lewis taught me. Just *do* something.

She put the clothes into the washer. A few residents wandered in and barely nodded their heads at her. Well, she wasn't exactly being friendly, either. She was too perplexed with the events of the day. The machines here were nicer than those in the old facility. They were brand new and gleaming white. There was a beautiful mural painted on one of the walls, depicting a meadow scene with a brook running through the middle of it. All along the banks were rocks of different shades of gray that were blurred by the water running over them. There were fish with yellow, orange, and green scales, also painted with a slightly blurred effect of everything being in motion. The trees were fir and cedar of many sizes. There were blue wildflowers in the foreground among the tall grass.

She stared at the mural for a long time and marveled at the artist's imagination and use of color. There was a lot of art in this new building. That was another difference from the old facility. More art to look at, as well as opportunities and places to make your own art. She had never thought she had any kind of creative ability except for playing the piano. "Well, we'll see," she told herself. She couldn't wait to see her finished egg.

Mary Jean took her clothes back to her room. After she put them away, she called her son again.

"Hi, Mom. How's everything?"

Mary Jean smiled and sighed.

"Everything's just fine. Next Saturday would be great for you to come by."

With that, Mary Jean got ready to head over to the cafeteria for lunch. She couldn't wait to taste the chicken pot pie. Oh, and the rhubarb pie, too.

28

Mary Jean listened to her phone messages as she made herself a cup of coffee the next morning. Shiela had called and postponed their shopping day. No matter, as she wanted to get back to her ceramics project. There wasn't anything she really needed that badly anyway. It was just an opportunity to spend more time with her youngest daughter. Shiela's busy vet practice gave her very little free time. And Mary Jean couldn't blame her for wanting to spend that time doing her favorite hobby, which was kayaking.

Mary Jean finished up her breakfast and headed out to the ceramics center. It was packed with residents glazing, sculpting, and carving their projects. Mary Jean sat down next to Arman.

"Hi, Mary Jean. How are you feeling today? We were all quite worried about you."

"I'm doing much better, thank you." She looked toward the shelf where she had left her egg, but it was cleared out and new projects were now sitting on the shelf waiting to be fired.

"Where is my egg, Arman? I don't see it on the shelf anymore."

"Oh, here, I'll show you where you can find the newly fired pieces."

He walked her around the corner to another series of shelves. She saw the swan and the horse, beautifully ablaze with color. The carved bowl had deep rust and green colors, and the mugs were earthy tones of cream, dark brown, and gray. They all looked amazing. She looked earnestly for her egg and finally saw it behind another sculpture. It looked exquisite in shades of turquoise blue and sapphire. She carefully picked it up and walked back to her table with Arman.

"It turned out lovely," said Arman.

"I never thought I could make anything so beautiful." Mary Jean turned it around and around in her hands, taking in the subtle change in colors. Parts of it were almost translucent while other areas were mottled, which created an interesting texture.

"What would you like to make next?" asked Arman.

"Oh, I don't know. I'll have to think about it for a while."

"I keep a sketchbook, and when I have an idea for something, I draw it out."

"That's a good idea. But I can't draw at all. It's as if I have two left thumbs." Mary Jean laughed.

"They teach drawing here. It's a real good class. It gives you the basics, and the rest is up to you."

He smiled, and his eyes were so full of life. It looked like he had found his passion in creating art. You are lucky if you find something you are passionate about in this life, Mary Jean thought. She could not say that she had for herself.

"Well, I guess there is a first time for everything." Mary Jean could not believe she was entertaining the idea at all. A drawing class? Just like yoga; another thing she never thought she'd find herself doing.

"I believe they have an Introduction to Drawing class late this afternoon. I'll go with you, if you'd like."

Arman waited while Mary Jean considered the idea. She'd probably make a fool of herself. But she found herself saying, "Sure, why not? I suppose there are other fools like myself also giving it a try." She laughed again and took note of the time the class began. As they were sitting there enjoying each other's company, Arman gave her a piece of his clay. This one was bigger than the first one.

"A little more of a challenge this time. I can show you how to make a mug, if you'd like."

"That sounds more technical than what I am up for. Is there something easier?"

"What about a small bowl? This piece is big enough for you to make a cereal bowl. You've already made two small bowls in your egg project. So this should be a piece of cake."

So they started the second project together, chatting away the morning. She learned how to build up the sides with coils of the same length and smooth the walls. By lunchtime, she had created a well-sized bowl with a pretty good shape.

"Now you can decide if you want to do any carvings on it. Or you can glaze it as-is. Some people draw on the clay when it has dried leather-hard. Or you can draw with an underglaze."

"Oh, hold on there, Arman. That sounds all too complicated for me. How about I just concentrate on what to glaze it with when it is bisque fired?" She cleaned up her area and placed the bowl on the bisque shelf. Then she turned to him.

"Thank you for a lovely morning. I learned so much. Now I know the excitement of waiting to see the final project completed. It's just like Christmas day when you are a child opening up presents—because you don't know what you're going to get! See you at 4 p.m. this afternoon for the drawing class?"

"I'll look forward to it." Arman waved.

As Mary Jean left, she thought, I'll look forward to seeing you again, too.

Mary Jean waited at the shuttle station. She decided to try the Italian restaurant on campus since she'd already eaten at the other Thai restaurant. She was in the mood for eggplant Parmesan. Every Italian restaurant served eggplant Parmesan as one of their specialties, didn't they?

The shuttle came, and she took a seat near the back. Several ladies were sitting in the front. It almost appeared like it was a birthday group. She overheard them talking about going to the spa for a massage and a pedicure. Wow, she'd have to try that. There was so much to do here. She also wanted to try the pool. There was a warmer pool where you could do aqua walking and other exercises, and there was also a hot tub. Mary Jean wasn't sure she wanted to get into her swimsuit, though. It had been ages since she had worn one. She wondered if others felt the same.

The Italian restaurant was located near the park. Large windows looked out onto the greenery. She worried the birthday group would take all the window seats, so she hurried ahead of them and got in line. She was lucky and was taken to a table for two right next to the windows. She should have invited Arman to lunch; that would have been nice. She felt self-conscious sitting there by herself. The birthday group was seated a few tables down from her. There were six of them, and they were loud.

Behind her, a voice said, "Is this seat taken by anyone?"

Mary Jean turned around to see a tall, dark, handsome man smiling down at her. It was George, the man whom she had had breakfast with the previous morning.

"Why, no, it's not. Would you like to join me for lunch?" Mary Jean felt shy, but what else could she say?

"I hope this isn't an intrusion. I know some people prefer to eat alone."

"Oh, no. I'm not one of those." Mary Jean smiled and looked down at her place setting. George sat down and deftly tucked his long legs underneath the table.

"How is your day going?" he asked.

"I made a bowl today at the ceramics center, but it's not finished yet. I have to put the glaze on once it is bisque fired."

"Whoa . . . what is bisque fired?" George leaned forward with his big brown eyes wide with interest. Mary Jean explained away and felt like a pro talking to a beginner.

For lunch, Mary Jean had the eggplant and George ordered the spaghetti and meatballs. They shared more of their day and their plans for the afternoon. Today, Mary Jean felt different. She felt like she was really living. Her world had opened up at Springfield Acres. Instead of focusing on a narrow point of view, which she had had at Kingsley, she now had more to talk about other than the food her old cafeteria served or the noise of the remodeling project that was going on in her old facility. Here, there was so much more yet to experience.

George and Mary Jean planned to get together for

dinner later that day in the main dining hall. With those plans in place, Mary Jean said goodbye and headed back to her apartment for a nap. She had to rest up before tackling her new challenge—her drawing class—at 4 p.m.

29

Mary Jean woke up from her nap just in time for class. There was a bank of dark clouds on the horizon, and it looked as though the wind had kicked up. She pulled her coat around her more tightly as she waited in line for the shuttle to arrive. Two younger women were also standing in line having a lively conversation.

They must be visitors, not residents, thought Mary Jean. She looked at her watch and saw that the shuttle was running late. She hoped she wouldn't miss her drawing class. She was feeling a little like canceling, but that was not her motto in life. Once you sign up for something, you follow through with it. The shuttle finally pulled up, and it was a packed house. The only remaining seat was beside an elderly man wearing a tweed wool beret, a gray chambray shirt, and gold corduroy pants that looked like they had come from an L. L. Bean catalog. His fine gray hair curled out from under his cap. He had friendly steel-blue eyes.

"Hello, may I sit here with you?" asked Mary Jean.

"Of course," said the gentleman as he made room for her on the seat.

"I am Mary Jean."

"And I am William," he said as he extended his hand. She took his hand and smiled and knew he was not a resident from Kingsley. She would have noticed him.

"Where are you going this afternoon?" William asked.

"I thought I'd try my hand at a drawing class. I have no creative skill except piano playing, but I thought, what the heck, why not give it a try."

"Well, I happen to be going to the same such class. I've always wanted to learn how to draw well, but I just never gave it much time. I tend to move on to new things a little too quickly, I guess. I hope I can have a little more patience this time. He chuckled and added, "I was an aeronautical engineer in my working life. I guess there is a degree of creativity in designing novel aircraft and missile designs." Mary Jean laughed, and said, "I would think so."

They sat quietly for a while, enjoying the scenery out the window.

"Have you looked into the ceramics center yet?" asked Mary Jean. This time, she looked at his weathered face and smiled timidly.

"No, I have not. Right now, the drawing class is all I can focus on. How about you? Have you had a look around there?"

"Yes. I've been twice. I've made an egg and am ready to glaze a handcrafted bowl. It's been fascinating learning about the process of building, glazing, and firing clay. You should visit just to look at the work of others. People make graceful animals and figures, as well as utilitarian objects like bowls and mugs. Some people paint and decorate their pieces with so much creativity and skill. It is so much fun to see what is new on the shelves."

"Well, it sounds like you've found a new hobby." William smiled again, and Mary Jean found herself relaxing under his warm gaze.

"Well, here we are. After you," said William as the bus stopped at their destination. When she stepped down the bus steps, he reached out to take her hand. Mmmm, very much the gentleman, she thought. She liked that.

The room was not crowded. There were perhaps about twelve people sitting at long rectangular tables facing a chalkboard in the front of the room. Several plants decorated the room, growing in pots. There were also vases filled with flowers and ceramic bowls piled with fruit. Big windows let natural light through as it looked out onto a meadow with a row of maple trees and the foothills to the west. Lots to draw around here, thought Mary Jean.

William and Mary Jean took seats next to each other. Mary Jean did not see Arman in the class. She wondered why he had not come. The teacher, a man in his forties, was sitting at the desk in front of the room. He was studying some notes in a black notebook. He was well dressed, wearing a crisp, red plaid shirt. He looked up and greeted the new residents as they found their seats. He had a sunburned face and shoulder-length brown wavy hair.

"Welcome, welcome everyone. My name is Ted. I will be your instructor for this class. This class is for *everyone* of all skill levels. How many of you got as far as drawing stick characters?" There was a few show of hands, including William and Mary Jean.

"Well, never fear! You will emerge from this class able to draw whatever you see in your own style. And style is something we will talk about. Drawing something realistically is not the only goal for you in this class—unless, of course, that is solely what you want to accomplish. We will talk about that further as the class progresses.

"There are paper and a few pencils in front of you. We will begin first by introducing ourselves. Say a bit about what you want to accomplish in the class and tell us a little about your experience."

The class was off to a good start for Mary Jean. She met new people, and she liked the informality of the class structure. Ted was friendly and outgoing, making sure each person felt comfortable. It was a relaxing and nurturing environment to explore one's creativity under some loose guidance.

The first class focused on materials and some basic shapes. Did you see a triangle, a rectangle, or a circle in the object in front of you? They practiced sketching pears, apples, and bananas. Mary Jean felt like she might get the hang of it after all.

The days turned into weeks, and the weeks into months. In later classes, Ted set up a few still life scenes and even encouraged people to gaze out the window to find a subject they wanted to draw. Just biting off a small piece of a scene, he explained, could set up a nice composition to be drawn.

As winter gave way to spring, the weather was getting nicer and the days were growing longer. Mary Jean was slowly picking up skills in both hobbies that were transforming into passions of hers. Working with clay and drawing had become activities that were part of her every day. She would sit downstairs in the glassed-in garden and sketch the chickadees that were feeding at the hanging bird feeder. She also looked forward to seeing what her new clay pieces would look like after the final firing.

During this time, Mary Jean often thought about

the garden project, which was due to begin this spring, and, of course, Derek. Would he be involved this year? How was he? She hoped everything was going all right at home. It seemed like it had been a long time since she had seen him. She decided to do some digging. She wanted to pin down exactly when they would be planning the next garden project meeting.

Mary Jean walked down the corridor by the garden, which led to the high-ceilinged office of the activities director. She knocked on the pine door and was told to enter.

Leslie was working at her desk.

"Hi, I'm Mary Jean. Remember me? We met when I first moved in. I was wondering when we would be meeting next for the garden project. You had mentioned that Springfield Acres would be participating in the project that Kingsley originally started. The student partner I worked with goes to Lafayette Elementary School. Last summer, we planted tomatoes and herbs, and he even made spaghetti sauce with his family. I was hoping he would be coming back."

"Well, it's nice to see you again, Mary Jean. I've been trying to contact the schools that want to participate. I'm sorry to say that Lafayette Elementary School is too far away. We are looking at Hoover Elementary School to possibly participate." She looked truly sorry for Mary Jean.

"I wonder if you could help me contact Derek's family so I could at least see how he is doing?" Mary Jean felt she had to try. After all, she and Derek had had something special. She just wanted to make sure everything was going all right with him at home with his family.

"I'll see what I can do. Do you know his last name?"

"I think it is Meyers."

"Okay. I will try and get their phone number. I'll have to check first if that is okay. Sometimes, the school may have privacy rules we have to abide by."

She smiled and held out her hand. Mary Jean clasped her hand and said, "Thank you very much for helping me. It means a lot."

Mary Jean turned around and headed back to her apartment. She couldn't help but entertain a nagging feeling that something bad had happened to Derek.

30

Winter had melted into spring, and little by little, Mary Jean kept widening her world with new activities and with her three new male friends, Arman, William, and George. Meanwhile, Lewis seemed to have disappeared into thin air. And Leslie never got back to her with Derek's phone number. It must have been against the school's policies to give out the children's contact information. Who knew . . .

It was now the beginning of March. It was still cold in the morning, sometimes as low as thirty-five degrees, and the days were getting longer. The sun did not set until around 6:30 p.m. or even a little later. Soon, summer would be here, and Mary Jean looked forward to getting outside more.

From time to time, she still had thoughts that she was living in a dream world. Who would have thought that she would get a new lease on life in her mid-nineties? That she would even have the energy and motivation to try new things, meet new people, and change herself? Every new day that she got up and out of bed was a gift. A gift not to be taken lightly. Until you've suffered hardship or come near death, how could you ever fully appreciate what you have? she thought. Sometimes the days were hard. She struggled to get up. But then she would recall the quote by the Roman stoic philosopher Seneca: "The world meets no one halfway. There is much good to life, but there will always be struggle." Though he had been born over two thousand years ago, his writings were both practical and timeless, helping people navigate the pitfalls of life.

Another quote she liked was: "The whole future lies in uncertainty: live immediately."

People were always searching afar for happiness, when really, it was right in front of them. Such as realizing how precious a day could be just by walking in the sunshine on your own, or eating a piece of fresh apple pie with vanilla bean ice cream.

I've reflected on this more than once before, she thought. It's good to come back to it, though. You have to. You have to keep remembering these things. Because, before you know it, it will be over.

Mary Jean thought about what "over" meant. Was there an afterlife? Sometimes, she thought she was going back and forth. Getting ready to be "over." But right now, at this moment, I am alive, she thought, and I feel like going outside this morning despite the cold.

That day, Mary Jean decided she would visit the therapy barn. Her daughter-in-law had always had horses throughout her life. They were her passion. Mary Jean's youngest daughter, Shiela, had also had a horse growing up. Horses never interested Mary Jean. She had always had too much to do in the house to even think about visiting her daughter in the barn to watch her ride. Lewis, her husband, did this, and he enjoyed it. Well, today Mary Jean was ready to continue expanding her world, and visiting the horse barn was on the list.

When she stepped off the shuttle, the sun was shining so brightly that she had to fish into her purse for her sunglasses. "I've forgotten what spring is like," Mary Jean said out loud. The stables were set up on a small hill, looking down on big, open pastures of green grass. At least the horses weren't shut up in little stalls like Shiela's horse had been. Mary Jean looked inside and found neat rows of open stall fronts so visitors and horses could get to know each other. Petting a fuzzy, white nose was encouraged, and a basket of red apples sat on a nearby hay bale.

There was an indoor arena with soft dirt, and an instructor was walking alongside a horse with a resident riding astride. She was talking softly to the rider and also to the horse as they walked slowly around in a medium-sized circle. The horse was a stocky, short, brown-and-white paint mare that was only fourteen hands but stout enough to hold someone quite big. Mary Jean remembered that a "hand" was a four-inch unit of measurement from the ground to the point of their withers, the tallest spot above the horse's shoulders. The horse had a long, broad white blaze on her face and a bit of pink on her muzzle. She seemed to know that the person riding her was new at this because she walked carefully with slow, determined steps.

"Hello," came a voice from behind her.

Mary Jean turned around. A young girl of about eighteen years old was standing behind her, wearing gray riding tights and a black sweatshirt. She held a halter and a lead rope coiled up in her hand.

"Oh, hi, you startled me!" said Mary Jean. "I was just looking around for the first time. I wanted to see what the therapy horse program was all about. My daughter had a horse when she was growing up, but he was quite feisty, and I would've been afraid to ride him if I had been so inclined."

"My name is Mindy. And you are?"

"Mary Jean. I'm in apartment #226. I was from Kingsley but am now a resident here."

"Oh, Kingsley . . . where some residents were poisoned, right? I'm glad you're here now. What can I help you with?" Mindy watched for any reaction in Mary Jean's face.

"I just wanted to look around and learn about your program. What services do you offer? Do you work with the residents and the horses?"

"Yes, I do. I care for the horses, feeding and watering them, cleaning the paddocks, and turning them out to pasture. I also give riding lessons and help some of the residents. Our program is also open to children with emotional or physical issues, and we help them bond with a horse. Sometimes, just spending time with a horse—brushing them and talking to them—can help alleviate their symptoms."

Mindy walked up to one of the stalls where a large, black Friesian gelding was standing. He was magnificent. He was very tall and muscular, with a thick, wavy mane and tail. His eyes were large, and he looked so intelligent.

"This is Soldier. He was rescued from a breeding farm where the owners could no longer care for their horses. He is eighteen years old and a true gentleman. He is tall, which is sometimes very intimidating for some people, but he will stand as still as a statue on the ground. Residents can walk all around him, petting him, even pull on his mane or tail, and he won't move. Dogs can run underneath him and around him. You can crash the wheelbarrow, and he still won't move. He'll only move if you ask him to. That provides a very safe equine for timid people to get to know. They can climb on a mounting block to brush his back. They can feel secure and marvel at his beauty and strength."

Mary Jean touched Soldier on his muzzle. He feels so soft, she thought. He was massive and a bit intimidating, but he was behind the door, so Mary Jean felt safe.

"I'll show you another horse in the corner stall."

Mindy led Mary Jean along the aisleway, and there in the corner was a dapple-gray Arabian mare. She was about 15.2 hands and a beautiful white color with splashes of rose-gray spots over her shoulders and haunches. It was as if an artist had applied watercolor dapples onto her graceful body. Her white, silky mane flowed off her tall, arching neck, and her long, sweeping tail was held high. Her large, liquid brown eyes, which were set wide on her dished face, caught Mary Jean's eye. She found herself being drawn into this horse's presence like a magnet.

"This is Dey Ash Marquise. She is a very special mare. She was given to the program because she can no longer be ridden very hard. She is fine at a walk and even a little trot. The owner thought she would make a great therapy horse because she is kind and very calm for an Arabian. She is only sixteen years old, which is quite young. She is great with the residents and will walk and stop calmly. She is very easy to lead and handle. On her own, she will walk very slowly, especially if she knows that the person riding her is inexperienced. She is the perfect therapy horse."

"Thank you for showing me around, Mindy. I can see these fine animals will work wonders for people who need a trusting and predictable presence in their lives. It's so wonderful that you offer these kind of services. I don't think I am interested in riding, but I can sure appreciate the beauty of these animals. I see they are well cared for and have room to run, too."

"Come anytime, Mary Jean. You never know. You may change your mind sometime. Being on top of one of these horses and having them move below you with incredible strength and gracefulness is like nothing else."

"Well, I don't doubt what you say, Mindy, but you will likely not see me getting on top of a horse at my age."

Mary Jean stroked Marquise's silky forelock and studied her face. Her large brown eyes showed such intelligence. It must have been a difficult decision giving up this horse. Mary Jean looked down the aisle. The shuttle bus was wending its way up the hilly driveway. She'd better get going.

31

Mary Jean sat sipping her morning coffee in her usual spot in the cafeteria. Across the room, Leslie was making her way toward her. Maybe she finally has some information for me about Derek, thought Mary Jean. She took a last bite of her oatmeal and waited while Leslie chatted with a couple of residents along the way.

"I believe I have some good information for you, Mary Jean," she said when she finally reached her table. "May I?" She motioned toward an empty chair.

"Oh, yes. Do sit down." Mary Jean sat up a little straighter, anxious to hear what Leslie had to say.

"I found some contact information for Derek and his family. They have moved into the school district for this area, so he will be attending the garden project after all!"

Mary Jean couldn't believe the good news. How things fell into place sometimes!

"Thank you so much for giving me this update. He's never left my thoughts. When is the first planning meeting? That's when we decide with our partner what plants we want to grow. We get assigned a plot, and at the next meeting, we pick up the seeds."

Mary Jean took out her small calendar from her purse.

"The first meeting is at the end of March. In mid-May, we will visit the garden plots and start planning each of our garden designs. We will start planting by the end of May." Mary Jean wrote down the dates in her calendar.

"I will look forward to the meeting coming up." Mary Jean thanked Leslie again and tucked her calendar back into her purse. She smiled.

She had the whole day ahead of her. Her hand-crafted bowl was finished. What else should she make? She also wanted to see Arman. He was such a kind man and so accomplished. At their last class, he had told her he owned his own little helicopter and had flown it himself until his late eighties. He had four older brothers, all in their late nineties, still living. At ninety-five, he was sculpting expressive animals. He had so many stories to tell. Don't we all, when we've lived so long? Mary Jean thought. But not all of us have such extraordinary stories.

Since Mary Jean had her red sneakers on this morning, she decided to explore the trails around the campus. There was that meadow with the tall cedar and fir trees that she had seen from the windows in her drawing class. She saw that the trail went through the meadow, perhaps to a pond. She would check it out. But first, she thought she'd ask George if he'd like to come with her. She didn't use her cell phone very often, but George had put in his number when they were having dinner the other night.

She dialed his number and reached his voice mail. "Hello? George? This is Mary Jean. I know this is last minute, but if you aren't doing anything in particular, I would like to invite you to come walking with me. I am at the shuttle station in front of the lobby. I think it would be fun to explore the meadow area and see if there is a pond up there."

She hoped he would quickly return her call. She put her phone in her pocket so she could answer it right away if he did. She found a bench and decided to wait for a few minutes to see if he would call back. The trees that lined the drive were in full blossom, and there were several birds among the branches chirping and chasing each other. She saw residents walking on the trails far away toward the barn. There was also a horse and rider out on a trail. That must be Mindy riding Soldier. The big, black Friesian was easy to spot even from a distance.

The phone rang, and Mary Jean answered, a little out of breath.

"Hello?"

"Hi, Mary Jean! I'd love to go walking with you. Just give me a minute to change into some good walking shoes, and I'll be right down."

"Okay. I'm right out at the shuttle station sitting on the bench in front of the lobby. See you soon."

The days were getting warmer. "I probably don't need this overcoat," mumbled Mary Jean to herself. She took off her coat and set it beside her on the bench. She was nervous. I can't believe I just invited a man on a walking date! she thought. They had had such a good time at dinner when they last met. A man and his white terrier walked by. He tipped his hat and made his way slowly down the path along the driveway. He was bent over, and his dog waddled next to him. They looked alike, the man and his dog. They say dogs resemble their owners, and vice versa, thought Mary Jean.

George appeared at the front door, dressed in

lightweight hiking boots and a dark-blue fleece jacket. He wore gray jeans and a broad-brimmed hat.

"I'm so glad you rang and invited me on your big adventure." His eyes crinkled as he smiled widely. They got in line, and what good timing that was, because the shuttle bus came by almost immediately.

The trail was muddy and a little rocky for Mary Jean. George slowed his pace and took her hand to steady her as they made their way down to the pond at the far end of the meadow. The trail wasn't steep, but the ground was irregular and they had to watch their step.

"This is turning into more of an adventure than I bargained for," said Mary Jean.

"It's a little tricky here, but it looks like they've graveled it up ahead. We've chosen the trail that is a work in progress," George said.

He let her go first, as a gentleman would, carefully steadying her when needed. The air was fresh, and birds were everywhere, digging for worms and singing in branches. The males were displaying themselves to the females in mating dances and song. The trail levelled out and became packed pea gravel, which immediately made walking easier. The pond was in sight. More of a small lake, thought Mary Jean. There were four mallard ducks and several Canadian geese swimming on the lake right in front of them. They made their way toward a wooden bench in a grassy area next to the water. Here they sat and listened to the sounds of nature—the outdoors in full concert.

The wind rustled the leaves in the branches of the trees nearby. The chitter-chatter of birds filled the air, and even the frogs had their own songs. Now and again, a fish would surface with a flicking sound in the water. A red-tailed hawk called to its mate in a nearby tree. Mary Jean looked out past the lake, and the sky was a deep, deep blue against the western foothills of the Oregon Coast Range. She breathed in the air and sighed.

"Smells good, doesn't it?" George breathed in too and let out his breath slowly.

"I used to stay inside all the time. A year or so ago at Kingsley, I rarely went outside. I forgot how being outside makes you feel. It brightens up the spirit, I think, because there are more things for your senses to experience outdoors compared to inside a building."

She sat staring ahead. She rolled up her sleeves so her pale, speckled forearms were exposed to the warm sunlight and breeze.

"I like the feel of the sun on my skin and the cool breeze, too." She reached down and floated her fingers along the tops of the tufted dry grasses next to the bench.

They stood up and walked along the edge of the lake. They followed the trail until it rose up out of the meadow and toward the horse stables.

"Are you up for the loop around the horse stables, or do you want to go back?" asked George.

"I want to keep going, though I will be a bit slower on this last loop. Hopefully, the trail remains in good shape."

They slowly made their way, winding around a couple of large oak trees. A gray squirrel scurried across the path. A woodpecker could be heard above them in a snag, the sound of his drilling echoing throughout the woodland. The stables were below them, and they saw four horses turned out in the pasture. They were grazing contentedly among the rich, green grass. Mary Jean could see Mindy cleaning some corrals, and another instructor was helping a resident groom a horse tied to the hitching post outside.

"Have you ever ridden a horse?" asked Mary Jean.

"Yes, I have. But I can't say I ever mastered that skill. My daughter had a horse for a few years during high school. She was on the drill team. She gave me one lesson once, and then we decided that would be the last lesson." He laughed and continued. "I like to be on my own two feet. I'm much more at home on skis or walking. How about you?"

"My daughter also had a horse. But I never rode. I just didn't have the interest. I was too busy keeping track of my four kids and taking care of the house. I worked in the local library, and later on in life when I retired, I worked in an artist co-op keeping their books. But no, horses never interested me." Mary Jean continued, "But I have to say, after visiting the stable the other day, I have a renewed appreciation for their beauty and the people who work with them. I know that their presence can have a profound, positive effect on people who have suffered trauma or who are severely handicapped."

Mary Jean was feeling pain in her hip, and she wondered if she would be able to make it to the stable where they could catch the shuttle back to the main building. She feared she had used up her day's allotment of energy and that she wouldn't feel like going to the ceramics center. Finally, the two reached the stables. Soldier was in the arena with a resident and an instructor. He stood stock-still while the resident climbed up a mounting block to get on him.

"That's it. Take it slow. Put your foot here in the stirrup. Now lift your other leg over. That's good. Just rest on your stomach for a while. Now try again.

You'll get it." The instructor was patient and kept her voice low and even. The resident struggled to get his leg over, and with a little push, he was in the saddle. George and Mary Jean sat down on a couple of hay bales in the stable to watch.

The resident held on to a strap in front of the saddle. These were special saddles equipped with extra handholds so the rider could feel safe. The instructor walked alongside Soldier while the resident held on tightly. Soon, the rider relaxed. He let go with one hand and stroked the massive shoulder of the horse. He whispered his name and continued to stroke him while the instructor walked Soldier around and around in the arena. Mary Jean noticed the man was crying. But he looked comfortable, not afraid.

"Well, I'll be. You can just see that man relax. What a sight to behold. It looks like it was quite emotional for him." George watched intently.

"I was told that some of the people who come here for the therapy service can't sleep at night. Some have seizures. But after spending time with these horses regularly, they seem to relax, and they learn to focus not on their problems but to stay in the moment. At night, they can learn with time to transfer those calm feelings to lying in bed, then relaxing, and finally falling asleep."

They watched in silence, and then Mary Jean added, "I also learned that riders use a lot of muscles to stay balanced while riding—both upper and lower body as well as their core muscles. I used to think that riding meant just sitting there and not doing much." George laughed, which caused Mary Jean to laugh, too.

It was time to get back to her apartment for a

much-needed rest. Both heard the shuttle as it drove up to the entrance of the stable. They made their way to the bus and found seats together. The sun was still shining outside, but clouds were beginning to form. Mary Jean folded her coat and placed it on her lap. As the shuttle made its way down the hill, Mary Jean thought about the rider on the horse. What must it feel like to get some solace? Finally relaxing after years of suffering from anxiety? We are only beginning to realize how complex and intelligent animals are, she thought. Horses as just beasts of burden? No, they are much, much more. She already knew dogs had innate skills, like detecting high levels of sugar in the body or when a seizure was about to take place. It was truly amazing.

George took Mary Jean's hand and said, "I've had such a good time this morning. Let's get together again soon. Maybe I could go with you to the ceramics center and try making a mug. I've broken my share of coffee mugs and could use another one. What do you think?"

"I'd like that," said Mary Jean. What was she getting herself into? What would Arman think when she brought George to the class? That is, if Arman showed up. She hadn't seen him in quite some time. And what about William? Life was getting sticky now, wasn't it? This was all new to Mary Jean.

32

Finally, the day of the first garden project meeting of the year had arrived. Mary Jean gathered together her notebook and pen and made her way down to the meeting room. She was going to see Derek! *I wonder how much he has changed?* she thought. *Has he grown much? How is his family?*

The large meeting room was cozy. It had a large, circular rust-and-cream rug and a big rock fireplace with a spitting fire that warmed the room. There were open-beamed ceilings and paintings of the local landscape on the walls. Rectangular tables had been set up and placed in a semicircle. This room was full of people: teachers from the participating school, students from the fourth and fifth grades, and many residents. Mary Jean searched the crowded room for Derek. It had been almost a year since she had seen him.

"Okay," said Leslie. "Let's get started. Please find your seats. We will begin by seeing how many students and residents are here. We'd like every student paired with a resident."

There was a rustle of moving chairs. Leslie looked flustered as she tried to count the residents and students. A teacher came up and provided a roster of student names. After a few minutes of confusion, the residents were paired with a student each except for Mary Jean. Derek was nowhere to be found.

Leslie noticed Mary Jean sitting alone. She came over.

"I don't understand, Mary Jean. Derek's father said he'd be here. Don't worry; I am sure there is an explanation why he is not here. I will check into it as soon as I can." She left to address the group. Mary Jean got up and left the room, feeling let down and disappointed. She had been so looking forward to seeing him! Whatever could have happened? I thought things seemed okay with his family when I last saw him, she thought.

She took the shuttle back to the main building and returned to her apartment. She looked out at the glassed-in garden and saw two residents sitting on a bench by the water feature. It was probably warm in there with the sun shining in. She sat down and picked up a magazine and flipped through the pages, not paying any attention to what she was reading. Then she got up and went to the kitchen and started putting away her washed breakfast dishes. She had eaten in this morning because she had wanted to make sure she had enough time to get to the meeting. She reached for the blue egg she had made that first day in the ceramics center with Arman. It took her mind off her worries about Derek.

Suddenly, someone knocked on the door. She walked over and opened it—and there was Derek! Only he was a few inches inches taller than she remembered.

"Hi, Mary Jean. I was late for the meeting. Leslie said I should come over and get you so we could decide what seeds we want to plant this year. We have to decide today and tell her so she can get the seeds for the next meeting."

"Oh, it's so good to see you Derek! Thank you for coming to get me. Let's go down to the meeting room and decide what we'd like to grow this year."

She took his hand, and together, they walked back to the meeting room. Derek told her about their move and where they lived now. It was only a few blocks away from Springfield Acres. His dad had found a job as a custodian at Hoover Elementary, and his mom did some sewing on the side at home. He was playing baseball now. His little sister was getting better at reading because he had worked with her over the summer. He seemed confident and talkative, unlike the last time she was with him. He sure was changing.

Derek decided to grow zucchini, carrots, and spinach. He knew the zucchini plant produced a lot of fruit, so he could give some to the food bank. Carrots were good for your eyes, and he had learned in school that spinach was one of the most nutritious greens you could eat. Kale was even better, he said, but he didn't like its taste. This year, they could pick flowers to plant, too, so they decided to plant two varieties of sunflowers and two types of marigolds. Derek wrote their choices down on the form provided and took it up to the front desk. Afterward, they drank red punch and ate some cookies next to the fire and shared their choices with the other students and residents. George was also at the meeting, and he had paired up with a little red-haired girl named Lilli.

"Hi, Mary Jean. This is Lilli, my partner in the garden project."

"Hi," said the girl.

"Hi, Lilli. This is Derek. Do you know him?" Derek and Lilli looked at each other shyly.

"No," she said.

Derek said, "I'm in fourth grade. I'll bet you are in fifth grade. That's why I don't know you. I've seen you out on the playground."

They discussed their choices for the garden and what their designs were going to be like. Mary Jean liked how encouraging George was with Lilli, letting her make the decisions and listening more than talking. These children were at the beginning of their lives. There was so much ahead of them. George and Mary Jean now had the privilege to spend time with the children in one tiny moment of their lives. Maybe they could even have a positive effect. Mary Jean knew that not all children were on an even starting ground, so it was up to others in the community to provide the opportunities that may not have come knocking for some kids. If people like her and George took interest, opened their doors, and provided encouragement, these kids could rise to the occasion as well as or better than those born into opportunity and wealth.

Hoover Elementary had its share of low-income families. Mary Jean knew Derek's family was working hard to make ends meet. And she knew that just working hard did not always get you out of debt or move you upward on the ladder. It helped, but it did not guarantee success. Luck and meeting the right people at the right time were certainly part of the success formula. The garden project was an early intervention community event that could provide the extra help some kids needed to get ahead.

Hoover also had a high school program for kids who did not show interest in going to college. It paired them with a mentor in a trade like carpentry, welding, or electrical engineering so they would be sure to have a well-paying job when they graduated. Mary Jean liked to think that she was making a difference in some young person's life. However she did it, it did not matter; she just hoped to contribute some of her time and impart her knowledge to the young.

At the end of the meeting, George and Mary Jean stood outside as they watched the yellow school buses take off. Their minds are like sponges, thought Mary Jean. So eager to learn. She thought about the future of these kids that she would not be a part of. She also thought about her time by the lake in the meadow with George. Drinking in the smells, the tall fragrant trees, the sound of the insects and the ducks. Would this all be here for them when they reached her age? There was so much to do before it was too late. They needed to be taught to take care of it all, or what they had now wouldn't be there for their children in the future.

"George, have you ever thought of what will be left for these kids when they are our age?"

"What do you mean, Mary Jean?"

"Remember our walk a few days ago by the lake—enjoying the outdoors, the trees, the animals, the feel of the wind . . . you know? Don't you ever wonder if it will all still be here as it looks now—for them?"

"Yes. I am very concerned. That's why I'm involved with the garden project. That's also why I continue to vote and try to put the right politicians in charge so they can form policies that will protect the environment."

"You know, that's a good point. It's one thing to do what we can as individuals. That helps a little. But what's more far-reaching is our ability to support the people who will make changes in our government and policies so we can all do the right thing for our planet."

Mary Jean made a mental note to herself to go home and write to her representative.

"Well, would you like to meet me at the ceramics center at 4 p.m. this afternoon?" said Mary Jean.

"Yes, I would. I'd like you to teach me how to make that mug." He smiled that big grin of his.

"But I think I know someone else there who would make a better teacher than I would." Mary Jean hoped that Arman would be receptive to her new friend.

33

That afternoon, George and Mary Jean met at the ceramics center as planned. Mary Jean looked for Arman but did not see him in his usual place. She and George took seats at the table where she usually sat with Arman. Mary Jean was worried.

Kia came over to her side. She looked very concerned.

"Mary Jean. I have some sad news. Arman is not feeling so well. He told me to tell you he would not be here today."

"Oh. I'm so sorry to hear about that. I was so hoping to see him. I've brought a friend of mine, George, to meet him. Arman was so helpful in teaching me how to work with clay. Maybe you could help my friend, George, get started? I'm going to check out some of the new projects that have been fired. I'll be right back, George."

Kia brought George a hunk of clay and showed him how to work the clay to soften it up. Then she showed him the technique that Arman had showed Mary Jean that first day. She formed a ball, cut it in half with a wire, them scooped out the inside, forming a little bowl.

"If you want to make a mug, you can use coils of clay, like this, to make the walls higher." She rolled up small coils of the rich, red clay, measuring them to see if they were the right length. She set them aside, then mixed some water and clay in a little bowl. She made little cuts on the surface of the bowl and one of the coils, brushed the gruel of water and clay on each surface, then pressed them together. Then she smoothed the coil edges onto the bowl. She repeated this process, building the walls up to form a cylinder.

"Now, you do the second half of the 'bowl' so we will be building two mugs."

"Okay. I'll give it a try." George followed the instructions and slowly built up the sides of the mug, being careful to "glue" the coils in place. Meanwhile, Mary Jean had brought over another resident's piece to show him. It was a bowl that had been thrown on a wheel, something Mary Jean had not yet mastered.

The glaze was a blue-black color with cream and brown mottling on one side. The light cream contrasted strikingly with the dark blackish blue. The bowl had been dipped in two glazes. The resident had waxed the bottom foot of the bowl first so that, when glazed, it would not stick to the kiln. It was almost perfectly symmetrical, which was quite different from a handmade bowl.

"I think I like that technique better," said George, looking up for just a moment from his work.

"Yes, you can get such uniform pieces this way. Still, the most difficult part is trying to decide what glaze to use." Mary Jean caught Kia's eye, and she walked over to see the bowl Mary Jean was holding.

"Whose is this?" She picked it up and turned it

around, inspecting the handiwork.

"I'm not sure. I picked it up from the shelf over there." Mary Jean wasn't sure if she should touch other people's pieces without their approval.

"It turned out wonderful. Look at the colors, how they contrast—I love how these two glazes work together. The symmetry looks good. Do you want to learn how to use the wheel?"

"No. I think I'll stick to handbuilding."

"Would you like another piece of clay to try something else?' asked Kia.

"Yes, I think I would," said Mary Jean. Kia disappeared into the storage room and returned with a large brick of clay covered in plastic.

"This is a lot of clay, but I think you will end up using it all." She smiled and motioned toward a bank of shelves along the wall.

"You can choose a cubby, put your name on it, and store your clay and unfinished projects there." She tapped George on the shoulder, who was deep in concentration working on his mug.

"You too, George. Pick out a cubby and put your name on it. I get the feeling you will be coming regularly, too." George looked up, said, "Thanks," and got back to his work.

The afternoon went by quickly as Mary Jean and George worked on their projects. They talked about the garden project, different glazes, what they were reading, and their kids and grandkids. Before she knew it, Kia had announced to everyone that it was time to clean up. Time had flown by, and Mary Jean scurried to put her clay away in her new cubby. She was beat. Luckily, the ceramics center had helpers who took over the cleanup for many of the older people in the room.

She and George waited together for the shuttle along with others from the class. She was ready to get back to her apartment and rest before dinner.

George turned to her and said, "I'm almost finished with my mug. I have no idea what to do next. But I can't wait to get back here and learn about the glazing process." George was animated when he talked, and she could tell he had caught the clay-making fever.

"It has to be bisque fired first. That's the first firing. Then you glaze it. Then it gets its final firing." Mary Jean and George found their seats and continued to chat about the possibilities for decorating and glazing George's project.

When they arrived at the lobby, Mary Jean promised to meet George for dinner in the cafeteria at 7 p.m. As she made her way to her apartment, she stopped. I wonder how Arman is, she thought. Maybe I should ask at the front desk if he is in. She turned around and headed back to the lobby.

"Hello. Can you tell me if Arman Kawowski is in his apartment? He was not feeling well, and I want to check on him." The lady called his apartment, but there was no answer.

"You might try the infirmary," she said. Mary Jean walked down the colorful hallway toward the infirmary. The paintings of the Oregon mountains that were hung along the walls were calming to her. Here was a meadow of wildflowers that overlooked the Columbia River Gorge. "I think that's Rowena Point where Marcus once took a photo," she said to herself. The yellow flowers filled the foreground, contrasting against the blue waters of the Columbia River below.

The infirmary was behind a double glass door.

A nurse was busy writing in a chart and did not see her as she came up to the desk.

"Hi. I am a friend of Arman Kawowski. I was wondering if he was here." Mary Jean showed her ID to the nurse. She examined it briefly and looked at her computer.

"Yes, he's here. He is being watched today because he had some serious symptoms this morning."

"Do you know what is wrong with him?" asked Mary Jean.

"We think he has the flu, so we are requesting that no one visits him for forty-eight hours until we can be certain that is what it is."

Mary Jean thanked her and left the infirmary. I hope he will be okay, she thought. He is older than I am, and I know the flu can be hard on us older folks.

She let herself into her apartment. It had been a long day, and she was tired. I'll just lie down for a little while, she thought. Mary Jean lay down on her bed and pulled the light comforter over herself. She listened to the classical music playing in the background that was piping through the intercom system; she could turn it off if she wanted, but she liked listening to it, especially when she was trying to sleep.

She thought about George and the mug he was working on. Then she thought about Arman's sculptures and her handbuilt mugs that were sitting in her kitchen. She heard Kia's comments about the beautiful bowl she had picked up off the drying shelf: "It turned out wonderful. Look at the colors, how they contrast . . ." She drifted off into another world.

She was floating above herself. She was hovering near the ceiling of her room, looking down at herself sleeping in her bed. The white comforter was pulled up to her chin, and she was lying on her back. She watched herself breathe in and out. Well, she was alive at least. She could see that from this perspective. What was she doing *up* here? As she pondered her situation, she watched as the woman below stirred, then went limp, not moving, not breathing. What was happening?

There he was. She had floated into the kitchen area, which looked out over the living room, and was startled when she saw him sitting in the living room, reading a book.

Lewis.

He flipped through the magazine pages and then put it down. He gazed out the window into the garden below. She watched him take out his pocket watch and look at the time. What was he waiting in here for? She called down to him.

"Lewis! What are you doing here? And what am I doing *up* here?" Mary Jean had her back to the ceiling and was looking down at him.

"Oh, I thought you'd show up about now. You can come down now. It's time."

Time for what? she thought. Mary Jean floated down very slowly until she could swing her feet underneath herself and stand up. She walked over to the couch and sat next to Lewis. "This doesn't mean what I think it means, does it?" asked Mary Jean. Lewis crinkled up his blue eyes and gave her a warm smile.

"You're with me now. That's all that matters." Lewis held her hand gently. She noticed his pocket watch on the coffee table. Time had stopped. She felt warm all of a sudden. All she was wearing was a cotton nightgown.

"I've missed you," said Mary Jean.

"I hear you are *the* woman around town here, if

you know what I mean. So many gentlemen calling."

"Well, you seem to know a lot about my life. Have you been spying on me?"

"Of course. Your happiness is my sole goal in this life."

"Why haven't I seen you?"

"You haven't needed me."

Mary Jean looked at him with a puzzled look on her face. She wasn't understanding any of this. Her mind was blurring the facts again.

"Can we go walking now?" asked Mary Jean. "I'm going to get dressed and put my red sneakers on. I want to show you the meadow I discovered on—"

She opened her eyes and felt the room swirling around her. Despite her condition, she knew exactly where she was because she had been there just this afternoon. The nurse picked up her hand and measured her pulse. She felt her head and said, "How are you feeling, Mary Jean?" Her eyes fluttered, and she tried to focus on the nurse in front of her, but she found it too difficult. She closed her eyes again and said, "I'm feeling a bit woozy."

"Well, just get some more rest, and I'll check on you again in a little bit. You seem to have come down with a very bad case of the flu." She hurried away to check on another patient.

Mary Jean closed her eyes and slept, but no dreams awaited her.

34

She heard some guitar music in the background, barely audible but beautiful to listen to. She opened her eyes and propped herself up on her pillows and looked around. She was in a room by herself. It was painted a very pale green. It had knotty alder wood cabinets and trim around the door. The rug was a brown tweed color. There were several potted plants and flowers in vases on a countertop along the wall. Light was streaming in from two tall windows, filling the room with a warm glow. She reached for a glass of water on the bed stand next to her. The water was cool, and she tasted a little lemon in it. There were two new paperback books on the bed stand, as well as two cards that were addressed to her. She opened the first, which read: "Get well soon! From your fellow clay students at the ceramics center." The second card lay next to a small vase of red roses in a lemon-yellow envelope, one of her favorite spring colors. "Am thinking of you. Love, George." He certainly is a romantic, thought Mary Jean. She thought about the friends she had made at Springfield and the new experiences she'd had, and she felt grateful. She wondered about Arman.

"Hi, Mom." Marcus and his wife were standing in the doorway. "How are you feeling? We just got a call the other day that you were down with the flu. The nurse told us to wait awhile before visiting you. She said you have been pretty sick."

He smiled meekly and looked anxiously for a good response. His wife, Kirsten, held back and let her husband approach the bed. One at a time seemed best.

"I'm doing better, I think." Mary Jean sighed and pulled the covers up a little tighter around her. "Does it feel cold in here to you?"

Marcus looked back at Kirsten. "No, Mom; it feels quite warm. But I am wearing this wool sweater, so I think I'll take it off." He removed his lightweight Smartwool sweater and laid it on the chair nearby. "Look at all these gifts. You must be quite popular here. We love the new facility, and it seems, from reports from your friends, that you do, too. We had no idea you were making things with clay."

It must be a shock to them, thought Mary Jean. She had never shown any inclination for doing art during her lifetime until now. Mary Jean thought about the clay she worked with and how it mirrored life. You could mold the clay into anything you'd like.

They chatted until the nurse shooed them away. They said they would have lunch at one of the campus restaurants and return afterward for a final short visit. After they left, Mary Jean picked up one of the books on the bed stand. Inside the cover was a handwritten note: "Thought you might like this, William." The book was entitled *Drawing with Style*.

How thoughtful. Mary Jean flipped through the book and saw it was full of illustrations and written in a fun, jaunty style. Yes, I have met some nice people here, Mary Jean thought. They have expanded my world and continue to surprise me.

Someone knocked on the door, which was ajar. "May I come in?" George walked through the door, holding a sweet carrot cake dessert. He set it down and took off his wool blazer. "Are you up for sharing a piece of cake? I had to just guess what kind you'd like. I can leave it here for later if you're not ready to eat it now."

"I'm so happy to see you, George. Thank you for the roses. They are beautiful."

"My pleasure, Mary Jean." He stood there, as if not sure if he should stay.

"Did you finish your mug?" asked Mary Jean.

"No. I need to pick out the glazes and decide if I'm going to try anything fancy. But I need your help. So, I can wait until you get better."

He cut the cake in two with a plastic knife he had brought with him.

"Do you feel like a bite now?"

"I think I can manage a small piece," she said.

They sat together, amicably eating their cake and discussing the weather, the student projects in the ceramics center, and all that their world contained. Then Marcus and Kirsten arrived with leftovers from their lunch, thinking Mary Jean would have liked some. George was introduced, and the three of them visited for about ten more minutes.

"We should head back, Mom. We've got horses to feed and dogs waiting for us at home. I'm glad you're improving. You should be out of here in no time." He and Kirstin gave Mary Jean a hug and left.

"He seems like a fine man, your son, Marcus.

And Kirsten, too. I'd like to meet your daughters sometime. I know they visit you fairly often. Maybe we could all have lunch together."

"Not just yet . . . but maybe soon." Mary Jean thought this was going a little too fast. One thing at a time, she thought.

George said, "Well, I'd better be going. You need your rest." He leaned over and gave her a peck on the cheek. "See you soon," he said. He picked up his coat, waved goodbye, and walked out the door.

Mary Jean was surprised by his kiss. She hadn't known that George felt so deeply about her. Was she making more of this than what it was? How did she feel? She hadn't known him very long at all. But when you are in your nineties, I suppose you can't waste time, she thought. Today may be your last day. Time was on Mary Jean's mind these days. Perhaps that's why she had dreamt of dying. She knew that all of the days from here on out were like icing on the cake. She would have to make the very best of them.

She picked up William's book on drawing and started to read. She wondered what he was doing right now. She felt confused about the two men's attention. They were both in good health and a few years younger than she was. We could all have several more years left, she thought. She wondered how that was going to play out. Well, she'd learned to not overthink things, to just take one day at a time. She read for about a half hour more and soon became sleepy. She shut her eyes and dozed off. The nurse popped in and closed the drapes so she could sleep. The last thing she heard was the guitar music and a duo singing in the distance.

35

What a cold spring this was turning out to be. Twenty-five degrees, with snow flurries to boot. And it was going to be like that all week, maybe warming up to forty. Mary Jean made sure to put on some warm wool socks before she laced up her red sneakers. Every time she put those shoes on, she thought of Lewis. She put on her warm winter coat over her wool cardigan. Everyone will think I am crazy to go outside today, she thought. It had barely been a week since she left the infirmary. They had kept her there for two days so she could get hydrated. They thought some visitor had brought it in, and it had swept through the facility like wildfire. Luckily, no one had died so far. Most of the residents had gotten milder cases and recovered well.

She needed to think. She still hadn't heard from Arman, and she was beginning to get worried. William had seen her at breakfast that morning and wanted to meet later in the afternoon to look at some drawings before drawing class. George had also asked her to call him when she was feeling better so they could go to the ceramics center to finish up their projects. How had life gotten so complicated?

She knew she should feel grateful for having these friends in her life, all vying for her attention. And then there was Lewis. But she kind of figured he didn't count since he had only last shown up in her dream. She felt he had moved on, having done what he had set out to do—to keep her safe and show her how to keep on living. How to make the best of these last months or years.

In the lobby, the person at the front desk looked at her inquisitively.

"You're not going out in this weather, are you?"

Mary Jean replied, "Oh, probably just for a few minutes. I need to get some fresh air."

As she stepped outside, the cold bit into her face. She pulled up her hood to block the wind. She walked slowly down the sidewalk looking up at the trees, which were bare and without leaves. Somebody had put some very fine gravel down on the sidewalk so people wouldn't slip. The clear-cuts in the foothills to the west were still covered in snow. She breathed in the crisp air and looked above her. Crystals formed where water had dripped down from a tiny shoot coming off a tree trunk.

She made her way a little farther down toward the outdoor pools. Steam rose from the water above the beautiful wrought-iron fence that surrounded the swimming area. It must cost them a fortune to keep these heated, she thought. She was surprised to see two women in the hot tub. They looked to be about twenty years old. They were talking softly and looking around every now and again. As she got closer, one of them noticed her. They both quickly got out of the tub, grabbed their towels, and left the enclosed area. Mary Jean walked faster, and as she rounded the corner of the pool area, she saw the girls running toward the parking lot. "Looks like someone is taking advantage of the amenities here," she said to herself. Mary Jean watched as the girls drove off in their Subaru wagon. "It must be spring break, and they thought they'd just have a little fun. How nice to be young and adventurous."

She turned right and continued back to the lobby around the other side of the pool house. It was silent. No birds were singing. The snow was melting below her feet as it crunched under her footsteps. She trudged through a small snowdrift on the grass. Once she was back on the sidewalk, walking became easier. She dug her hands into her pockets to warm her fingers. She felt refreshed. Now she could tackle her social problems and enjoy the rest of her day. She laughed at this thought. Who would have thought the last chapter of her life would be so exciting?

The building felt too warm. Mary Jean took off her jacket and sweater when she saw William walking up the stairs. She took the elevator up, and when it opened, she saw him heading toward her apartment. He knocked at her door and waited.

She walked up behind him and said, "Well hello, William. How are you today?"

Surprised, he turned with a start and said, "I know we were going to meet later in the afternoon, but I thought I'd bring these drawings over now. I hope that's all right." He looked sheepish as he stood there clutching his sketchbook.

Mary Jean quickly said, "Come in, William. I'd love to see your drawings."

"Thank you." He sat down on the couch in the living room while Mary Jean hung up her garments in the closet. She scurried around the kitchen, making a pot of coffee the two of them could share. She brought out some scones Marcus and Kirsten had brought her when she was in the infirmary. They might be a little stale but they would do. The smell of the coffee soon filled the little apartment. She poured two cups.

"Do you take cream?" she asked.

"Yes, please," he said.

Mary Jean brought over the coffee and sat down next to him.

"William, I decided I am not going to the drawing class tonight. I feel like I need a little more rest. I was just outside for a short walk, and it was so refreshing. But I think I need to take it easy. I wanted to thank you for the drawing book. It's been such a pleasure to read and learn more about the different styles."

William sipped his coffee as they chatted about the book and what their plans were for the day. Then she told him about George and Arman, and William shared more about his family. By the end of their conversation, she felt that they both had a common understanding that there was always room for one more friend in each other's lives.

After William left, Mary Jean decided to go to the library for a change of scenery to read more of the drawing book. She tucked the book into her purse and headed to the large library in the east wing of the building. She loved taking her time while strolling down the halls so she could stop and admire the paintings on the walls. She stopped to study a large canvas on her right. The subject was a barn scene. It was acrylic, and the colors were brilliant. The peak of the white barn could be seen at the top of the painting against a sky of cerulean blue. In the background were large trees on either side of the barn, almost black and somewhat abstract. The middle of the composition was a blend of golds, yellows, and creams depicting a field of corn. A meandering dark-green line ran through the center of the painting, horizontally, suggesting a creek. The colors below the creek turned into greens of all shades, with a spot here and there of golden yellow. The overall effect was beautiful.

By the time she got to the library, she had spent nearly forty minutes looking at paintings on her way there. Mary Jean walked through the large glass doors of the library and looked for a place to sit. She chose a love seat in the back for some privacy.

She got comfortable and took out her book. As she was beginning to read, she noticed a woman across the room who was crying softly. Her hair was braided and pulled up around her head like Mary Jean's grandmother used to wear hers. No one was paying any attention to her. Mary Jean sat there awhile, watching her. Finally, she decided to walk over and introduce herself to find out what was so terribly wrong.

"Excuse me, but I couldn't help noticing that you were crying. My name is Mary Jean. Is there anything I can do to help?"

The woman looked up, and Mary Jean could see she was clearly embarrassed.

"Oh . . . thank you . . . I . . . I . . ." She started crying again, and Mary Jean asked, "Would you like to get some tea in the cafeteria with me?" The lady stopped crying and looked down at her shoes. "Yes," she said. "That would be nice."

On the way to the cafeteria, Mary Jean learned that the woman's name was Emily. She had recently lost her husband to a heart attack. He had been eighty-two years old. She couldn't live by herself anymore, and her kids had brought her here after selling everything in her home. Springfield Acres was new and had so much to offer, they said, but she was so sad all the time that she couldn't notice all its benefits. She didn't care; she just wanted her Henry back. Mary Jean told her what it had been like when Lewis died. After moving to a condo, where she lived for five years, she moved to Kingsley, where things had not gone so well.

The cafeteria was nearly empty. They found a table by a potted palm and sat down. They ordered tea and some muffins. Soon, Emily was talking more freely about the last two terrifying weeks before Henry had died. It had happened so fast, she said. He hadn't been feeling well. He complained of indigestion and was staying in bed all day. Finally, she got him to the doctor, and soon they were doing various tests. It went on for weeks—the waiting for the results and then more tests. At one point, she had to be hospitalized for a nervous breakdown. Her daughter sat with her in the evenings, and they hired a caregiver to come by three times a week. Henry hated the intrusion and was so rude to the caregiver that she left. Finally, Henry had a full-blown heart attack and died on the way to the hospital. Emily looked down and sipped at her tea. She left the muffin untouched.

"I know change is hard," said Mary Jean. "I was lucky to have my four children available to help me. Even so, the adjustment to living alone was so difficult. You are grieving now, and it's only been a few weeks. It takes time to come to grips with everything."

Mary Jean sat with Emily quietly and let her be. By helping others, we can help ourselves, she thought. Sometimes, just having someone close by who can listen is a comfort. After a while, Mary Jean suggested a short walk in the glassed-in garden. Exercise was another way to improve your mood, she had learned. Together, they walked down the stairs and through the double doors to the garden.

36

This was a garden like no other. Mary Jean had often looked down into the space through the tall glass windows, but she had not been able to appreciate the scale of the garden until she was actually standing inside of it. The ceiling was very tall, high enough for a forty-foot tree to be very happy. There were northwest natives like ash, cottonwood, pine, fir, and birch trees, as well as smaller plants like the ficus usually used for patios. Avocado and Meyer lemon trees flourished here, as well. Because the garden was enclosed in glass and heated, it was warm. Mary Jean and Emily walked along the pathways, stopping every now and again to look above them and around them.

Mary Jean couldn't believe the variety of plants that were here. The design of the garden was captivating. It had pea gravel paths that intertwined with resting areas and wooden benches. Water features were an integral part of the design, and the sound of water flowing, trickling, and dripping filled her ears. There was a large, rolling glass door that could be opened to let in fresh air when the weather was good. Birds flew within the garden, and some were busy making nests for their future broods. Residents had filled some of the bird feeders with nesting material like yarn, straw, and grass clippings to help them out. What a clever idea, thought Mary Jean.

"I still wonder if I am dreaming sometimes," said Mary Jean aloud. She and Emily were sitting down at one of the benches.

"This must have been very expensive to build," said Emily. "I know," said Mary Jean. "How ever could they have afforded to make something so large and extravagant?"

An employee was picking some lemons. She used a small ladder to reach the fruit. When her baskets were full, she carefully climbed down, placing one foot after the other on each rung. The lady gathered up her baskets and made her way along the path toward the two women.

"Would you like a lemon?" The woman smiled and put the basket of fruit in front of them.

The woman had long black hair and wore a red embroidered blouse. Her skin was brown and she looked Hispanic. Mary Jean had noticed that the staff here was very diverse—Asian, Hispanic, African American, and Native American. The management seemed to be progressive and inclusive. It sure wasn't like that when I was working, thought Mary Jean. Everyone at the library where she had worked had been white. It's about time things changed. Kingsley had mostly employed Hispanics, and Mary Jean was certain they had probably paid them minimum wage and never promoted them above the status of house cleaner. Here, everyone was friendly and polite, and she'd heard that they were paid well and had health insurance covered by the retirement center.

Emily and Mary Jean each took a lemon. The fruit

was small but heavy, and it smelled delightful. They talked about the lemon meringue pies they used to make. Emily had also always made lemon bars for her kids when they were little. Mary Jean was careful to pause and listen while Emily told her story. She knew that would be the most healing.

"Have you heard of the garden project?" asked Mary Jean.

"No. I haven't been here very long, and I haven't felt like looking into any of the activities yet." Emily fished in her purse for a Kleenex to blow her nose.

"You are paired up with a student, and together, you decide what you want to plant in a garden plot. Last year at Kingsley, a third-grade boy and I planted tomatoes, basil, and oregano. He and his family made spaghetti sauce with the tomatoes and herbs he grew. If you are interested, you can sign up with the activities director, Leslie Drake. She will find a student for you to work with."

"I will think about it." Emily forced a smile. She stood up.

"Thank you for your kindness. I really do appreciate it. I think I'll go back to my apartment now. Maybe I'll see you at the dining hall later tonight."

Mary Jean got up and said, "I'll walk you to your apartment."

"No need. You've done enough. I'm sure you have a busy day ahead of you." She picked up her purse and walked back down the path toward the door to the building.

That poor woman, thought Mary Jean. It's so hard to move on. I hope her family comes to visit her soon.

Mary Jean decided to see if she could find George. She guessed he was probably at the ceramics center. He had been visiting the center almost daily. The day was proving to be a sunny one. She headed toward the shuttle stop, where six others were already in line. Soon, she was making another friend or two. A short woman in her eighties was going to the pool. She had been a swimmer all her life and did laps regularly. She was slim and looked ten years younger than her age. Obviously, her lifestyle kept her young. Mary Jean had never been much of a swimmer; in fact, she was a little afraid of the water. She had taken swimming lessons as a child but had never learned to be proficient at it. She and her husband, Lewis, had taken the kids to Paulina Lake every summer, but she would just wade.

"How many laps do you do?" asked Mary Jean.

"I do about forty laps. It takes me about an hour. I'm slow, but it's a great way to start my day."

Her friend who was standing in line next to her nodded and said, "I do the same. We've been swimming together for twenty years. I can't believe how the time has flown by."

It seemed like it was a common phrase that people used around here: time flying by. How do you slow it down? she thought. There are times in our lives when we want to speed things up, like when our children are toddlers and in diapers. We can't wait until they are older. Then we can't wait until Friday, when the weekend will be here and we can do something fun. Or maybe it's when your child is learning to drive; you can't wait until they finally master that skill so you can breathe easier. Then they are graduating high school, and you then wonder where the time has gone. Now they no longer need you, or so it seems, and you are left alone in your too-empty house, and it is difficult to find a new way of living.

Mary Jean's mind was running rapidly backward

then forward in time as she contemplated that phrase. Where had the time gone? She knew where it had gone. It had been a life well-lived with many ups and downs. With brief moments of happiness, satisfaction, love, and anger—a spectrum of emotions and events all adding up to what it meant to live. Travelling had filled her and Lewis's retirement years. They had travelled the globe. She thought of all those photo albums filled with pictures from their trips. She had gradually gotten rid of some of them. She knew she couldn't leave too much of her belongings behind because who would want them? Her kids all had busy lives and were making memories of their own—only now it was digital stuff all stored on the computer.

She thought about all these things as she sat on the bus. She had whittled down her material possessions to just what would fit in her small apartment. Having just moved from Kingsley, she had gotten rid of even more. It was freeing, in a sense. There was more space, less clutter. And that was peaceful.

The shuttle pulled up to the ceramics center, and Mary Jean stepped off. She spied George's lanky figure through the windows and felt a flutter of excitement in her chest. She took a deep breath as she pulled open the door.

37

There weren't many people in the class, maybe just ten. George was busy working on a sculpture of a dog. He had it on a wheel of sorts so he could spin it around and look at it from all angles. He had been working on it for a couple of days, and she could see how his skill had grown from his first project, the mug.

"Hello, George." Mary Jean took a seat next to him. She had picked up her stash of clay from her cubby. She had no idea what she would make next.

"Well, how are you, Mary Jean? So glad you could make it! It's good to see you."

He stopped what he was doing to look at her. His hair was neatly combed, still with some black mixed with gray at the temples, and trimmed short. He was dressed in a simple, blue cotton shirt tucked into clean, well-fitted jeans. He wore a leather belt with tooling and a silver buckle, giving him a kind of Western look. His shoes were brown leather lace-ups, and he wore navy-blue plaid socks.

"I'm fine, George. And you?" She looked at his sculpture and said, "Well, I do believe that is a dog. But I'm not sure what breed."

"Well, that's okay because it is a mixed breed. It is my dog that passed away before I came to Springfield Acres. He was a collie mix, black and white. His name was Keegan."

He stopped and looked down. She could tell he was reliving a moment of sorrow, remembering his old companion. "He lived a long life of sixteen years, pretty long for his size as he was a large dog, about sixty-five pounds."

"I'm sorry. I can tell he meant a lot to you." Mary Jean could read his face, see the sadness in his eyes.

"I know nothing about sculpture, but Kia said to just rely on your memories . . . and instincts. The feel of his coat, the determination in his eyes, his lithe and agile body, his playfulness and joy of exploring . . . she said to close your eyes and imagine all these things, and it will come into your hands as you work the clay."

"It sounds mystical." Mary Jean took her clay out of the plastic and cut a piece off. She would think outside the box, this time, and make a small elephant.

I still don't see Arman here, she thought to herself. She didn't remember seeing his name on the get well card from her ceramics center friends. Oh, I hope he is okay. She never checked to see if he had left the infirmary. Now she truly felt alarmed. She got up and approached Kia.

"Is Arman Kowalski still enrolled in the class?"

Kia looked puzzled, then surprised. "Oh, I'm sorry. I thought you knew because you were in the infirmary with him."

She hesitated until an awkward silence hung between them, and then she continued, "He passed away two days ago."

Mary Jean opened her mouth in surprise. "No,

I did not know. I remember going to see him, but they wouldn't let me in because he had the flu. The next thing I knew, I had the flu and was back in the infirmary." She couldn't hold back the tears as they slid slowly down her face. She was overwhelmed with grief as the memory of him washed over her.

Kia took her hand and said, "He had been ill for a long time, even when he was coming to the classes. He was weak, but clay-making was therapy for him, so he kept coming."

Mary Jean sat there, wiping the tears from her face. George consoled her, and they talked quietly for a while. She would miss that dear man who had introduced her to clay and encouraged her through her first project. She knew she could no longer count on people being around. His warm friendship would be missed.

This was the last chapter in her life, and no one knew when it would end.

She wrapped up her clay and put it back in her cubby. She no longer felt like creating anything today. She wanted to be alone, so she told George she would see him later that evening for dinner.

She walked down one of the paths and headed out on a new trail. She always found that fresh air and being outside brought her spirits back up. Walking was a way to work through one's difficulties. She noticed the begonias just starting to flower. There were a row of pink ones and some oat straw grass along a berm. A cottonwood tree was just ahead, and the white fluff from the tree was floating through the air and covering the path with white. She wended through some groves of birch and came upon a cedar fence and an arbor. Upon the arbor was a red flowering rose. The aroma of the buds was intoxicating.

She stopped and sat on a bench made of stone. An inscription was on the bench. It read, TIME IS OF THE ESSENCE. Indeed, so it was. She had missed her chance at a last goodbye with Arman.

One of her new friends at Springfield, Ann, had such a good attitude about death. She would tell Mary Jean how much she missed the person, say a sentence or two about what she loved about them, and then move on. She would change the subject and focus on what she was doing next. She always had something going on—new places to go and people to meet. She did not dwell on the grief. Of course, if it were someone in her family, she would spend a longer time grieving. But you could tell, even then, that she loved life too much to spend a day sadder than she had to. Mary Jean thought about this. Move forward, she thought, and she continued down the path.

Plans. It was always a good idea to have plans. A change of pace, a new location, something to look forward to. She thought she'd call her Marcus and ask him to pick her up and take her to see her great-grandson. Better not waste any time. He was almost one year old. The hat she had bought him last Christmas probably did not fit him anymore. Maybe the adults could do a short walk in Peavy Arboretum together with the baby in a backpack carrier. She used to love walking on the paths there among the trees. It had been ages since she had visited the park. It was close enough for her grandson and his wife to meet them there.

She hurried along, and as the path wound back toward the retirement center, she noticed two hawks above her calling to each other. She looked up and searched the trees for them. She finally spied the nest they were building. Ahead of her, she saw a couple looking through binoculars at some birds in the meadow. They had a small book with them that they referred to every now and again. They chattered away excitedly, taking turns to look at the birds. Across the way, she could see someone in the arena at the stables. Life was taking place all around her.

When she reached the lobby, she took the elevator up and headed back to her apartment. She thought of the inscription on the bench. When she let herself in, she sat down on the couch and picked up the phone. She dialed her son's number and waited impatiently for him to answer.

"Hi, Mom. Is everything all right?"

"Oh yes, Marcus. I'm glad I got you. I want to know if you could pick me up sometime next week. I want to visit Ivan. I bet he is so big now. I want us to go for a walk at Peavy Arboretum. I haven't been there in years and years. Do you think they would like to do that with Ivan?" Mary Jean knew she was talking too fast.

"Well, I sure can call them and see if I can set something up. Are you sure you are up for walking there? There are gravel roads, and some of the paths are uneven . . ." Marcus didn't sound very encouraging. It was not like him.

"Yes, I'd sure like to try. I've been walking the paths here at Springfield Acres and have worked up to two miles, believe it or not."

"Why, Mom, that's great! I can't believe it. You know Peavy Arboretum is one of my favorite spots, so I'll call up Finley and see what I can do. I'll let you know tomorrow."

"Okay then. I'll wait to hear from you. Bye for now."

"Bye, Mom."

Well, that was that. Now, what else could she plan? Mary Jean sat back and thought about her opportunities. Soon, the garden project would begin. Only another two weeks to their second meeting to choose their seeds in mid-May, and then planting time would be two weeks later at the end of May. She could hardly wait.

38

Mary Jean got up early the next day. She wanted to check out the pool. Although she had never been much of a swimmer, she thought she'd at least see what the pool area looked like. It was on her to-do list: explore Springfield Acres thoroughly and see firsthand all that it had to offer. She would even bring her swimsuit so she could sit in the hot tub for a while.

The building was very large with a ceiling that could be opened up when the weather was good. The ceiling was made of a clear material, which let in a lot of natural light. The space was organized into several pools. The largest was a lap swimming pool, and she could see people slowly making their way down the lanes using a variety of strokes: some were using breaststroke, while more proficient swimmers were doing freestyle or the crawl, as she used to call it. That was the stroke Mary Jean could never master.

There was a shallow pool designated just for swim aerobics and therapy. Residents were walking in place in the water and using flotation devices on their arms. She saw a wheelchair by the poolside. *I guess water therapy is good for those with a handicap*, she thought. You can feel weightless in the water and as if you can walk again. Mary Jean saw another pool in the far corner. There were at least eight people sitting in a soaking tub. Jets of water broke the surface, and Mary Jean decided to check this out first. She headed into the dressing room and put on her suit. "Haven't been in one of these in years," she said to herself out loud. She put on some rubber sandals and wrapped a large blue towel around herself. She looked in the mirror. Why, I look younger today, she thought. She studied her face, and it seemed her skin was a touch smoother. A few less wrinkles. Her legs looked not so bad for a woman in her nineties.

She walked over to the hot tub and stepped in. Four of the residents had left, so there was plenty of space. It was hot, so she had to take her time. She waded in up to her knees, then very slowly sat down on one of the seats. She breathed in deeply and exhaled like they did in those yoga classes. She felt her muscles relax, and she closed her eyes. She knew there was another hot tub outside where she'd caught the two teenage girls during spring break when it had been closed for maintenance. How they'd managed to climb over the fence she did not know. But she thought how nice it would be to sit out there in the evening with the stars out. Maybe she'd have to try that out.

After about ten minutes, Mary Jean got out and decided she'd try the large lap pool. She dipped her foot in to test the temperature. Brrrrr . . . too cold. She probably should have gone in there first. She waded in and put both feet on the first step and waited while her body adjusted to the cooler temperature. She took a few more steps until she was standing waist-high in the water. A young woman walked toward her as she sat down on the step.

"Hello. My name is Laura. I'm one of the instructors here. How are you this morning?" The woman was in her thirties and slim, with long blond hair pulled back in a ponytail. She was wearing a turquoise one-piece swimsuit. She had strong, muscular arms and legs.

"I'm fine, thank you," said Mary Jean. "This is the first time I've been to the pool. I'm not much of a swimmer. In fact, I would love some lessons. I want to be able to swim like that woman over there."

She pointed to a woman a few lanes over who was swimming powerfully down her lane, then gracefully turning and pushing against the wall to head back. She was doing the freestyle stroke and was so smooth that she barely broke the surface of the water.

"Just kidding. If I could manage just a few yards, that would be something." Mary Jean managed a bit of a smile.

"Well, I'm sure we can help you out with that. When would you like to begin?"

"There is no better time than right now." Mary Jean was on a mission to not waste any more time. She was surprised by herself; she had not planned to swim at all just an hour ago. She adjusted her suit.

"Well, you are in luck. I have a fifteen-minute break right now. Let's see what you know, and we'll start from there."

Laura asked Mary Jean to run through the basic strokes so she could evaluate her skills at each one. Once her assessment was complete, Laura had Mary Jean build her strength by holding a floating device and kicking to move through the water for a short distance. They practiced for ten more minutes.

"That's good for today. Come back Wednesday

morning around this same time. We'll build up your strength a little at a time. Then we will focus on learning a new skill."

Laura was very patient. She helped Mary Jean relax and kept the session short.

Well, scratch that one off the list, thought Mary Jean. She liked how it relaxed her and took her mind off worrying.

The woman a few lanes away had stepped out of the water and was towel-drying her short gray hair. Her body was lean and still had tone. She glanced over at Mary Jean and gave her a big smile.

"Hi, I'm Maggie. I saw you taking lessons from Laura. She's great. You looked like you were really enjoying yourself. Before you know it, you will be improving, and it will make you feel so good. Swimming stretches out the whole body and is easy on the joints." It was nice to be encouraged.

"Thank you for the support. I'm Mary Jean." They talked awhile and then headed toward the dressing room to shower and change.

Mary Jean learned that Maggie was a retired teacher. She had always loved to swim and had been on the swim team in college, but now she just swam to stay healthy. Her family lived close by. She had two daughters who rarely came to visit her.

"They have busy lives. Both have three kids and work full-time jobs. I don't know how they do it. I had my kids late in life, around forty. I had summers off, thank goodness."

Mary Jean did not want to share how lucky she was to have her children visit regularly, so they talked about Springfield Acres and its amenities. Had Maggie been to the stables or walked on the paths around the meadow? Maggie's interests were narrow, and

Mary Jean found out she only went swimming. Maggie had only arrived a week ago and didn't know anyone at the facility. She confided in Mary Jean that she felt lonely. She loved the new facility but suffered from bouts of depression. Swimming helped her mood, which explained why she did it most days of the week.

What Mary Jean loved about Springfield Acres was that it attracted people much younger than the usual age of retirement home populations. Also, other members of the community used the facilities like the golf course, stables, and the pool. Even the ceramics center had some young students from Maple Grove. We so often isolate the elderly from the rest of the population, thought Mary Jean. Being around the little ones gives us a chance to rediscover that sense of play. And intergenerational programs, where older adults and youth are paired together, have been shown to decrease the social isolation that elders experience. The children also benefit by improving their social and emotional skills while reducing their fear of aging people. At Kingsley, she rarely saw little kids. And when they did visit, some of them would cry out of fear when they saw their great-grandparent.

Besides frequenting the ceramics center, Mary Jean had been to the stables and hiked several, though not all, of the trails on the property. She had taken drawing classes. Now she had taken her first lesson at the pool house. She had also visited the two on-site restaurants. All that was left to explore was the theater and the golf course. She'd leave those for another day. The garden project wasn't far away. She had plans.

39

Arman's memorial was to be held in a few weeks' time. She missed him. She knew he would have wanted her to be happy, not sad. Go make something, he often told her. So, she would follow suit. She would create something for him and bring it to the celebration of his life and give it to his kids. She would tell them of his kindness and show them what a good teacher and friend he had been to her.

The ceramics center was crowded with people that morning. Mary Jean could hardly find a seat. She brought out her clay from her cubby and put it in front of her. What would honor Arman's life? What would his family like to take back with them? She sat pondering this for a while. Outside, the sun was shining, and she knew it was going to be a warm day. She knew how Arman liked to sit outside with his shirt off, soaking up the sun on his outside balcony. He always said he was getting his vitamin D. That's it, she thought. She'd make a type of gazing ball or sphere that radiated energy and vitality, just like the sun.

Mary Jean started by making coils of clay, building

it up layer by layer in a circle like Arman had showed her that very first time. She used a mixture of water and clay to help seal the edges. Slowly, the piece took shape, and now she was reducing the length of the coils to curve it into a ball shape that was hollow inside. It couldn't be too wet or too dry. She remembered his words: "Too wet and it will collapse; too dry and you won't be able to form it correctly." She held it in one hand, and with the other, she patted it with a wide wooden spoon, shaping it into a smooth ball.

When she was finished with the orb, she made a small square pedestal for it to sit upon. She engraved her initials in the bottom and set the pair on the drying shelf. She thought of the colors she wanted it to be. She would need to apply multiple glazes in layers to get the effect she was thinking of. She tidied up her work station and put everything away in her cubby. It felt good to express herself with clay, and it helped her work through her sorrow. But she knew that death was part of the circle of life and that she was not far from it, either. Each day that she got up, she cherished it; even if there was pain in her hips or feelings of loneliness at times. Here at Springfield, she had places to walk where she could listen to the birds, take in the green meadows, feel the lovely shade of the trees, and share all these things with a friend. Her family also visited and took her places.

The class was dispersing, and people went their separate ways, but not before sharing a smile, a goodbye, and a how-are-you. There was always a friendly atmosphere at the ceramics center, and it seemed that creating art brought out the humanity in people. She waited in line for the bus and chatted with Ann, a member of the class.

Ann had a girlfriend, Donna, who also lived at Springfield. This was new for Mary Jean. She had never known any gay couples before. The couple often held hands as they walked to the dining room. They laughed and touched each other when they were talking. Mary Jean had become more tolerant over the years. She thought about the young people she often saw with rings and tattoos on their bodies. There were young women with pink hair and men with sagging jeans. There were even men who wanted to be women and women who wanted to be men. She now saw the value in diversity, in being open to new experiences, even those that were foreign and that she didn't understand.

The bus stopped, and the line of people slowly boarded. As everyone settled into their seats, Mary Jean looked out the window. A younger couple was walking down one of the paths. The man was African American and the woman was Asian. Her long black hair fell in a straight ponytail down her back. His was in short dreadlocks. They ambled along, obviously not in a hurry. Just enjoying the moment.

When Mary Jean approached the door to her apartment, she noticed a small basket at her doorstep. The basket was covered with blue tissue paper. "I wonder what this is?" she said out loud. She let herself in and placed the basket on the table in the living room. She tore the tissue open and pulled out two books. One was entitled *All You Need to Know about Dying* and the other was called *Sweet Dreams: The Lull before the Last Day*.

"This is shocking!" said Mary Jean to herself. "Why would anyone leave these on my doorstep? I know I am no spring chicken, but really, this is a little presumptuous, I think."

Mary Jean thumbed through the books and dropped them back on the table. Was this Lewis? Of course, her last recollection of him was in a dream. *Is he helping me get ready for the inevitable?* she thought. *Maybe that's why these books have showed up. I suppose I have been thinking of this topic myself.* But she was tired from the day's activities and decided a nap would do her good. She would look into this when she had more energy. She got a drink of water and made her way to her bedroom. Her bed was neatly made, but the white knit comforter enticed her to curl up in it. She lay down and pulled the blanket over her shoulders. She was soon fast asleep.

40

Mary Jean had never played golf. Her husband, Lewis, had gone once a month to play nine holes with his buddies, but it was mainly a social get-together. She took the bus to the golf club meeting room. People were coming and going. Golf carts were whizzing around the paths, and people, mostly men, were teeing off out on the greens. Mary Jean shook her head and said out loud, "I've seen it, and that's all I need to do. I don't think I'll start playing golf at my age." With that, she turned around and waited for the next bus to arrive. At least she could cross it off her list.

It was windy out, so she took her blue windbreaker out of her cloth shopping bag and put it on. Marcus, Finley, and Lisa were coming to visit in the afternoon at 2 p.m. with Ivan, her great-grandson. Though they had previously arranged to go to Peavy Arboretum, she had decided not to be a burden by asking Marcus to drive the hour and a half to come pick her up and then an hour and a half back, so she suggested they all meet at Springfield Acres instead. She was stiff today, and a little tired.

While she waited, she decided to visit the theater to see what was playing. She thought she'd give George a call to see if he'd like to go see a movie this week. She took the shuttle bus to her destination and was glad to be inside; the weather was looking ominous, and tree branches were swaying in the wind.

The theater was small. It had four small rooms to accommodate four different movies playing at the same time. It was decorated in plush red carpet and velveteen blue curtains. There were antique carousel horses in the lobby and vintage black-and-white pictures of old movie stars. They served popcorn, ice cream bars, candy, and soft drinks at the concession stand. They also had pizza, wine, and beer. Moviegoers were allowed to eat and watch the movie, something they never had in her day. The theaters were cozy and seated about thirty people. The seats were nicely padded and had beverage holders for drinks. She liked the feel of the place.

She hurried back to her apartment to wait for Marcus and the others to arrive. What a treat; a visit from her son, grandson, and his wife—with her great-grandson! They were going to take her out to lunch at one of the nearby restaurants. When she entered the lobby of the main building, she decided to pay a visit to Leslie to get any updates on the garden project. Leslie was busy at her desk when she arrived.

"Hello, Leslie. I wanted to double check when the next meeting is for the garden project. I'm excited to get back to reconnecting with Derek."

"We are planning to choose seeds in less than two weeks. Just check the daily calendar of events for the exact date and time." Leslie picked up some papers and shuffled them. She seemed anxious to get back to her work.

"I'll do that," replied Mary Jean. She thanked her again and turned to leave.

"Wait," said Leslie suddenly. "Did you say Derek? Derek Meyers? I think I heard that the family split, and he is living with his mother now. I believe they are living out of her car. Such a sad situation . . ."

Mary Jean was shocked. What had happened? He had seemed happy and well-adjusted during the last meeting back in March. She had hoped their partnership throughout the garden project over the summer would allow her to check in on how he was doing. It seemed even more important now that things had changed in such a bad way.

"That is terrible. Can you tell me more about his situation? Is he still going to school? You say he is living out of the family car? Where is it parked, do you know?" Mary Jean couldn't believe how quickly someone's life could turn around for the worst in such a short period of time.

"I think he is still going to school, but I don't know where their car is parked or anything else about it. I sure feel sorry for him and his family." Leslie looked truly concerned.

"Well, thanks for the information. I'm going to have to find out more. Maybe I can be of some help." Mary Jean then left and hurried to her apartment.

Marcus, Finley, and Lisa were waiting for her at her door. Baby Ivan was cooing and making loud noises while Lisa swung him up and down.

"Hi, Mom. Is everything all right? You look stressed about something," said Marcus.

"Oh, I just found out that Derek, my garden partner, and his family have split up. Derek, his sister, and his mother are living in their car." Mary Jean motioned them in and they all sat in the living room together. Ivan looked sleepy as he lay in Lisa's arms.

"That sounds pretty bad. But there's nothing you can do about it." Marcus fidgeted and looked at his watch. Finley took the baby out of Lisa's arms because she was getting tired holding him. He started squirming.

"Well, I just need to give it some thought," said Mary Jean.

"I think we'd better get going or we're going to have a screaming, hungry baby on our hands," said Finley. With that, they all headed out to try one of the nearby restaurants.

They spent the afternoon having a late lunch, followed by dessert. Time flew by, and before she knew it, they were in the parking lot saying goodbye. Ivan had grown so much since she had last seen him. She observed that her grandson was a patient and involved father. She was so proud of him.

It had been a long day. As she hurried up to the dining room to meet George for their regular dinners, she thought of Lewis. She thought of him at the most random times. During their last conversation, he had said that she was out of danger now. That his work was done . . .

Mary Jean was thinking more and more about the afterlife. She had already read those two books that had been dropped off in front of her door. What did she believe would happen after she died? She considered her Presbyterian upbringing and what the Presbyterian Church (USA) taught: "If there is a Presbyterian narrative about life after death, this is it: when you die, your soul goes to be with God, where it enjoys God's glory and waits for the final judgment. At the final judgment bodies are reunited with souls, and eternal rewards and punishments are handed out."

Mary Jean pondered this. She wasn't sure what she thought about it. Her encounters with Lewis over the past year had upset her views on all of this, but she waved those thoughts out of her head. It wasn't important. Right now, she was alive and going to have dinner with a dear friend.

41

There were about twenty-five residents in the room waiting for the second garden meeting to start. Mary Jean looked around and saw that there were some new faces in the crowd. She saw George and waved to him. Leslie came through the door in a whirl and spread an armful of folders out on the big desk in the front of the room. She adjusted her glasses and cleared her throat.

"Hello, everybody. I'm glad you could make it. The students will be arriving in twenty or so minutes. Before they arrive, we have a little paperwork to get through. We need to register everyone, and you will need to sign some releases so the institution is not held responsible if you were to be hurt."

There was always so much bureaucracy with these organizations, thought Mary Jean. Things were always so slow to get started.

Leslie passed around a form for all to sign. Soon, they heard voices coming down the hallway outside. The students filed into the room, accompanied by a teacher from the school, and sat on the other side of the room. Mary Jean watched carefully as the students were seated, searching desperately for Derek.

The door closed, and it seemed all the students had already been seated, with no Derek. Mary Jean's heart sank.

But just when she thought she'd never see Derek again, the door cracked open and in walked Derek. He was skinnier. He wore jeans that were too short and a dark blue T-shirt. His hair was longish, and his shoes were scuffed. He looked in her direction, as if searching the group of older people. He caught her eye, and she thought she noticed the smallest smile form on his face.

"Thank you all for coming. I'm going to pass around a piece of paper to the students. Find your partner's name and write your name down next to it." The students filled in their names next to their partner's, and that was that. Derek made his way over to Mary Jean and sheepishly said hello.

"How have you been, Derek?"

"Okay." He looked down at the table.

"I know things have been rough. I was told you are living with your mother now." Mary Jean decided to tread carefully. She did not want to be judgmental. She gave him time to think about his response. How could she help him to open up?

"Yeah, my dad left us. He lost his job. My mom is waiting tables and doesn't make much money now." He looked down at his scuffed shoes. Mary Jean could tell he was embarrassed. She thought she'd better change the subject.

"What do you think you can make with zucchini?" asked Mary Jean, remembering the selections they had made previously.

"I don't know. My mom has never cooked with it." His long hair flopped in his face, covering one eye.

"Well, zucchini is great because you can make bread and pancakes out of them and also stuff them with different things."

"That sounds good." He smiled shyly and then said, "We also have carrot and spinach seeds. What meals have you made with those vegetables?"

"I've made a 'Best of Show' carrot cake that I entered in the state fair one year." Mary Jean beamed.

"That's cool. I love the cream cheese frosting on carrot cake," he said. That familiar smile was there.

"And my spinach lasagna is a favorite with my children. It has cheese in it. I bet you like cheese." Mary Jean kept studying his face.

"Yeah, I do. It is probably a good idea to hide the spinach in other foods though. I know it's good for you, but I'm not sure I really like it." He crinkled up his nose.

"Well, it does taste pretty good in a lasagna." Mary Jean laughed and knew that things would be back to normal between them.

They talked about Derek's mom, and he asked her whether she liked her new home at Springfield Acres. Mary Jean talked about the new facility and all that it had to offer. She mentioned a few of the friends she had met and then asked him about his friends. He told her that it had been hard making friends because of his predicament. Kids made fun of him, and he missed his dad.

"I can't have anybody come over to visit. We live in my mom's car now and eat at the shelter. My mom tells me it's only temporary until she can find a different job that pays more. My little sister cries a lot because she is scared of the sounds at night."

Mary Jean kept her cool and just tried to listen.

She knew she had to help Derek and his family. But how? She would talk to George and Marcus. Maybe they would have some ideas.

The meeting wrapped up after Leslie reminded everyone that they would meet in two weeks for the planting at the end of May. They were to meet directly at the garden plot in the park the next time. Compost would be delivered, and they would work it into their plots and then plant their seeds.

"Take care of yourself, Derek. I will see you in a couple of weeks." She rested her hand on his shoulder lightly and smiled. He nodded and followed the rest of the students out of the room. She heard them talking excitedly, their voices echoing down the hallway.

Mary Jean was determined to make a difference however she could. But she felt she had to act quickly. Somehow, she knew her time was running out.

42

The little dog came scratching at her door early in the morning. Mary Jean was half awake and didn't want to get out of bed. But when she heard the little bark, she knew instantly that it was Spot! She threw the covers off of her body and wrapped her robe around her as quickly as she could. When she finally opened the door, there sat a curious Spot all by himself. Where the heck had he come from? Did that mean Lewis was around? She looked both ways down the hallway to make sure no one had seen her or the dog, then coaxed him in and closed the door.

"Where in the devil did you come from?" she asked. He looked up at her with his inquisitive, liquid brown eyes as if trying to decipher her words into something meaningful.

"Well, where is your owner, Lewis? Have you been with him?" Spot gave her a low bark, jumped up on her, and wagged his tail.

"Now, none of that stuff," she said. "You need to stay down and behave yourself." She got a bowl down from a cupboard in the kitchen, filled it with water, and set it down for him. He lapped it up like he had not drunk in quite a while.

"You sure are a thirsty little thing. I wonder if you are hungry. I'm not sure I have any food for you to eat." She opened the fridge and took out some leftover meatloaf from the previous night's dinner. It was a good thing she didn't have a very big appetite these days or she wouldn't have had anything left to feed the dog. "Here you go, boy." Spot gobbled up his food, wagging his tail with enthusiasm.

Once Spot was done, Mary Jean had to think about what she was going to do with him.

"Usually, Lewis shows up right about now," she said aloud.

Mary Jean waited to see if her intuition was right. She decided to make a pot of coffee while she contemplated what to do with the little dog. She sat down on the couch in her living room while Spot lay down at her feet, content to take a little nap while she sipped on her coffee. She looked out of her sliding glass door to see what the weather was like. The sun was peeping up over the horizon, and she knew it was still early. Her stomach was growling, so she fixed a quick piece of toast and a soft-boiled egg for her breakfast.

As she ate, she thought about Lewis. She still felt as if she had dreamed all of it. The resemblance to her late husband, the familiar face, the twinkle in his eye. She'd been so busy with her new life at Springfield that he had faded away like her memories of being a toddler.

"Well, maybe I can take you out for a walk. Then I'll need to check on my sphere in the ceramics center and finish that up." Arman's memorial was tomorrow, so she didn't have much time left. Spot had a little red collar on but no tags. She found some twine in the kitchen cupboard and fastened it to his collar.

"Okay, now mind your manners. We are going to go see if your owner is around."

They stepped out into the hall and proceeded to the stairway down to the main lobby. Spot trotted obediently by her side as if he knew the importance of being good. The lady at the front desk was answering the phone when Mary Jean and Spot arrived. Spot sat next to Mary Jean's legs and did not move a muscle.

"Can I help you?" the lady said when she finished her call.

"Do you know who owns this dog? I mean, I know who owns him, but I haven't seen him around. His name is Lewis Weeks. Is he registered here?"

"Let me look." She fiddled with the computer. Mary Jean looked around the lobby and out the big glass doors. People were coming and going, but there was no sign of Lewis.

"No, I'm afraid there is no one by that name here." The lady looked concerned and stared down at Spot. "What are you going to do with that dog?" she asked.

"Oh, I'm not sure. I may be able to give him to one of my daughters. She is a vet, and she often finds homes for strays."

Mary Jean looked down at Spot who had started to squirm and whine a little. "But I may just decide to keep him. He's a really well-trained dog. Someone really loved him and spent time with him. You can tell." Mary Jean smiled. Spot stopped whining and sat very still as he looked up at her.

"Well, look at that. He understands what I'm saying."

"You will have to register the dog with us and be sure he is up to date on all his vaccinations."

"Oh, I think he is already up to date on all that. Look, he has some information on his collar." The lady nodded and then watched Mary Jean and Spot walk out the door to wait for the shuttle bus.

When the shuttle let them off at the meadow trail, Mary Jean let Spot off his leash. She called after him as he ran off to chase a bird. He came back immediately, so she felt it was safe to keep him off the leash for a while so he could run and get some exercise. Why had Lewis left Spot all alone? she thought. Or maybe he had left him on my doorstep on purpose because he knew I would take good care of him. Well, he could have asked first.

The clouds filled the blue sky with white cotton candy, and the wind blew the leaves of the birch trees, filling the air with a sound like fluttering wings. Mary Jean noticed she was getting slower. Her joints ached more than usual, and her arthritis seemed worse. Still, it felt good to be outside and have some company—a little package of joy leaping around and chasing butterflies and sniffing up rabbits in the grass. Just watching him play made her feel younger.

They were at the top of the knoll that overlooked the small lake. Spot ran down to the water. She didn't know if he knew how to swim, so she stiffly reached down and picked up a stick. Spot got excited. She tossed the stick into the water just a few feet away from land. He quickly waded in deeper until he was swimming. The ducks quacked noisily, making it clear they were not happy with his presence, and flew off to find a safer place. Mary Jean and Spot were immersed in their little world of splashing water, warm sunshine, and companionship.

Finally, Mary Jean said, "Spot, we have to go now. I need to finish the sphere for Arman's family." Spot stopped in his tracks and came to Mary Jean's side, pricking his ears up and licking her hand. They slowly walked back to the shuttle pickup area. Two more people were waiting there, and she became engaged in a lively conversation about dogs and their silly antics.

Mary Jean soon discovered from their conversations that there was a doggie daycare on the campus. Apparently, lots of residents had pet dogs; in fact, the establishment encouraged it. They also had a dog therapy program, where therapy dogs would visit residents who were lonely, disabled, or in hospice. Animals were so sensitive to people's emotions, Mary Jean thought. They could sense when you were unhappy. Just their presence, and letting people stroke their coat and talk to them, was soothing. In fact, she had read somewhere that science had proven that petting animals reduced people's blood pressure.

She found the dog daycare and decided to check out the facility before dropping Spot off. The dogs had large runs outside in the grass. Employees were working with groups of dogs, engaging them with toys. The dogs were barking and running around, looking as though they were enjoying themselves. In another space, owners and an instructor were taking their dogs through their paces. It seemed like it was a class on obedience. There was a little water pool in another area where dogs were retrieving floating toys and splashing about.

"This seems like a good place," Mary Jean told Spot. "The people are smiling and treating the dogs kindly. The dogs seem to be enjoying themselves, and there is plenty of room to play and run." She took Spot to the front desk and signed some papers. She was lucky that the girl who was checking them in was new and had not asked for a copy of Spot's latest vaccines. She needed to get to the ceramics center to finish up her project today.

Only three people and Kia were at the center. It was lab time, where anyone could come in and work on a project for a maximum of four hours. Mary Jean got her sphere from the bisque fired rack and took it back to her table. She selected two underglazes and some paintbrushes. She decided to paint a design on the orb with the underglaze, then use another glaze that would go on top. The design would show through.

She got lost in her project, and time flew by. When she was finished, she put it on the rack for the final firing phase. Kia had mentioned that it would be fired by tomorrow morning. She could hardly wait to see what it would look like. That was what was so exciting about ceramics; she never knew for sure how her piece would turn out. Sure, she had an idea, but anything could happen, and most surprises were welcome.

Mary Jean picked up Spot just in time before the daycare closed. If she hurried, she could still meet William for dinner at the Thai restaurant. She had been making this a regular thing, always having dinner with either George or William. She found she enjoyed the diversity of each man's history and felt stimulated by the different conversations they provided.

43

William looked dapper in his gray slacks and mustard plaid shirt with the sleeves rolled up. His hair was trimmed and neatly combed. He was gazing out the tall windows overlooking the water fountain outside.

"Hello, William," she said as she slowly sat down on the chair opposite him.

"Good to see you, Mary Jean." He smiled broadly, and the edges of his blue eyes were crinkled.

They busied themselves with small talk and studied the menu. After selecting their entrées, they settled into that familiar space that comes with knowing each other for a long time. Only, they had only recently met, thought Mary Jean, so maybe these things sped up as you got older.

"William, I need your help on something." She filled him in on Derek's family situation. William listened intently.

Mary Jean pulled her sweater over her shoulders and said, "Derek is such a kind and hardworking boy. I hate to see his future cut short because of his circumstances."

William was silent for a while before replying.

"I think you need to get more information. How long have they been living in her car? Why did they separate? Was there any abuse going on, and does she or Derek feel threatened?"

Mary Jean felt somewhat overwhelmed. These things were never black and white. There were always two sides to the story. But still, living in a car? At the very least, she wanted to make sure they could have a safe place to stay.

"Maybe I can meet with Derek's mother. I can find out more information. Or I can wait another week or so until we meet with our students at the garden site. Maybe she will be there and I can talk with her."

"That sounds like a good plan, Mary Jean. Would you like me to come with you?" William seemed genuinely concerned as he searched her face.

"No, thank you. I think it would be less threatening if I talked with her first while Derek is there. We'll just have to see how it goes." They finished up their dinners and ordered a berry cobbler to split for dessert.

After dinner, William and Mary Jean walked outside to catch the shuttle back to the main building. They talked about their families and what they were all doing. Marcus was coming to visit the day after the next to help Mary Jean with some of her finances. She had been slowly gifting each of her children and grandchildren money. She was so lucky to have Marcus helping her with all of this. Her memory was still surprisingly sharp, but things bothered her more, and she still had a bad habit of worrying too much. So much so that some nights she had trouble sleeping. She had become obsessed with dotting every *i* and crossing every *t*.

Mary Jean had been feeling more tired these

days, and trying to plan too much was a bad idea. Sometimes she just felt like sleeping all afternoon. She was surprised that she had had a good appetite at dinner with William because she was noticing that she had been eating less and less the past few days. Well, I don't walk much anymore, so I guess it shouldn't be such a surprise that my appetite is falling off, she thought. She wondered how she was going to keep Spot exercised. That last walk with him had really pooped her out.

The next day, Mary Jean took Spot to the dog daycare. She heard him whimper as the staff walked him back to the large and spacious play area, which had a water ditch running through it, tall bunches of reed grass, and a few shade trees and bushes. The employee took the leash off Spot's collar to let him run free. Mary Jean waited and watched to see if he would engage with some of the other dogs. A smaller dog, a corgi mix, picked up a stick and ran in front of Spot. Spot scampered after the little brown-and-white dog, and together, they leaped over the ditch and ran circles around each other playing keep-away. Satisfied that Spot would be happy here, Mary Jean headed over to the ceramics center.

Mary Jean had learned that it was hard to know how the varying glazes would react to the fire and smoke in the kiln. A lot of it had to do with where it was placed in the kiln and what it was next to. Mary Jean searched for her sphere among the numerous pieces on the cooling shelves. Finally, she found it! The rusty orange and marine blue colors amid the black areas were stunning. She never imagined it would turn out this beautiful.

She picked it up and headed back to her table. She set it carefully in white tissue paper and rolled it up. Then she placed it in a decorative box she had brought from home. She tied a dark blue ribbon around it and attached the card she'd bought at the store with one of her daughters. "There," she said. It was all ready for the memorial.

44

The memorial was being held at the chapel at 10 a.m. Mary Jean tucked Arman's package into her bag and hurried to the chapel.

A large group of people were milling about in the room, looking at photos on long rectangular tables draped with white cloth. It was a display of Arman's life and his achievements, and by the size of the group in the room, she could see that he had touched many people's lives.

The two-hour service was filled with many voices telling stories of Arman and their connection to him. Mary Jean was filled with emotion and willed herself to muster the courage to say a few words about her friend. When the moderator asked if there was anyone else who wanted to say something, Mary Jean held up her hand timidly and walked to the podium.

"Hi, I'm Mary Jean." She coughed a little, clearing her throat before continuing.

"Arman taught me to be brave, to take chances on learning new things. He said that you are never too old to challenge yourself. He encouraged and taught me how to be creative and to feel the joy of making something with clay."

She felt a tear slide down her face as she stepped down from the platform. Two men rose to take her arms on either side to steady her. There. She had done it. She felt relieved but very happy to have told everyone what Arman had done for her.

Music played as people hung around, some eating and some laughing together as they shared the happy memories of their father or dear friend. When people started to leave and lined up to pay their respects to the family, Mary Jean got up with her gift and stood in the receiving line. When it was her turn, she handed the gift box to Arman's daughter.

"Here is a little something I made for you in honor of Arman."

His daughter replied, "May I open it now?' She looked young for her age, a lot like Arman had.

Mary Jean nodded while the daughter moved to a small table to unwrap her gift. Two other family members crowded around her. When the colorful sphere was revealed, there were oohs and aahs and murmurs of "very beautiful." Mary Jean told them she had tried to catch the light from the sun because Arman had told her he felt the sun was energizing and always made it a point to sunbathe a little each day. "He will be missed deeply," she said.

"Well, I think you've captured some of that energy, Mary Jean. Now we'll have to fight over it to see who gets to display it in their house. Thank you so much. We will treasure this."

Mary Jean smiled and said goodbye, and then she headed back to her apartment.

Marcus was coming to help with some of her investments and savings the next day. She thought about Derek and his plight all night. She tossed and turned and did not get much sleep at all. But before she closed her eyes, she finally came up with an idea of how she could help him.

The next day, Marcus knocked on the door, and it took her a while to get up off the couch to answer it.

"Hi Mom, how are you?" he asked.

"I'm okay. I'm a bit sad. I went to my friend Arman's memorial yesterday morning. I'll miss him."

"I'm sorry about your friend. I remember you telling me about him. He was an amazing guy, flying helicopters in his later years."

"Yes, he did that. And a lot more."

"Would you like some coffee while we look at these numbers?"

"Sure."

They gathered around her small table and got to work. Marcus was always so prepared. Things went smoothly, and they finished up her business pretty quickly.

"Can I take you out to lunch, Mom?"

"You know, that would be nice, Marcus. But let's just stay in the building. William and I were just eating dinner the day before yesterday at the Thai restaurant, so I'd just like to eat here this time."

"Sure, Mom. We can do that. Are you feeling all right?"

"I'm fine. Just stiff, and my hip is hurting more than usual. Stop worrying. Let's just go eat lunch now, okay?"

They walked down the hallway to the little deli on the same floor. They chose a table in a corner next to a large potted fig tree. A waitress brought them menus. Mary Jean chose the salad with chicken and Marcus a burger and fries with his usual IPA.

"Marcus, I want to discuss something with you."

The waitress filled their water glasses and scurried

away. Mary Jean filled him in on Derek's situation, the garden project, and her connection to the boy.

"I want to help. What do you think about me setting up a small trust fund for him and his little sister? First, I want to feel out the situation a little more by meeting with his mom. I know this is highly unusual. I wonder if I could keep it anonymous? I could give his mother rent without her knowing who it is coming from. That way, they wouldn't have to live in their car, and Derek and his sister would have some lasting security."

Marcus looked a little blank. He was sometimes hard to read. Mary Jean guessed that he thought this was a bad idea. However, she knew what a big heart her son had.

"Um, well, it's your money, Mom, and you certainly have enough. You have been very generous giving us gifts, and, well, I can't see what better gift than to give it to some family in as great a need as they are."

Mary Jean was delighted. They discussed the details, and she told Marcus that she would get more information to see if this would be a good solution to the problem. When they were done, Marcus walked Mary Jean back to her apartment.

"Thank you for being so supportive of my wishes, Marcus. We will talk further after I meet Derek's mom. We are planting seeds tomorrow, so I should know something soon."

Mary Jean watched from her balcony as Marcus drove off into the May sunshine. She needed to get a lot of rest so she'd have enough energy to participate in the garden activities and talk with Derek's mom the next day. She had a reservation for dinner tonight with George this time but decided to call him and cancel. She would stay home and make something in her apartment since she wasn't that hungry anyway. She could make a grilled cheese sandwich in her toaster oven with a can of tomato soup on the side. That would be plenty.

The rest of the afternoon, she stayed inside and read her new novel. She wrapped herself in a shawl and curled up on the couch with a cup of tea. She quickly dozed off and found herself in one of those surreal dreams of other places and people.

When she awoke, it was 7 p.m. She slowly got ready for bed without eating dinner. She brushed her teeth, used the bathroom, and then slipped into bed. Well, I definitely will have enough rest for tomorrow, she thought as she drifted back to sleep once more.

45

Her head was thick and heavy. She felt dizzy as she swung her feet out of bed. It was 8 a.m.! She had overslept. She dressed as quickly as she could. Her body was aching and slow to move, and she wondered how she was going to make it out the door. Breakfast was a must, and she also had to place an order for a boxed lunch to take with her to the garden. She prepared her usual breakfast: coffee with cream, poached egg on wheat toast, and a small glass of apple juice. She couldn't drink orange juice anymore because it was too acidic. For the same reason, she only drank half a cup of coffee with mostly milk.

    She picked her boxed lunch up from the cafeteria, took the elevator down, and waited for the shuttle as a line formed. People wore their garden hats and outdoor clothes that they did not mind getting dirty. She hadn't thought of that as she had been in too much of a hurry to get going. It wouldn't matter. Derek would do all the dirty work, literally. She picked a seat in the back where she would be unlikely to have to share a seat. She did not feel like talking much this morning.

It was late May, and the sun was out in all its glory. The breeze was a bit cool, but the day was going to be unseasonably warm. The bus rumbled along, and Mary Jean took in the sights of spring. The tree blossoms were in full bloom, and the grass fields were tall and a deep yellow-green. Bulbs were a bit past blooming, but along the roadway she could still spot blue irises, yellow daffodils, and some orange California poppies.

They arrived almost at the same time as the students' school bus. Derek was heading her way. He wore the same clothes he had had on the last time they met. His hair looked greasy, and his face mirrored his plight.

"Hi, Derek," said Mary Jean.

"Hi." Derek looked down and seemed very quiet.

"Is there something wrong, Derek?" she gently asked.

Derek didn't reply right away. He looked down at his shoes.

"Let's get our plants and seeds. Then we can find a spot over there and talk," said Mary Jean.

She slowly led the way over to the organized tables with blue-and-white checkered tablecloths. The ladies were chatting away and helping students pick up their orders. Mary Jean and Derek picked up their zucchini and spinach starts and carrot seeds, then they headed to a private spot with a cement bench. The bench was a memorial to a young man who had died in a car accident in the community.

"What a beautiful thing to do to remember a loved one," said Mary Jean as she read the inscription on the bench. As they sat down, Derek was still very quiet. Mary Jean looked at him and noticed a tear rolling down his face.

"Whatever is the matter, Derek?" Mary Jean urged him to explain.

"My father died a couple of weeks ago. He hurt himself. I stayed home for two weeks, and this is my first day back to school. My mom thought it would be a good time to get me back into school."

"You poor dear! I can't imagine how awful you must feel. Do you want to talk about it?"

He shook his head and said, "I miss him."

"You will always have your memories of him. He will always be a part of your life, but in a different way. He will be in here."

She touched her heart, then his chest.

"Like my friend Lewis once told me, your loved ones will always be with you."

She held his hand and watched as the tears continued to come. They got out their lunches and ate in silence for a while. He looked up at her, and his eyes said thank you. They picked up their seeds and starts and got to work. Derek did all the digging and planting with some supervision from Mary Jean. She told him when to dig a little deeper, to pat down the dirt so the roots would be well covered, and to water them afterward. They put two little stakes in the ground and fastened a string in a line so Derek could sow his seeds in a straight row. Mary Jean told him that half the fun was making a neat garden; however, it by no means had to be perfect.

After they were done, they walked back to their spot on the bench. A small shade tree protected them from the sun as the day was turning out to be quite hot. Yellow jackets were buzzing around, looking for spilled morsels of turkey from their sandwiches. A red, old Subaru drove up and parked across the street from the garden. A short, athletic woman with dark brown hair walked toward them.

"Derek, it's time to go," his mother called. Mary Jean had Derek help her get off the bench.

"Hi, I'm Mary Jean, Derek's garden partner." Mary Jean held out her hand.

The woman looked her up and down, took her hand tentatively, and said, "Hi, I'm Natalie."

"Won't you come sit with us for a moment? Derek has shared some news with me about your late husband. I am deeply sorry for your loss."

Mary Jean made some room for Natalie on the bench and Derek sat under the tree on the grass.

"Yes, it was quite a shock to me and the kids." Natalie stifled a rush of emotion and wiped her eyes.

For the next half hour, the two women talked under the shade of the little tree. They shared their losses and information about their families and hardships. At the end of their conversation, Natalie seemed, in Mary Jean's assessment, to be a very hardworking, intelligent woman who had just had bad luck with no family support to dig her out of her hardship.

"I would like to make an offer to you that I know will sound highly unusual. I would like to set up a trust fund for Derek and his sister to help you out. Please do not make up your mind today, but I'm asking you to think about it. I am old and am not going to need this money; and my family members are well cared for. I would like to die knowing that I helped someone in need whom I care for greatly."

Mary Jean looked at Derek. He was also looking at her with wide eyes.

Natalie was weeping silently. Finally, she said, "This is absolutely the kindest thing anyone has ever offered to me. The burden of providing for my children would be lifted. But I simply could not accept your offer."

Mary Jean took a deep breath and said, "Please, just think about it. We need to also get you out of your car and back into some housing. I would be glad to meet with you and try to find some resources that can get a roof over your head." She thought this was a better approach then also offering to pay her rent.

Natalie looked off into the distance. She watched the other kids and their elderly partners working in the garden. The seniors were helping the children with the spacing and planting of seeds.

"I guess that is what community is about. Helping . . . and receiving help from others.

Sure. Let's meet again and talk about this. Just knowing someone cares gives me hope and lifts my spirits."

They arranged for a time to meet again. Marcus would be invited, too, to help them wade through the legal matters. Marcus had always dabbled in the stock market and had also taken classes on finance in his spare time. He had been a great help to Mary Jean as she slowly gifted some of her money to the grandkids. With the help of a lawyer, he and his wife had set up a trust fund for Finley, so she felt confident he would know what to do. And if not, he would know who to contact for help.

As Mary Jean rode the bus home, she mulled over her thoughts. I know this sounds rushed, and I hardly know this woman. But I know Derek pretty well. I know the potential that is there. He needs the infrastructure to come into his own. I can provide that. She listened to the conversations around her on the bus and closed her eyes, smiling, thinking about the step she had taken.

46

Marcus was on time as usual. The three adults sat together in Loafer's Cafe, a popular eatery in Springfield while Derek and his sister slurped down some milkshakes at the end of the table. They had brought games for the kids to occupy themselves while they worked to set up the trust fund documents. After three hours, they had a plan that spelled out the money that would be made available and a third party who would administer the payments. Natalie would have a certain amount for rent, the kids would have money for clothes, and everyone would have health care. Mary Jean was so glad that Natalie had agreed to let her help. She knew it certainly could have gone another way. All that was needed was for their lawyer to look over it.

Mary Jean was very weary when the meeting was over. Natalie, Marcus, and the kids were heading out to look at a couple of apartments. They would soon have a roof over their heads.

Over the next few weeks, Derek and Mary Jean met a couple more times at the garden to tend their plot and talk about his new life. He looked neater and had new clothes. His shoes were clean, and most of all, he had a positive outlook on things. He shared with her his dream of becoming a firefighter. He said he wanted to help people—and it would also be cool to put out fires. He said his sister was doing better in school and that she could now read almost as well as he could.

Mary Jean had one more thing to take care of before she left this world. Spot.

"Derek, have you ever wanted a dog?" she asked him one day while picking the zucchini in the garden. She had brought Spot along on this particular trip to the park so he could meet and play with Derek.

"Are you kidding?!" Derek shouted. "I've always wanted a dog. And the apartment we live in now allows us to have one! We are on the ground floor, and it has a small enclosed yard. Are you looking for someone to adopt Spot?" he asked.

"Well, yes. And I can't think of anyone more suited to owning a dog than you! Spot needs someone who is responsible, who will take him for daily walks, who will teach him tricks, and who will love him, most of all. Do you think you can handle that kind of responsibility?"

"Oh, yes! I take out the garbage at home and clean my room—though I am not great at it, I have to confess. And I water the houseplants when they need it. I also do the dishes at night for my mom when she is tired."

"Well, let's talk with your mom next time and see if she approves."

Mary Jean sighed and looked down at Spot. He was curled up sleeping at her feet as he often did whenever she sat down. She knew it was important to increase the bond between Spot and Derek because Spot loved her and would miss her when she was gone. Derek knelt to the ground and tickled Spot's ears. The little dog woke with a start and jumped up to lick Derek's face. Mary Jean knew she needed to talk with Derek about when he would get Spot.

"Derek, you know I am getting older every day," Mary Jean started out simply. She tried to think of a way to gently tell him about what was going to happen to her someday in the not-so-distant future.

"Yes. I know that." He looked at her inquisitively while scratching behind Spot's ears.

"Well, when I am tired of living, and, well, when I die . . ." Mary Jean's voice trailed off, and Derek interrupted by shouting, "I don't want you to die!" He ran over to her and put his arms around her, squeezing hard. Tears began to trickle down his cheeks. Mary Jean hoped she had done the right thing by talking with him and getting him ready for the inevitable.

"I know this is hard for you to think about. But when I am gone, Marcus will bring Spot over to live with you. Think of Spot as a continuation of our friendship. He will keep you company, and it will be as if I were there with you." Mary Jean took a deep breath and thought about what she had said. It brought her some comfort to know that the two of them would help each other during the sad and difficult transition that was coming.

The weeks rolled by. By the end of fall, Mary Jean and Derek's family were getting to know each other well. They often picked her up and took her to the park, where she could sit comfortably and watch Derek and his sister play with Spot. Natalie would pack a lunch of potato salad, cold fried chicken, coleslaw, and sometimes baked beans. She also made homemade lemonade mixed with iced tea and brought ice cubes in the cooler.

Over the next few months, Natalie went to the local community college with Mary Jean's help and took courses to become a medical office assistant. Now she no longer needed help with rent and was looking to buy a house. The women talked about the books they had read, how their families were doing, and the challenges of raising kids. Mary Jean did not tell Natalie about the books she'd received from an anonymous person about what happens at the end of life. She was sure she knew who the mysterious donor had been. Those books had given her some closure on what the last day might look like. It was not something she wanted to dwell on—but she wasn't afraid now. She felt certain she would not be alone.

One night, Mary Jean was getting ready for bed. She slipped in between the cotton sheets and felt warm and secure. This past year had been full of good memories with her own family as well as Natalie's. Mary Jean knew she was getting weaker day by day. Soon, she would no longer have the strength to go out at all. She heaved a sigh of relief as she closed her eyes and thought of all the experiences she had had since coming to Springfield. She'd tried new things, met new friends, helped a family in need, and even adopted a dog. She felt complete as the years flipped by like a motion picture on fast forward in her head. She could no longer get around without a walker now.

The following morning, Mary Jean woke up with the sun barely peeking in through her window. It was very early. She slowly moved the covers aside and went to the restroom. Spot, who was sleeping by her bed, got up and stretched. When she had dressed, she walked to the kitchen and fed Spot. While he was eating, she sat down on her couch in the living room. She looked down, and on the floor, her red sneakers were peeking out from underneath the couch.

She slowly bent down and pulled them out. With difficulty, she put one on, then the other. She tied them up and sat there thinking of all the places these shoes had taken her.

Mary Jean got up stiffly and shuffled over to her walker. She opened the door and shuffled toward the elevator, with Spot following closely behind. They walked out to the courtyard garden, and with slow determination, she followed the path to the fountain. She sat down while Spot jumped up and sat with her on the bench.

Mary Jean closed her eyes and listened to the birds twittering in the branches above her. The water from the fountain made a lovely trickling sound. She could hear the buzzing of the bees as they worked the flowers around her. A soft, cool breeze caressed her face.

The gardener found her.

Spot's whining had alerted him, and when he walked toward the noise, Mary Jean was slumped over with Spot licking her face. What was odd, though, was that Mary Jean was in her socks with no shoes on.

Her family was called, and Marcus took charge. He set up the memorial for the following week. All sorts of people turned up. Her children and grandchildren, Derek and his family, William, George, and all the other friends she had met at the retirement center. Some had died before her, but all who had met her remembered her empathy for others, her interest in life, and her appreciation for her family. It was a beautiful ceremony with her favorite songs and yellow roses. Afterward, the crowd enjoyed some of her best recipes, like her spinach lasagna and lemon meringue pie.

Natalie gathered her two children and offered her condolences to Mary Jean's family. Marcus took her aside and told her that he would bring Spot over the next day, if that was all right. The poor dog could sense something was up, so Marcus was keeping him tonight at his house. Natalie told him that was fine; Derek would be overjoyed to be reunited with him. And she knew Spot would help to comfort him.

That night, Marcus took Spot home. The dog was subdued and never left his side. He followed him around the house, but when Marcus called him, he would not respond. Marcus talked to him about Mary Jean, and when Spot heard her name, he pricked his ears forward and wagged his tail. Spot slept at the foot of his bed. The next day, Marcus packed him up and headed to Natalie's house.

When he arrived, he put the car in park. Spot stared at him from the passenger's seat.

"Well, this is goodbye, Spot. You're going to have a really nice home with Derek. He'll take really good care of you." Spot continued to stare at him quietly.

Marcus went around to the side of the car and got the dog out. Together, they walked up to the family's new house, which had a yard. Derek answered the door and scooped Spot up into his arms. Natalie invited Marcus in and the two of them talked briefly while Derek and Spot tore around the house together.

Finally, Marcus said goodbye and headed home, all the while thinking back on the events that had unfolded. He missed his mother greatly, but somehow, he felt she wasn't far away. He knew he would be visiting Natalie and her two kids now and then—and of course Spot, too. Somehow that just felt right.

Author's Note

I was inspired to write this book based on my observations of my husband's Sunday evening talks with his mother. She is turning ninety-six years old this year, during a pandemic, holed up in her apartment away from danger. She has a good memory and is an avid reader but is walking less. Her world is confined to the spaces around her and is enriched by the love of her family who stay in touch often.

I've been able to form a picture of how her world is shrinking. When my husband shares with me the nature of their conversations, I find them funny but, at the same time, sad. The bunny trails she goes on lead to unrelated topics, and it is sometimes hard to interact with her in a satisfying way.

In this country, we shy away from discussing aging and what that might look like for all of us. We hear sad tales of parents being put in nursing homes, only to wither away and die alone. Some of us try to keep our parents home for as long as possible, bringing in help that is usually rejected.

As a dietitian, I worked in nursing homes

in Oregon for five years during the 1990s. I was appalled at the dark buildings devoid of color, the unappetizing food, and the dreary atmosphere where most residents sat around doing nothing in their wheelchairs. There were no garden spaces, very few visitors, and if a child were brought into the building, I am sure he or she would feel like it was a very scary place indeed.

What if we could reimagine the spaces where we put our elderly?

What makes us happy in midlife probably still makes us happy at the end of our lives—like spending time outdoors in the sunshine, walking among the trees, hearing the water rush over the rocks, and listening to the birds singing in the trees above; or forming close relationships, spending time being creative, enjoying the arts and music, or bonding with an animal.

If you could imagine your last few years, what would they look like? That is what I've tried to do here: to paint a picture of what could be possible. I hope the people who build spaces for the elderly will take this message to heart and begin building places where they would like to live out the rest of their lives.

To get in touch, please contact me at www.rainbowdunstudio.weebly.com.

Acknowledgments

I want to thank Mark, Carol, Suzanne, Chris, Sharon, and Steve for reading the first draft of my novel. Each person gave their own thoughtful comments and suggestions, which helped me to form my final draft.

Sheridan McCarthy was a godsend, providing me with guidance and so much useful information as I travelled down the path of self-publishing.

My editor, Kimberley Lim from New York, did an excellent job keeping my timeline accurate and giving me insightful examples of how to improve the pacing and clarity of the story.

I am so grateful for Alexis Spakoski, my book cover designer and long-time friend. She helped incorporate my red shoes painting, selecting great backdrop colors and a fitting design.

And lastly, I thank my husband, Mark, for believing in me and supporting me along the way.

CPSIA information can be obtained
at www.ICGtesting.com
Printed in the USA
JSHW031913110222
22660JS00003B/6